A Series of Rooms

A SERIES OF ROOMS

A.J. BARLOWE

Copyright © 2024 A.J. Barlowe
All rights reserved.
ISBN-13: 979-8-218-51974-2

Cover design by Jessica Sherburn (@Ouijacine)

CONTENT WARNINGS AVAILABLE ON THE BACK PAGE

*To the ones who believed in this story,
from the very first draft.*

"I'm going to base this moment on who I'm stuck in a room with. It's what life is. It's a series of rooms, and who we get stuck in those rooms with adds up to what our lives are."

- House, M.D.
One Day, One Room

CHAPTER 1
Liam

Liam was only halfway through his first legal drink when his friends abandoned him.

If he were the kind of person with a backbone and a shred of self-respect, he might have left the bar after that. Better yet, he might have tracked Ben and Nathan down and confronted them, unleashing a decade's worth of grievances with a drink to their faces. He might have left the bar on his own, caught the L to the last commuter train of the night, and left them behind for good.

But he was the person that he was, so instead, he shouldered his way through the crowd and planted his back against the first open patch of wall he could find.

It was Liam's twenty-first birthday, and he wanted nothing more than to go home.

The exposed brick was sticky in a way that made his skin cling where it touched, but it was better than being surrounded by a sea of sweaty bodies on all sides. The deafening pulse of music he couldn't escape was bad enough, vibrating through the floor, up his legs, into his bones. He considered retreating to the back patio for a break in the noise, but a quick assessment of the distance between points A and B, and the massive wall of people in between, held him in place. He felt briefly, absurdly, like a castaway on an abandoned island, stranded in place until help came.

The sharp prickling sensation in his palms was the first tell-tale sign of impending panic. Liam pulled in a deep breath, but the air was thick with booze and sweat and it did nothing to ground him. The drink in his hand was not the comfort he'd hoped it would be, either: an overpour of vodka, with the barest essence of cranberry, that burned going down. Still, he forced himself to drink like he knew what he was doing, and he did feel a bit warmer with every sip. That was probably a good sign. He wouldn't know. It was something he might have asked Ben and Nathan about, if they had bothered staying in his line of sight.

He only got in a few more sips before a stray elbow knocked the icy shock of liquid down his front. No apology, no offer to replace the spilled drink, no acknowledgement at all from the cluster of sequin shirts that pushed past him as if he didn't exist. For a moment, he was too stunned to react, just frozen in place with his white shirt—because, sure, of course he had worn white tonight—plastered to his stomach.

His buzz wasn't strong enough to dull the indignity of walking to the bathroom covered in cranberry juice and vodka, so he kept his eyes down as he fought through the crowd and hoped his apparent invisibility would hold up just a little longer.

The bathroom walls were more sharpie and faded stickers than paint, and the room was lit by a singular bare bulb. The urinal looked like it hadn't been cleaned since its installation, and the smell supported that theory. One of the three stalls was missing a door. It was becoming more apparent by the minute that Liam was not compatible with bar life.

He stood in front of the mirror, studying the stain on his shirt through the cracks and grime. *Happy birthday*, he thought.

The drink covered too much of his shirt for him to accomplish much by leaning over the sink. Mostly, this just resulted in sending rivulets of water dripping into the waistband of his jeans. Liam shut off the water. The only thing that could make this night even more pathetic would be crying in the bathroom about it, so he took a deep breath and closed his eyes.

Okay. *Okay.* This was salvageable. With a sideways glance at the door, he reached behind him to pull the shirt over his head.

When the wet material slipped past his eyes, Liam let out an embarrassing yelp. A man had come out of the half-shut stall and was now standing behind him in his reflection, looking equally startled. Whether by Liam's presence or his reaction, he wasn't sure.

"Sorry," Liam apologized, despite the fact that he had done nothing other than take up space in a public restroom.

The man, who looked to be about Liam's age, said nothing. He quickly recovered and stepped up beside him at the trough-style sink.

"I thought I was alone," Liam said, because he was suddenly hyper aware of his semi-nudity and felt the need to explain. "I just need to clean this. I. . . spilled my drink."

More silence.

Okay, then.

Liam flipped on the faucet and began to scrub cold water into the stain.

When he glanced up at the mirror, he saw, now at closer range, that the man next to him was crying. Or, at least, he had been recently.

Liam knew he was staring but couldn't make himself look away before he was caught. Reddened eyes caught his own for half a second, then they both looked down again. Liam worked faster, desperate to extricate himself from an awkward encounter of his own making. Beside him, the stranger was splashing cold water on his face, no doubt trying to reduce the swelling around his eyes.

When the water shut off, the space between them felt too quiet, despite the muffled bass coming through the door. Liam stole another glance at him in the mirror.

"Are you okay?" he decided to ask.

The man, who was now gripping the edge of the sink, stared dead-eyed into the basin. He didn't so much as glance in Liam's direction.

Liam looked away and wrung out his shirt. It was only slightly pink-tinted now, which was probably the best he was going to get. Maybe the dark lighting would work in his favor, and no one would notice. Resigned, he stepped away from the sink and over to the air dryer. He pushed the large silver button and... nothing.

You've got to be joking.

He pushed it again.

Not even a sputtering attempt at a startup.

He punched the button one last time, though that one was mostly an act of aggression rather than an earnest attempt.

"It's broken."

Liam swiveled around slowly, startled to hear the stranger speak. He was looking at Liam now, too—directly at him, instead of through their shared reflection. His dark eyes were still swollen despite his efforts.

"You know, I was just starting to gather that," Liam said, feigning the casual coolness of someone who wasn't standing half-naked in a bar bathroom.

If he was someone who enjoyed showing off his body at the best of times, maybe this wouldn't be half as awful, but here he was. And now his options were down to hiding in this cesspool of a bathroom until his shirt dried on its own, or stepping out into the club as a one-man wet t-shirt contest. Nathan and Ben were sure to have a field day with that, whenever they deigned to find him again.

That was the deciding factor.

Liam squeezed his shirt one last time, then glanced at the stall with the missing door. He didn't allow himself to linger on the thought of the bacteria that clung to every square inch of this room and draped his shirt over the wall.

For the second time tonight, Liam found himself on the verge of freefall. It was harder to ignore his exposed state when he had nothing to do with his hands, so he settled for crossing his arms and sinking into a crouch by the wall. If he was going to be here a while, he might as well get comfortable. He focused on breathing and wondered if it would be worth dipping into his savings to call a cab back to the hotel. *To which Nathan and Ben had the only keys.*

"Are you okay?" the stranger asked. Liam looked up to find him still standing there, witness to his downward spiral. There was a begrudging quality to the question, as if he'd had to force himself to ask. Liam tried for a smile, but it felt more pathetic to pretend.

"This wasn't exactly the twenty-first birthday I'd imagined."

Though, perhaps if he had been more realistic about his expectations, it should have been. Really, Liam was partially at fault for the position he found himself in now. He should have leaned into his own suspicions when his friends offered to take him to the city for his birthday. He should have realized that this weekend was always about finding an excuse to get drunk and run up a hotel bill on Nathan's dad's credit card, and not a sudden interest in celebrating Liam.

"Where are your friends?" The man turned to face him, leaning back against the sink.

And wasn't that the million-dollar question? He opened his mouth to say something witty and biting, but what came out was, "I'm starting to think I don't have any." Then, trying to save face, "Do you want to talk about yours?"

"My what?"

"Your reason for hiding out in the bathroom?"

Liam regretted it immediately, when the small opening that had been pried open between them slammed shut. The man turned back to the sink.

"Sorry," Liam said again. "I didn't mean to pry."

The other man was quiet for a few more seconds, then shook his head. "Just a bad night."

Liam curled his fingers around his own upper arms, slippery with humid sweat. He didn't know what kind of comfort he could give a complete stranger, nor how much weight it would hold coming from someone crouched on a bathroom floor, but at least he could offer solidarity.

"I'm Liam," he said lamely.

The stranger looked back at him, and for a moment it looked like he might actually respond. But before he could speak, the bathroom door burst open, and the stranger flinched like he'd been struck.

Two drunk guys stumbled in, one of whom was still holding his open container of beer as he approached the urinal. Neither of them paid Liam or his quiet companion any attention, but it seemed to take a moment for the tension to dissipate. He shook his head, then tossed a fleeting glance at Liam.

"I need to go," he said.

Before Liam could so much as utter a goodbye, the door swung open, letting in a swell of bass and liquor, and he was gone.

"Cassidy, where have you been?" Ben was drunk and sweaty when he threw an arm over Liam's shoulder, yanking him close. "Wait, why are you wet?"

Not so long ago, the casual act of affection might have done something for Liam. Now, he shoved out of Ben's hold, knocking into a wall of dancing bodies behind him. He ignored the shouts of protest and held out his hand.

"I need the key card," he said.

"What? Why?"

Nathan, pulling his face out of the crook of a girl's neck, finally looked at him. "Why are you wet?" he asked. Liam felt like screaming.

"Give me the key," he repeated.

"We've only been out for an hour and you want to leave?" Nate said.

Would you have even fucking noticed? Liam wanted to shout back.

"I have a headache," he lied.

"Don't be a buzzkill," Nate said. "We brought you all the way out here for your birthday, and you're going to bail on us?"

The lights, the bass, the sweat, the damp cloth clinging to him—Liam was crawling out of his skin and ready to snap. "I haven't seen you since we got here," he yelled back, struggling to be heard over the music. "Just let me leave and you guys can hang without me, which was clearly the plan all along."

Ben seemed to sober a bit at the accusation, almost looking genuinely hurt. "Come on. You know that's not true. It's easy to lose people in here. I lost Nate for a minute, too. It's fine. We're all good now."

"Whatever." Nathan put a hand up, digging into his pocket with the other. He flipped open his wallet and shoved the hotel key at Liam. "If he wants to be a little bitch about it, let him go."

Liam reached for the key, but Nathan dropped it before he made contact, letting it clatter to the floor. He turned his attention back to the girl without sparing Liam a second glance. Ben looked away, pretending to be distracted by something across the room. Liam swallowed back his anger and hurt and dropped to a crouch. The card was sticky when he finally pulled it off the floor.

"Hey," Ben called after him as Liam turned to leave. "Happy birthday."

***

Liam forced himself to stay awake long enough to shower when he got back to the hotel. His stained shirt, mostly dry after the long walk, lay in a heap on the bathroom floor. His mood had already improved after rinsing off the grime of the bar bathroom and other people's sweat, but the exhaustion lingered. It didn't take long after his head hit the pillow for him to drift off.

When he woke, it was to the harsh overhead light and the ungraceful entrance of his friends. Ben was drinking something wrapped in a brown paper bag and stumbling into walls. A quick glance at the alarm clock told Liam it was a little after one in the morning. He had only gotten an hour of sleep.

"Rise and shine." Nate pointed at him. "Night's not over yet."

Liam blinked at them, pulling the comforter closer to his chin. "What's going on?"

"What's going on," Ben echoed, "is we got you a birthday present."

Something light and flat landed on Liam's stomach. He peered down over the blanket and saw a hotel key card. "I don't get it," he said.

"It's a surprise."

"It's a key to a room I'm already in, but thanks," Liam countered.

"Check the room number," Nate said, stealing the bottle from Ben's hand to take a swig.

Liam did as instructed, flipping the key around to see the number "336" scrawled at the top of the card. "That's not our room number," he observed.

"Oh, he's quick."

"I was sleeping."

"And now," Ben said, bouncing onto the bed and jostling him, "you're awake."

Liam—begrudgingly—sat up and lifted the key card. "What is this? You got me a different room?"

"We wanted to make it up to you," Ben said. "We were assholes for losing you earlier, so take this as our apology."

"You do understand how exiling me to a room by myself might not send the right message for that?"

"Who said you'd be by yourself?" Nathan said, smiling. "The room isn't the surprise. It's what's waiting for you there." He sounded very satisfied with himself, which had Liam tensing. It wouldn't be the first time Liam was the butt of one of Nathan's great ideas, and he was really not in the mood.

"Just tell me what it is."

"That's not how surprises work," Ben chided. "Up you go." He followed up by bodily shoving Liam until he rolled off the bed in a tangle of blankets.

"What is wrong with you?" Liam stumbled to his feet. "I just want to sleep."

"There are beds in the other room," Ben said.

Nate's shit-eating grin widened as he added, "Though sleeping is optional."

Liam bent over and picked up the card from where it had fallen. He studied it, then looked up at Nate. "If I go look, will you let it drop?"

Nate's answering gesture of surrender was no answer at all, but it was the best he was going to get. Liam huffed out a breath and shoved past him, toward the door.

"This better be good," he said.

In the hallway, he had the fleeting thought that he should go sleep on the couch in the lobby and avoid Ben, Nathan, and their dubious surprises until morning. But it was his own curiosity that had him taking the elevator down to the third floor instead.

Possibilities flitted through his mind, none of them good, each of them worse than the one before. His leading theory was that they had found this hotel key card on the floor somewhere and were setting Liam up to walk in on some poor, unsuspecting tourist couple. A quick breaking-and-entering charge for the sake of a quick laugh. He wouldn't put it past them. Liam had a decade of experience paying the price of Ben and Nathan's attempts at humor.

By the time he reached the room, his palms were damp. He wiped them on his pants and hesitated outside the door. He entertained the lobby option one last time before mustering the courage to tap the key against the digital lock.

He held his breath as the light turned green.

Liam clutched the door handle, turning it downward before it had a chance to lock up again. He stayed like that, frozen and squeezing the metal as it grew warm under his palm, listening for signs of life. When it was only silence, he pushed into the room.

It was dark, save for a sliver of bronze light from a streetlamp shining through a slit in the curtains. He stepped tentatively into the corridor that separated him from the rest of the room, letting the door click shut behind him. He bit back the urge to call *"hello?"* into the empty room, like the first person to die in a horror movie, and instead felt along the wall for a light switch. He found one at the mouth of the hall, just as it opened to the room.

When he flipped on the light, he couldn't process what he saw right away. He stumbled back a step, convinced that he had wandered into a strange dream. Because of all the things Liam expected to find waiting for him in the dark, the stranger from the bar bathroom had not been one of them.

CHAPTER 2
Liam

He looked different in the light. That was the first coherent thought Liam was able to string together. The second thought slipped out of his mouth before he could filter himself:

"What are you doing here?"

The man stood slowly, rising from his perch on the edge of the bed. He was just as guarded as before, but even so, it was apparent that he was processing a shock of his own.

"Sorry," Liam said. "That was rude. I just meant. . ." *What the fuck are you doing here?* "No, that was pretty much what I meant. Just with a little more. . . decorum."

Something twitched between the stranger's brows. "Decorum," he repeated, unsmiling. "Liam, was it?"

Liam blinked, surprised at his memory of what he was sure had been an insignificant part of this guy's night. "I. . . Yeah. Sorry, you left before I could get your name earlier."

From the answering hesitation, the way the man watched him, Liam almost regretted asking for it now.

"Leo," he said finally, and then Liam's mouth was moving faster than his brain again.

"Oh. Leo, Liam. We're sort of like. . . Phonetic fraternal twins." *Please stop speaking.*

The man—*Leo*—crossed his arms tightly over his chest and offered the barest approximation of a smile at the mass-produced wall art, but there was nothing amused about it. The hardness in him that Liam had encountered earlier had now been replaced with something more impenetrable. It was nearly hostility.

"I think I'm missing something," Liam confessed, adopting a defensive posture of his own. "My friends said there was some sort of surprise?"

"I thought you didn't *have* friends," he replied sharply. "You must have been mistaken, though, because I don't come cheap. I would say your friends must like you very much."

Sleeping is optional, Nathan had said. *We wanted to make it up to you*, Ben had told him.

Any disbelief Liam might have felt, any benefit of the doubt he might have afforded his friends, vanished before it could fully form. Because they would, in fact, go this far. If there was anything about them that Liam could always count on, it was Nathan and Ben's propensity for taking a joke too far.

And it been a joke, once upon a time. He remembered, with sudden clarity, the night they'd learned that their *good pal Liam* had never slept with anyone before. They had been a few beers deep at the time and couldn't stop pissing themselves over the proposition of getting "hired help" to get his first time out of the way. For Liam, it had been humiliating and invasive, and he had tried hard to shut them down and never think about their commentary on his sex life again. For them, apparently, their "joke" had planted the seed of an idea, nurtured by years of unchecked behavior and a warped sense of humor, all leading to the perfect punchline.

"Oh my God," Liam said, feeling faintly nauseous. "You're...?" He didn't know how to finish that with any amount of propriety, so he gave it up, shaking his head. "Okay. Listen, I had no idea about any of this. I'm not... Whatever they told you, I'm not interested in... I mean, not that I have any moral objection, or anything. I swear I'm not casting judgment on your line of work. There's nothing wrong with—" Liam broke off. He was too busy stumbling over his messy rejection that he didn't notice the crack in Leo's stony mask right away. Then he registered the look of panic. "What?" Liam asked. "What's wrong?"

Leo kept his eyes downcast and pulled in a breath. "I think," he said through gritted teeth. "We got off to a bad start. I'm sorry." The forced softness of his tone, almost contrite, was a jarring change of pace. "I was just having a bad night. We can start over."

A bad night, he had said when Liam asked him before. The redness around his eyes had mostly faded since their bathroom encounter, but in the light, there were more prominent signs of distress: dark circles under his eyes, a grayish pallor to his skin. There were loose fringes of thread at the hem of his shirt, small tears in the fabric, and an air of hunger radiated from his frame.

"You were crying," Liam said softly. "Was it. . . ?" He gestured uncertainly. What was he even trying to say?

"It doesn't matter." The tight press of Leo's lips formed an even less believable smile than before. "I'm fine now. Let's just start over." With what appeared to be great effort, Leo uncrossed his arms and took a step toward Liam.

Liam, instinctively, took a step back. "I think you're misunderstanding," he said.

"It's fine." Leo took another step forward, a lithe, syrupy grace to his movement that hadn't been there before. He moved close enough to touch Liam's hand, to take it into his own. "We can do this however you want." There was clearly an attempt at seduction in his voice, but Liam could hear the tremor underneath. He could feel it where their fingers touched.

Liam pulled his hand free and Leo froze, reducing him to the rapid rise and fall of his chest.

"I'm sorry," Liam said again. "I don't want to."

Leo was still for a long few seconds. Then, to Liam's horror, his eyes filled with a glassy sheen. He turned away before tears could fall, swiping at his face.

"Oh, hey. That sounded bad. I'm sorry." Liam started to reach out a hand but retracted it before he could make contact. "It honestly has nothing to do with you, I—"

"Fuck." The word was whispered into the palms now covering his face, so quiet Liam almost didn't hear. Then, louder, "*Fuck.*"

"What's happening?" Liam said. He was beginning to get the feeling that whatever this was went deeper than hurt feelings. He waited out the tense silence, helplessly watching this almost-stranger fight to control his breathing.

"Please," came his muffled whisper. "I need the money."

A sick feeling lurched in Liam's stomach. "They didn't pay you?"

That was the wrong thing to say. Leo dropped into a crouch so fast that Liam thought, at first, that he had fallen. Leo pushed his hands into his hair, blunt fingernails scraping over his scalp hard enough to leave marks.

"I messed up," he said, over and over. "I know better. I know. *I know.*"

Liam felt the uptick in his own anxiety, watching him fall apart with no idea how to help.

"Listen," Liam said, kneeling beside him. "You'll get the money. All of it, okay? I'll make sure of it. It's not your fault my friends are assholes." When Leo didn't immediately respond, or even look up at him, Liam continued. "You can just take the money and go. Consider it a paid night off."

Bloodshot eyes peered up at him, wary and tired. "I'm booked for the night," Leo said.

"You'll get the full amount," Liam promised. "How much is it?"

For a few long moments, the hum of the air conditioner was the only sound in the room.

Leo pulled his eyes away before he answered, as if bracing for a negative response. "Five hundred," he said.

Fucking Nathan.

"Okay. That's fine. I'll get it for you. I'll go now. Wait here?"

Leo hesitated for a moment, then nodded.

Liam waited until he was seated back on the bed before he left. He spent the walk to the shared room dreading the altercation ahead of him, and still reeling from the one behind him. He really wasn't in the mood for whatever rehearsed commentary they had planned for his return. He could already hear it, predictable as ever: *"Jesus, Cassidy, we knew you'd finish quick but that's gotta be a world record."*

But when Liam opened the door, their hotel room was dark and empty. He stopped short, pulling his phone from his pocket. There was a singular text from Ben waiting for him.

Meeting friends in Wicker park, it said. *Have fun, killer.*

It shouldn't have stung. He didn't want to admit that it did, but he found himself momentarily frozen by the hurt. It hadn't been enough to lose him at the first bar of the night. Now they had created a diversion that allowed them to leave him behind without feeling guilty, if they were even capable of such a thing. Had this been the plan all along? To use

Liam's birthday as a viable excuse to borrow daddy's credit card for the weekend, then ditch him for their real friends?

He clicked his phone off without responding.

Any hesitancy he might have had about digging through Nathan's bag had faded, at least. He dropped onto his knees by the duffel on Nathan's side of the bed and tore through the pockets. Nathan always carried cash, and thankfully he carried extra when he was out of town. Liam counted out four-hundred in large bills and sighed. He pulled out his own wallet, already knowing it was a bust, and found two twenties. It was the best he could do for now.

As he made his way back down the hall, drafting mental apologies for the shortage, a bleak possibility dawned on him: What if Leo had nowhere else to sleep tonight? What if this overnight job, this hotel room purchased as a joke at Liam's expense, was his only opportunity for shelter? It was early October, and the night-time temperatures in Chicago were beginning to drop. He thought about the clothes Leo had been wearing. Short-sleeved cotton and ripped jeans. Not a jacket in sight.

The more he considered it, the more the fragmented pieces of the evening came together to form a clearer picture. He didn't want to project his own assumptions onto this stranger, but it was obvious something was off. Whatever questions Liam had, whatever pieces of the story were missing, he didn't need all the information to understand what was right in front of him: that this person was in desperate need of a break, and Liam was in a unique position to grant him one.

He knocked when he got back to the room, waiting on the uncertain call of approval before keying himself in. Leo was waiting right where he'd left him, hunched over at the foot of the bed. His posture stiffened when Liam entered.

"It's a little short," Liam prefaced as he held out the wad of cash. Leo unfolded the bills and began counting as soon as they were in his hands. "My friends went out, and this was all they left behind. We can go to an ATM for the rest if you want. Or I can transfer you the money. Do you take—?"

"Cash only," he said without looking up.

"No problem. We'll sort it out." Liam rocked back on his heels, shoving his hands into the pockets of his sweatpants. "Um, so listen. About tonight—and please, feel free to tell me if I'm overstepping or whatever—but, would you. . . maybe like to stay?"

Leo's hand stuttered midway through tucking the money into his front pocket. He looked up at him slowly, wary once again.

"I know I said you should just take the money and go," Liam said, eager as ever to fill the silence with nervous rambling. "But I was just thinking, the room is already paid for, and not on my dime. Why let it go to waste?"

Leo narrowed his eyes, searching. "You want me to stay?"

"Yes? I mean, yes. Only if you want to, though."

After another beat of silence, Leo nodded. "Okay."

"Okay," Liam echoed on the exhale, grateful for some silver lining to this disaster of a night.

Leo stood and pulled the wad of cash out of his pocket again, depositing it onto the nightstand. This was probably Liam's cue to excuse himself, slip out, and let this guy enjoy his night, but the idea of slinking back to his empty hotel room and waiting to be woken up in the middle of the night—*again*—by a drunk Nate and Ben wasn't exactly appealing. It was his fucking *birthday*, after all, and Liam didn't deserve to be miserable either.

He was about to pitch the idea of a joint room service dinner on Nate's tab, but Leo turned back to him and spoke before he had the chance.

"How do you want to do this?" he asked.

Liam stared at him. Leo stared back with the resolve of a man on a gallows march. Then it clicked.

"No!" Liam blurted. "Sorry. No, that... I promise, that was not intended as a proposition. I'm still not... I don't want to..." For a lack of words, he gestured vaguely toward Leo's body, which, justifiably, earned him a blank look. Liam closed his eyes, took a breath, and started again. "I just meant that you could stay here tonight, keep the money, and everybody keeps their hands to themselves. Thoughts?"

"Why?" The word slipped out of Leo like he had been holding it back and couldn't anymore, putting into a single word every suspicious glance and weighted silence.

"Because I know a thing or two about having a terrible day." Liam tried for a smile. "If you don't mind the company, maybe we could both hide out here for a while?"

"And do what?"

Liam crossed the room to the desk in the corner and picked up a laminated menu.

"This could be a good start," he offered. "Are you hungry?"

"I don't have any money," he said, then winced. "I mean, I can't spend. . ." He gestured vaguely toward the cash on the nightstand.

"It's on the room," Liam interrupted before he felt the need to explain further. "They owe us dinner, I think."

Despite his reassurance, Leo ordered the cheapest item on the menu. In turn, Liam ordered a few extra appetizers and hoped his intentions wouldn't be so obvious as to embarrass him.

When the food arrived, they each claimed a separate bed. Liam turned on the TV and tossed the remote to Leo, hoping that a little background noise might lessen the self-consciousness of eating with a stranger. Still, he couldn't help but notice the way Leo shoveled spoonsful of his chicken noodle soup into his mouth, as if it would be snatched out from under him any moment. He felt guilty when Leo caught him staring and slowed his pace.

"Sorry," they said at the same time.

Liam cleared his throat. "When was the last time you ate?"

Leo shrugged one shoulder as he took another bite, slowly this time, keeping his eyes trained on his food. Wordlessly, Liam reached for the platter of wings and fries he had left on the nightstand and held it out. Leo took a single fry from the end of the plate with shaky fingers.

"It's yours," Liam said, leaning forward to place the whole platter on the bed beside Leo.

They were quiet for the rest of their dinner, but Liam found that it wasn't the uncomfortable kind.

"Tell me to leave if you would rather be alone," Liam said when they were finished, gathering the empty containers. "But to be honest, I'm in no hurry to go back."

"It's not my room to kick you out of," Leo said. He must have sensed that wasn't the kind of enthusiastic consent Liam was looking for, because he amended his statement. "I don't mind if you stay."

"Are you sure?"

Leo narrowed his eyes. "You ask a lot of questions."

"I talk when I'm nervous."

"I hadn't noticed."

Liam looked up from the trash bin in time to catch the fleeting wisp of a smile. Despite himself, he mirrored the expression. "Yeah, well, I've never been accused of being subtle."

"Would you mind if I took a shower?"

The sudden change in topic, or perhaps the fact that he was asking Liam permission for such a menial task, caught him off guard.

"Sure," he said. "Yeah. Go for it."

Leo wasted no time climbing off the bed and crossing to the bathroom. He stopped for just a moment as he reached the corner, looking back at Liam as if to say something more. Liam watched him patiently, giving him time to find his words, but after a beat he seemed to decide against it and disappeared into the bathroom.

Alone, Liam collapsed back onto the bed. He hadn't realized just how much tension he was holding in his body until then. When he heard the water splashing against the shower floor, he pushed himself onto his elbows, debating whether or not he should grab his duffel bag from Nathan and Ben's room. Maybe he could get his laptop, give himself something to do. Maybe he could lend Leo something clean to wear out of the shower. The thought had him reaching for his key card.

Much to his relief, Ben and Nathan were still gone for the time it took him to slip in and out.

The shower cut off shortly after Liam returned, but not before he placed a stack of clean sweats just inside the bathroom door, which had notably been left ajar. He tried not to read the gesture as a misplaced invitation, closing it gently behind him before he returned to the bed he'd claimed.

When the bathroom door creaked open again, Liam looked up to find Leo standing in the doorway, a towel wrapped around his waist. He held up the wad of Liam's clothes, looking unsure of himself.

"They're mine." Liam explained, making a conscious effort to keep his eyes above Leo's neckline. "For you."

"I have clothes," Leo said, bristling.

"You don't have to wear them if you don't want to," Liam said. "I just thought it might be nice to have something more comfortable to sleep in." He left out the fact that Leo's clothes were visibly unwashed, and he wanted him to feel refreshed after his shower.

Wordlessly, Leo stepped back into the bathroom. When he reappeared a minute later, he was wearing the sweats.

"Thank you," he told Liam.

"All good."

"For the food, too."

"It's on the room." Liam reminded him.

Leo remained standing in the empty space between the beds and the bathroom, looking uncertain about his next move. When Liam made no effort to direct him, he settled for the empty bed, this time scooting back against the headboard and drawing his legs up to his chest.

"I'm sorry about earlier," Leo said suddenly. "I made you uncomfortable."

"Don't worry about it." Liam opened his mouth, then closed it. "Do you want to talk about it?"

"Why?"

"I don't know." Liam shrugged. "You seemed really freaked out."

He turned away from Liam, facing forward. "I'm fine," he said. Any of the soft sincerity he'd earned retreated again behind an airtight seal. For a minute, Liam thought he might have lost him completely. Then, tentatively, Leo asked, "You said it was your birthday?"

"It is," he said. "Or, it was. I guess it's technically a new day now."

"Sorry you didn't have a good time."

Liam shrugged. "It can only be uphill from soggy-and-naked-in-a-bar-bathroom, right?"

Leo huffed a quiet laugh of agreement. "That place is a shit hole," he said.

"Do you go there often?"

Leo shifted, the bed springs creaking under his weight. "Often enough," he said eventually.

"My friends chose it because it was a gay bar and they wanted to be supportive of my *lifestyle*," Liam emphasized with air quotes. "But I'm pretty sure Nate was making out with some girl from a bachelorette party most of the night."

"Your friends," Leo said, pausing to consider his words. "They seem... different from you."

"I'm sorry for whatever they said to you. They can be assholes."

Leo shot him a sideways glance. "You don't like them?"

"No," Liam said, then quickly backtracked. "I mean, yes. It's not that I don't like them. It's complicated." Liam drew his legs up in a mirror of Leo's position. "Our parents have been friends since we were kids. We were sort of grandfathered into it, but it became apparent early on that we didn't have much in common."

"But you keep them around?"

"I think most people would see it the other way around." Liam laughed, a bitter sound. "For me, they were a survival tactic. Not that it's much of an excuse now, but being in their orbit got me through school mostly unscathed." Liam returned Leo's questioning glance with a knowing look. "I've never been very good at making friends. Being the weird religious kid would have been bad enough without the glass closet I was standing in."

"Religious?" Leo asked.

"Past tense," Liam said. "But I grew up that way. It kind of sticks with you, though. No matter how far you run."

Leo rested his head on top of his knees, his face turned toward Liam. He blinked slowly, exhaustion lining his features. "Yeah. It does."

"You too?" Liam asked.

"Past tense," he echoed. "Pentecostal. Strict. Fire-and-brimstone."

Liam wanted to press for more, but something in the way he spoke, the careful avoidance and carefully chosen words, told him to ease up. "Pop quiz," he said instead. "Heathen to heathen—what was the first gruesome bible story to traumatize you as a child?"

Leo gave a small snort. He thought about it for a second, then a twitch pulled at his mouth. "Jonah and the whale," he said. "For obvious reasons."

Liam tilted his head. "Obvious reasons?"

In an instant, the soft smile was wiped from Leo's expression. "What's yours?" he asked a little too quickly.

"Sodom and Gomorrah." Liam said. "Also, you know, for obvious reasons."

Leo laughed. The sound, low and rough and sudden, seemed to surprise even him. "It's hard to believe you're bad at making friends," Leo said.

"That's because you don't know me," Liam said, horrified to hear that his tone hadn't come out as lightly as intended.

If Leo heard how close he was to cracking, he gave no indication. He only shrugged, eyelids finally losing their battle against sleep.

The drone of the television was the only sound in the room after Leo drifted off. Liam assumed he wouldn't be far behind, given the long night in the rearview, but he was wrong. Minutes strung together into a full hour, his eyes glazed over as infomercials flickered across the screen. His thoughts centered solely on the stranger in the next bed over.

Not so much a stranger anymore.

The conversation about their upbringings had Liam wondering what Leo's childhood might have looked like compared to his own. Perhaps not that different at all, though somewhere along the line their paths had diverged in a significant way. He didn't know Leo's story. He didn't know his past, or even have a good grasp of his present, but the details he had gleaned so far did not add up to something good. It had only taken a couple of minutes with Leo to feel the fear that pulsed beneath every action and word. He was terrified of something or someone, and Liam didn't know what role he was supposed to play in holding that information. Or if he was to play any role at all.

It was closing in on 3 a.m. when Liam finally grabbed the remote from the nightstand and turned off the television. Just as he was about to click off the lamp, though, a small noise from the other bed drew his attention.

Leo was flat on his back, just as he had been the last time Liam looked over, but this time his eyes were wide open, darting across the ceiling as if they were the only part of him capable of movement. His body was rigid, convulsing around each gasp for air, none of which were deep enough to fill his lungs. A particularly strangled sound from his throat prodded Liam into action.

"Leo?" he said, scrambling out of bed. "Hey. Are you awake?"

Liam's sudden proximity must have triggered something, because from the corner of his eye, Liam caught a flash of movement. Leo's hand twitched against the duvet like it was being electrocuted; quick, desperate jerks of motion from a body that was otherwise out of his control.

"Leo?" he tried again, louder, but nothing seemed to break through.

Taking a chance and praying that he wouldn't make things worse, Liam reached up and clasped Leo's hand between both of his own, squeezing tight.

"It's okay," he repeated. "You're okay. You need to wake up. Please, wake up."

Finally, *finally*, Leo's frantic eyes cut over to catch Liam's. The moment of connection seemed to bring him closer to the surface.

"There you go," Liam encouraged. "Can you move? Can you nod your head or something?"

Slowly, as if afraid to find out the answer for himself, Leo jerked his chin up then down. Just once, but it was enough to break whatever paralysis had been cast over him. Leo came back to himself in a rush, scrambling to a half-sitting position against the headboard. Liam rose to his feet and hovered nearby, unsteady and unsure. At his side, his fingers throbbed from the strength and sudden release of Leo's grip.

Leo drew in a few more ragged breaths, though they were beginning to level out, each one pulling deeper than the last.

"Are you okay?" Liam started to ask, but before he could complete the thought, both of Leo's arms shot out toward him, clutching Liam around the middle. Leo buried his face in the material of his shirt, which soaked through with tears in seconds. Liam could feel Leo's whole body shaking. Slowly, carefully, he raised his hands to rest on Leo's back.

There was a snapshot of a moment, frozen in time, where Liam marveled at the path his night had taken: from catching a stranger's eyes in a dirty bathroom mirror, to holding him as he fell to pieces in a hotel bed.

When his back began to ache from the angle, Liam lowered himself onto the edge of the bed, watching for signs of distress. Liam couldn't see the clock from where he sat, but they stayed like that long enough for Leo's panic to subside to a steady baseline.

He had been sure that Leo was asleep again when Liam felt the soft vibration of murmured words against his chest.

"What?" he whispered, blinking back to awareness.

"I said my name isn't Leo." He fell quiet again for so long that Liam thought that was the end of the thought. Then, even more quietly, he added, "It's Jonah."

Liam let his head fall back against the headboard, turning this new piece of information over in his mind.

His lips parted in sudden realization.

Jonah and the whale.

When Liam woke, it was to an empty bed and, upon further inspection, an empty room.

He turned over his shoulder, the sheets falling away as he blinked the sleep from his eyes. He strained to listen for any sound coming from the bathroom, and when he found none, his eyes shifted to the nightstand.

Leo's—*Jonah's*—sparse personal items were gone. In their place was a single sheet of hotel stationery with a note written in pen, resting on top of a neatly-folded pile of borrowed pajamas:

Liam,
Thanks for everything.
Happy birthday.
Your friend,
Jonah

CHAPTER 3
Liam

The car ride home was stuffy with tension and the aftermath of bad decisions. The smell of liquor and misery permeated the air around Ben and Nathan, strong enough still to make Liam grab for the keys before they left. Nathan had refused and climbed into the driver's seat anyway.

Ben was in and out of consciousness in the passenger seat, the window fogging where his breath ghosted from his open mouth. Twice, they'd had to pull over when his dry heaving came a little too close to the real thing. Predictably, Liam took the backseat. He hadn't uttered a word to them all morning, and he had every intention of continuing that trend all the way home.

Jonah's note burned a hole through his pocket, the memory of the night before clinging around him like a dense fog. The domino line of red flags had toppled to a cataclysmic finale, leaving Liam wide awake in the aftermath of Jonah's breakdown. He'd hardly slept at all. He had too many questions. Would he have even been brave enough to ask them, if Jonah had stayed until morning? Would it have been his place? How thin was the line between one person's responsibility to another and a breach of boundaries?

Liam had no business casting himself as anyone's savior, nor projecting the role of a victim onto someone he had known for a single night, but their encounter left him aching for reassurance.

Not for the first time, Liam felt the burn of Nathan's gaze in the rearview mirror. This time, Liam stared back, willing him to be the first to look away. Instead, Nathan's eyes hardened.

"What's your problem, Cassidy?"

Liam turned back toward his window, resolute in his silence.

The car switched lanes so aggressively that Liam had to cling to the door handle to keep from swaying over. Ben let out a groan, bracing himself on the dash.

"Chill, Nate," Ben said.

"No, he's been a broody little bitch all morning. Just say what you want to say."

Anger heated Liam's blood, curling his fingers into fists in his lap. Ben turned halfway in his seat, looking back at him. "Is it because we went out again last night?" he said, looking maybe genuinely remorseful—or maybe it was just the hangover. "I really didn't think you would mind."

"You seemed pretty content with your own company," Nate said. "You're welcome, by the way."

"What am I supposed to be thanking you for?" Liam snapped. "I didn't ask for that, and you didn't even *pay* the guy."

Ben turned to Nathan. "I thought you got cash out."

"Must have forgotten to give it to him before I left." It was the dismissive shrug, the flippancy with which he said it, stark against the memory of Jonah's desperation for the same sum of money that was meaningless to someone like Nathan Scott, that broke Liam's last thread of composure.

"What is wrong with you?" he shouted. "Was this really your idea of a joke? That person you *rented* for me last night is a human being with a life outside of whatever joke you thought you were trying to land."

"I'm failing to see how I'm the bad guy here. He offered a service, I took him up on it. Is this all because I forgot the money? I can send the fucking money."

"This," Liam seethed, "is because you have spent this weekend proving to me how incapable you are of caring about anyone other than yourselves."

"What are you talking about?" Nathan said. "We brought you to the city, we bought your drinks, we paid for the hotel. What more do you want?"

"*Drink*," Liam corrected. "You bought me *one* drink, because that's all the time it took for you to ditch me."

"Hey, you're the one who decided to leave early," Ben interjected, but Liam steamrolled past him.

"And your *father* paid for the hotel," he continued. "You don't get points for being a trust fund baby. How did you even know this kid was a prostitute?"

"What? It was on his profile," Nate said, like it was obvious.

Liam closed his eyes, shaking his head. "What profile?"

"I don't know. Some app for gay guys."

"Why do you have an *'app for gay guys,'* Nathaniel?"

Nate met his eyes in the rear view with a mean smile. "Don't say I never did anything nice for you."

"What are you on about? He was just some guy at the bar."

Nate's expression tightened. "You knew him?"

"I didn't *know* him. I just saw him there before I left."

Nate's eyes moved back to the road. He shrugged. "I don't know what to tell you," he said. "I searched by location, so I guess he was already at the bar when I messaged him."

It took a beat to process, but Liam stopped short when he made the connection; a profile meant a means of contacting Jonah. "Show me," he demanded.

Nathan laughed, a cold, condescending sound. "Planning the second date already?"

"Show me his profile."

"Fuck off."

Moving purely on rage instead of thought, Liam lunged between the gap in the seats and snatched Nathan's phone out of his hand. The auxiliary cord ripped out of the socket, the sharp cut-off of music plunging the car into silence. The car swerved.

"What the fuck!" Nathan yelled at the same time Ben cried out in surprise. A horn blared past them, but Liam was too absorbed in his task to care. He scrolled through the homepage until he found a symbol he recognized, hidden inside a folder, and opened the app. It was easy enough to find him from there: the only message thread Nate had was with "Leo's" account.

Liam held the phone out of Nathan's reach and began typing. He only got partway through a sentence before Nathan's hand closed around his wrist. They wrestled over it, fingers jamming keys at random, but he managed to hit send before the phone was ripped from his grasp.

For a long moment, the only sound in the car was their labored breathing, joined quickly by the roar of acceleration as Nathan blew past the speed limit. Ben was gripping the handle above his seat, looking green in the face.

They all lurched sideways as Nate swerved onto the nearest exit ramp, and again when the car jammed to a stop on the shoulder.

Nathan was out of the car in an instant. Before Liam could process what was happening, he had pulled Liam out and slammed him into the side of the car.

"What the hell is wrong with you?" Nathan's face was red and furious, inches from his own. "Are you out of your mind?" He emphasized the question with a hard shake.

Fueled entirely by adrenaline masquerading as courage, Liam placed both hands against Nathan's chest and shoved. "Send me his profile," he said.

"I'm not doing anything for you now."

There was a short, silent standoff before Liam sprang forward again, grabbing for the phone a second time. It was Ben who interfered, appearing between them and throwing his arms out. "Woah, okay. Everybody needs to relax. Nate, just give Liam his number."

"Are you seriously siding with him? He almost killed us just now."

"Come on," Ben said. "Clearly it's a big deal to him."

"I don't care. If he wants to see his fuck buddy again, he can track him down himself." Nathan checked Liam's shoulder on his way back to the car, slamming the door behind him.

Ben sighed, looking between them, then retreated to the passenger side.

Liam stood still.

"What are you doing?" Ben called out his window. "Get back in the car."

And suddenly Liam was very tired. As he stood on the side of the road, shaking from the crash of adrenaline and a severe lack of sleep, he couldn't help but feel like this was some sort of karmic retribution.

Maybe this was exactly what he deserved for keeping their company all these years. A stronger man might have fought harder, but Liam had done enough fighting for one weekend. He just wanted to go home.

He avoided their eyes as he climbed into the back seat, pulling the hood of his sweatshirt over his head. Nobody spoke for the rest of the drive.

CHAPTER 4
Jonah

Jonah blinked awake when the car rolled to a stop, lifting his head away from the window. The short hair at his temple was cold and damp from the condensation of an unseasonably cold morning. He swiped his hand across the moisture on the glass, and the knot in his stomach pulled tight. They were already at the house.

"Does he know?" Jonah asked, avoiding the driver's eyes peering back at him from the rear-view mirror.

Marcus, a man of few words at the best of times, didn't reply. Jonah knew better than to push, but he couldn't help but ask again. It would be better if he knew what he was heading into.

"Did you tell him already? About the money?"

It wasn't as if he had forgotten about the cash shortage last night, but it seemed that his client had. Jonah had intended to wake him this morning to ask for the remaining sixty dollars, but as he'd hovered over Liam's sleeping form, shifting on his feet, guilt had locked the words in his throat.

Liam hadn't gotten anything from Jonah worth paying for. He hadn't even *wanted* him.

Jonah had stood there for several minutes while the beginnings of sunlight trickled in through the window, while the clock on the nightstand ticked closer to Marcus's arrival, but in the end he hadn't been able to bring himself to do it. It was only when the hotel door had closed behind him, putting a lock between Jonah and his only chance at salvation, that regret had settled in.

"Go," Marcus said. He barely turned in Jonah's direction, just enough to show a sliver of a dark-stubbled jaw. His leather jacket creaked against the seat when he moved. "Being late won't do you any favors."

Jonah opened the door and climbed out onto unsteady legs. Before he closed it behind him, Marcus leaned back in his seat, catching his eye through the opening.

"Eight o'clock tonight," he said. "I'll be outside."

Jonah pushed the door shut and turned down the cracked pavement toward the house.

House was an unseemly term for it, but on a structural level, once upon a time, that had been its intended purpose. The evidence was there in the bones: a two-story graystone building with weathered brick along the flat side, a concrete porch with fist-sized chips in the steps, and a rusted-iron fence along the perimeter. The inside, which might have once housed a single family a century before Jonah was born, had been divided into rental units, and then reconstructed once again a few years ago to accommodate seven dormitory-style rooms. And below them, as Jonah knew well, a stone cellar.

He tried to avoid his reflection in the glass as he slipped in through the front door. There was no masking the groan of the hinges, but he pressed down on the knob out of habit, muffling whatever sound he could. In theory, the house should have been empty. The morning shift at the meal center down the street would have started already, and attendance was mandatory. He stood still in the front hallway for a moment, listening for creaks in the old wood floorboards. Hearing none, he slipped into his room behind the staircase—the only one on the first floor, and the only one built for single occupancy.

Jonah peeled off his shirt, grateful to avoid the communal shower after his hot one the night before, and grabbed his volunteer tee from where it hung on the doorknob. White lettering on the breast pocket spelled out *Shepard's Fold*, and beneath it, in smaller print, *Guiding the Way Home*. He pulled it over his head and discarded his only other shirt on the bed to deal with later.

He broke into a jog outside the house. Marcus was right: being late wouldn't do him any favors.

The kitchen was empty when he entered the meal center through the back entrance. Breakfast hours would be starting soon, and he was sure there was already a line forming out front. Everyone else was already in the cafeteria, setting up.

Jonah slipped one of the last remaining aprons over his head and went to join them.

No one looked up when he entered. By now they were used to Jonah showing up late.

He kept his head down and went to the first empty station he saw, then shook the coffee carafes. They were still empty, so he went to work on starting a fresh batch. As the machine heated up, he scanned the room. No sign of Shepard yet, but it was only a matter of time.

At the serving table, the other residents worked in pairs, scraping pans of eggs, bacon, and potatoes into large aluminum vats. An electric griddle was set up at one end, where someone was flipping pancakes.

A couple of the new boys, whom Jonah only knew vaguely by name, messed around at the other end, flicking spoonsful of food at each other when the coordinators weren't looking. The sharp howl of their laughter echoed across the large room. When one of them turned—a boy with tight, dark curls—Jonah accidentally caught his eye. There was a fleeting moment of uncertainty when Jonah lifted the corner of his mouth in greeting before the boy flattened his expression and turned back to his friend, picking up where they'd left off.

Jonah returned to his work.

He was used to the others keeping their distance. On paper, they were all part of the same program, and they all lived under the same roof, but the rules—spoken and unspoken—weren't the same across the board. Jonah was an outlier. No one knew specifics about what went on behind closed doors, but Shepard's claim on him was like a plague. His mark on Jonah clung to him wherever he went, following him like a dark cloud. He couldn't blame the others for wanting to keep their heads down and their hands clean. For not wanting to make themselves known by association.

He picked up the shakers of sugar and powdered creamer and saw that they were almost empty. A glance at the clock told him he still had a few minutes before the volunteers unlocked the front doors. Jonah grabbed the containers and headed back toward the kitchen.

Grateful for the momentary solitude, Jonah unscrewed the caps and set them on the counter before ducking into the pantry. It was a closet bigger than his room at the house, with shelves of bulk ingredients for the daily meals they served to the community. Jonah yanked the cord that turned on the light and dropped to his knees in the corner. His hand had just closed around the box at the back of the shelf when a voice from the doorway made his limbs go numb.

"There you are." His voice in the confined space was too close, too loud, even if the words were spoken with saccharine softness. "Hiding?"

Jonah's fingers bit into the cardboard hard enough to dent it. He turned around, unwilling to have his back to Shepard for long, and found him leaning against the doorframe. His stance might have seemed relaxed to an outside observer, but Jonah saw it for what it was—an obstruction. He had him cornered.

Ross Shepard wasn't slight in stature. The top of his head missed the doorway by inches, his shoulders broad enough to create a solid barrier between Jonah and the kitchen. Still, he wasn't the kind of person you would be scared of unless you knew to be. Intimidated, maybe, but his friendly affection had kept him high in the public's opinion for years.

From an outsider's perspective, he was the Patron Saint of Wayward Young Men. He had started Shepard's Fold, working closely with Chicago PD and the court system to find rehabilitative alternatives to incarceration for those just above the juvenile age limit. On paper, he was doing a public service—providing free labor for charitable causes and keeping troublemakers off the street. In reality, his position gave him unfettered access to and power over a group of vulnerable young people, year after year. He was careful about which ones he chose to do his under-the-table work. Very few people ever got to know the danger that lay beyond the façade. Jonah was unfortunate enough to be one of them.

"No." Jonah swallowed, keeping his eyes on the box in his hands.

The squeal of hinges preceded a soft click, Shepard sealing them in. Jonah pressed his back against the hard shelf, grounding himself with the pain as footsteps crossed to him, slow and taunting. He came to a stop inches from Jonah's knees, a looming shadow blocking out the light.

"Where's my money?" he asked.

No point in delaying the inevitable. Jonah put the box down and stood, half expecting to be shoved back to his knees, but desperate to lessen their difference in stature. He reached into his pocket and withdrew the cash, handing it over. He kept himself pressed into the corner as Shepard counted.

When he reached the last bill, his fingers stuttered, flipping over the stack as if there would be more hiding underneath. A dangerous, familiar anger stirred beneath the surface as he leaned into Jonah's space.

"And the rest of it?"

Jonah recoiled from the stench of his cologne. "He didn't have it," he said, resenting the break in his voice.

"Are you lying to me?"

"No."

"Empty your pockets."

"I'm not lying," Jonah repeated, scrambling to obey the command. He barely had time to pull his front pockets out before Shepard lost his patience. He grabbed Jonah by the waistband of his jeans and yanked him around, shoving him face-first against the shelf. Rough hands patted him down, digging into his pockets and lingering in places that had Jonah squeezing his eyes shut. When the search came up empty, Shepard released him and took a step back, leaving him frozen in place.

"We'll talk about how you can earn back that money later," he said. "I'm sure we can figure something out."

Jonah, desperate to take that as a dismissal, reached for the box again, but a hand wrapped around his bicep.

"One more thing," Shepard said, deceptively casual. Jonah clenched his jaw and forced himself to meet his eyes. "Tell me your name."

The question stopped him short. "What?"

"When you go out on a call," Shepard emphasized slowly. "What is your name?"

His stomach pooled with icy dread. One thought played on a loop, a haunting incantation: *how does he know?*

There was only one right answer, and somehow there were no right answers at all. Whatever came out of his mouth next would be like stomping on a wide-open bear trap, but his silence wasn't an option.

"Leo," he whispered.

"See, that's what I thought." Shepard's grasp dropped away, leaving a pulsing ache in the shape of his hand. He pulled his phone out of his pocket and flipped it around for Jonah to see. A message illuminated inches from his face.

Jonah, the message said, his own crucifixion in black and white. *Can we talk,* followed by a string of incoherent letters.

The floor dropped out from under him. When the screen clicked to black, Jonah's petrified reflection stared back at him.

"So, what do you think your new friend wants to talk about, *Jonah?*"

His pulse beat wildly in his ears, his throat, his fingertips. Jonah had messed up. He couldn't call it a slip, because it wasn't an accident; he had given away his real name with intention. Liam had been kind to him. He had shown Jonah the sort of thankless compassion he didn't believe in anymore, and Jonah had very little he could repay him with except that small token of good faith. But it was a mistake he would not make again.

"I'm sorry," he whispered.

Any remainder of Shepard's false calm slipped in an instant. He took a step toward him and Jonah stepped back, but not quickly enough to avoid a hand on his throat. His vision went fuzzy at the edges when his head collided with the shelf behind him. Several cans of vegetables crashed to the ground at their feet.

"Do you need a reminder of the rules of our arrangement?" His breath was hot and damp against Jonah's cheek.

Jonah had a plea locked in his throat, but before he could even attempt to voice it, the hand around his windpipe disappeared, leaving him breathless and shaking. It took him a moment to register the sound of movement from the kitchen.

"Jonah?" He recognized the voice of one of the volunteer coordinators, accompanied by a knock on the door. "You okay in there?"

Shepard shot Jonah a look that communicated his wordless threat, then reached for the pantry door. His public persona was a skin he slipped into with effortless ease.

"He's with me, Molly," Shepard said, crouching to pick up the fallen cans for show. "Jonah had a spill, but we're taking care of it."

Molly shifted her gaze to Jonah, who quickly looked away. He waited a few terse seconds, feeling the radiation of Shepard's quiet rage beside him.

"Alright," she said after a moment. "It's filling up out there, kiddo. We need you on the line."

Jonah nodded, not trusting his voice, and watched her retreat through the swinging door and into the chaos of the cafeteria. As soon as she was gone, Shepard shoved the cans against his chest, making him flinch.

"Clean this up," he said. "And come find me after your shift. We aren't done talking."

CHAPTER 5
Jonah

A tinny thump from the dumpster startled him. Jonah looked up to find a rail-thin cat balancing precariously on the edge, its spine curved in a perfect arch. Fresh rain soaked his hair—both the cat's and Jonah's. Even sheltered beneath the overhang of the brick building, the wind carried the spray onto his huddled form, a cool mist that countered the early summer air.

The park was mostly empty at this hour. He didn't know what time it was, but he was pretty sure it fell somewhere in between the late-night partiers closing down bars and the early-shifters swatting at their alarm clocks. Shortly after sunrise, the city park workers would be by to unlock the bathrooms, and Jonah could sneak in to wash up at the sink before anyone else arrived. Until then, at least the building itself provided some meager shelter from the worst of the storm.

"Hey, buddy," Jonah called up to the stray. The cat froze, startled by the presence. "It's okay, I'm not gonna hurt you."

Maybe the cat found something trustworthy in his voice, or maybe, more likely, he was drawn to the half-eaten tuna sandwich on his lap. Either way, he bounded down from the lip of the dumpster in a graceful leap, landing next to Jonah on silent paws. He kept a skeptical distance, his pink nose twitching. Slowly, carefully, Jonah extended a hand, palm up and fingers splayed. After a moment of indecision, the cat took a step closer, stretching his neck forward. The tip of his nose bumped against Jonah's index finger and jerked back.

Jonah looked down at his soggy sandwich, the first meal he'd seen in two days. He swiped his finger along the crust, collecting a bit of tuna. Even more slowly than before, he held the offering out, smiling as the bait worked, drawing the cat closer. After a few hesitant sniffs, a tiny sandpaper tongue poked out, cleaning his finger in three swipes.

The sensation brought back memories he couldn't afford to think about. Because thinking about Mittens was a short jump to thinking about his mother, and how she would scold Jonah for sneaking him scraps of human food, back when Jonah's greatest infraction had been a stray piece of chicken under the table. Back before he had shattered the illusion and brought everything crumbling down.

"You want more?" Jonah asked, already scooping another clump onto his fingertip. "You look hungry."

His suspicions were confirmed when the cat licked his finger clean. He was going in for scoop number three when something changed in the stray's posture, his wiry muscles tensing as he crouched low, ears perked. It took Jonah an extra second to register the sound of approaching footsteps, but by the time he did, his new friend had already disappeared into the darkness. Jonah let the scoop of tuna fall to the pavement.

He wiped his hands against his jeans before taking another bite for himself. Sanitation was a luxury he couldn't currently afford to care about.

The second thump against the dumpster was nowhere near as light as the one before.

Jonah dropped the remaining half of his sandwich onto the wet ground with a start. When he looked up, there were three men—boys, really, not much older than himself—standing over him. Jonah tensed, feeling like he had suddenly switched places with the cat; he was the one on the defensive now, and he had a feeling things wouldn't work out so well for him.

Aside from the incident with his father, Jonah had never been in a physical altercation. Somewhere beyond the panic of trying to wrap his head around what was happening, Jonah found it within himself to be genuinely shocked at just how much it hurt. He could do little else as a means of defense other than curl his body in on itself, trying to shield his more vulnerable parts from the worst of the blows.

It didn't last long, he didn't think. It was hard to tell, when time could be measured only by how much of it he had to suck in a breath between kicks to the stomach. Eventually, he felt a hand reach into his pockets, one by one, presumably looking for something of value that simply didn't exist. A small wad of what Jonah was pretty sure were three crumpled dollar bills was all they could take.

Three dollars was the price he paid for his beating. He only hoped it would be enough to make them leave.

Jonah groaned as a final boot contacted his back, unable to scream when his lungs felt like they were deflated. He curled in tighter on the ground, preparing for another onslaught, when another voice added to the mix.

The newcomer drew closer, and Jonah could make out some sort of shouting through the echo of the falling rain that muffled all other sound around him. Was he dying? Was this what dying felt like? Had they killed him for three dollars and a laugh? He couldn't open his eyes to find out.

Not until a soft hand touched his face.

He jerked back.

"Hey." The voice was quieter now, gentler, dipping into his personal space. "Are you okay?"

Jonah dared to peer up from behind his arms. The man who had chased off his assailants looked to be a bit older than Jonah, kneeling in front of him with shaggy blond hair and a full face of piercings. Something in Jonah's mind supplied that he looked like the type of person that would attract all the wrong attention in his hometown. Someone his own family would turn their noses up at.

"I don't. . ." Jonah swallowed, bringing his hands up to cover his ribs. He winced at the contact. "I don't know."

"Let's get you out of the rain. Do you think you can stand?" He was already extending a hand to help him up, but Jonah shrank back.

"I don't have anywhere to go."

He wasn't sure why he said it, but it was true. Even so, a part of him regretted it when the look of concern turned to something more like pity.

"A hospital, maybe?" His voice was light, as if trying to take the edge off of a humorless situation.

"I don't have money."

"I can't just leave you here." He sighed, tilting his head down at Jonah. It reminded him of the way the cat had looked at him just minutes before. The boy turned over his shoulder, toward the building across the street, where he had presumably come from. Distantly, Jonah could make out the muffled sound of music, loud and heavy. After a moment, he looked back at Jonah, pressing his lips together, then nodded decisively. "Alright. You're coming home with me."

Jonah blinked. "What?"

"Just to get you cleaned up. You don't have to stay," he said, then smiled. "But you're welcome to, for the night. If you want. The rain isn't stopping anytime soon."

Jonah struggled to push himself into a sitting position, using the side of the dumpster as leverage. "You don't even know me," he said. Something about the stranger's kindness was almost as off-putting as it was comforting.

A dazzling smile pulled up the corner of the boy's mouth, tugging a black studded piercing with it. "That's an easy fix," he said, extending his hand again. This time Jonah took it, hesitantly. "My name is Dominic."

He could tell something was off.

An overnight call almost always meant a wealthy client with too much cash to spare, and a ritzy hotel to show for it.

Jonah had come to associate overnights with luxurious high-rises along The Loop, floor-to-ceiling windows overlooking Lake Michigan, and room service that included champagne more expensive than an entire night of Jonah's company.

Tonight, Jonah stood in front of a five-story chain hotel, a faulty vacancy sign flooding him in a neon glow.

"I'll be in the lot near the end of the block at ten tomorrow." Marcus spoke through a crack in the driver's side window, eyes straight ahead.

Jonah nodded and watched the car pull away from the sidewalk.

He kept his eyes low as he passed through the lobby. If the night shift desk attendants ever had any suspicion of what he was, they never said anything, but he had been on the receiving end of enough contemptuous stares to want to avoid them altogether. In the elevator, he uncurled his palm to check the smudged ink for the room number. He hit the fourth-floor button and watched the glowing red light ascend.

The room was at the end of the hall. Jonah approached with soft footsteps, closing his eyes for just a moment. It never did any good to try and predict what the night would hold, but the images flashed before him anyway: faceless figures, fragmented memories of strangers in leather seats and hotel beds. Age-spotted hands extending a glass of champagne, a thumb-sized glass bottle, a leather belt twisted into cuffs. He had come to expect a few constants from client to client, especially those who paid for an entire night of his time, so when he finally knocked on the door the person who answered caught him off guard.

"Liam?" The name surfaced easily in his memory.

"Hi," Liam replied.

A cold, achy feeling settled over him, a mix of dread and disappointment that he should have been immune to. For the week since their first interaction, the memory of that night had been a warm flame he'd kept shielded between his palms, a singular moment of reprieve like a pinhole of light in the dark. Was a week all it took for him to change his mind?

Liam's soft smile crumbled when his eyes fell to Jonah's cheekbone.

"Jonah," he said.

He cringed at the use of his real name. The bruise on his face still throbbed as a reminder of what that piece of information had cost him. He knew by the look on Liam's face that it hadn't faded as much as he hoped.

"What happened?" Liam asked. The concern in his voice carved Jonah's hurt into something sharper.

"Does it matter?"

Liam seemed taken aback. "Of course it matters."

Jonah's shoulders rose in defense. He tossed a look over his shoulder, checking that the hallway was clear.

"Sorry," Liam said. "Do you want to come in?" He stepped aside, allowing Jonah a glimpse into the room behind him.

What choice did he have?

The chill from the air conditioning covered his skin in goosebumps as he entered. He wrapped his arms around himself, rubbing his palms over his arms as Liam closed the door behind them.

"Too cold?" Liam asked, already moving across the room to switch off the unit.

"I'm fine," Jonah answered automatically. He kept his posture rigid, every nerve in his body on high alert. He didn't believe that Liam had any desire to hurt him physically, not really, but he had made the mistake of trusting kind men before. Jonah kept his back to the wall.

Liam hovered several feet away, eyes lingering on the bruise. Jonah waited for further questioning, but it didn't come. Part of him wished Liam would just skip the false niceties and get to what he'd come here for. It would be less of a mind-fuck if he didn't insist on pretending he was the person Jonah had thought he was a week ago.

"What made you change your mind?" Jonah asked, ripping off the bandaid.

Liam stopped picking at his nail and dropped both hands to his sides. "What?"

Jonah crossed his arms over his chest, guarding himself from the look of genuine perplexity. "You were pretty insistent last time that you weren't interested."

Liam's eyes widened. "I'm not," he blurted. "I mean, I'm interested in *you*, obviously, as a person. But not. . . Is that what you thought? Is that why you're upset?"

Jonah felt himself flush, unnerved by his own transparency. "Why am I here?" he asked, ignoring the question.

"Because I couldn't get you out of my head," Liam admitted with a level of candor Jonah hadn't expected. "I don't know. I guess I just needed to see that you were alright, after the way things ended."

Jonah looked away, exposed by the memory of his vulnerability. "I told you, it was just a bad night."

"I get the feeling you might have a lot of those."

"Spare me the savior complex." Jonah was quick to sidestep the dangerous territory he was approaching.

Liam took a step toward him but stopped when Jonah flattened himself to the wall, raising his palms in a gesture of surrender. "Jonah," he said. "Is someone hurting you?"

The blood drained from his face. "No."

"Did someone give you that bruise?"

"Don't ask me that." Jonah pushed off the wall and paced to the other side of the room. He scraped his palms over his face. "Why are you doing this?"

The footsteps on the carpet were slow in their approach, and they didn't come within touching distance. "I want to help you."

"'*Help me*,'" Jonah scoffed.

"If you're being hurt, we can go to the police. I'll go with you."

Jonah turned around. "No. No cops."

"If someone is forcing you, or. . . or coercing you–"

Panic took over before he could even finish his sentence. Jonah turned and beelined for the door, slipping past Liam. He didn't know what he would do, or how he would make up the money he was skipping out on from an overnight call. All he knew was that whatever happened to him tonight would be much better than what had happened to him last time he had been careless enough to—

"Wait." Liam stepped in front of him before he could reach the door. Jonah flinched back, genuinely startled. A flash of regret passed over Liam's expression. "Sorry. I'm not going to hurt you."

"I didn't think you were going to hurt me," Jonah snapped.

"Okay," Liam said, raising his hands. "Listen, no cops. I understand. I'll respect that. Just... Please stay."

Jonah blinked, his chest and shoulders moving with the labor of his breathing. He forced himself to look into Liam's eyes. "What do you want from me?"

"Your company?" he said, a little uncertain. "If that's on the table?"

Jonah eyed him warily.

"I arranged for an overnight stay," Liam continued. "I have the cash this time—all of it, plus what I owe you from last time. Whatever it is you don't want to tell me about, whatever you do outside of here... It just seems like you could use a break."

A *break*.

Jonah stared at the man in front of him, searching his face for all the signs he had missed the last time he'd decided to trust a stranger. Liam had been good to him before, but so had Dominic. There was one distinct difference, however, separating the past from the present. Before, his misplaced trust had cost him everything. This time, he had nothing left to lose.

The realization stung almost as much as the one that followed: that it didn't matter if he trusted Liam or not, because really, there was no choice. Whether Liam's intentions were genuine or not, he was Jonah's client. He had paid for a night—a full one—of Jonah's company, and so Jonah's fate had been decided the minute the door closed behind him. And really, long before that.

CHAPTER 6
Liam

Liam was trying not to stare.

A tense silence filled the space between their beds, a mirror image of the position they had found themselves in last time. He had just barely managed to talk Jonah into staying after a near panic attack, but now that he was here, Liam had no idea what to do.

The past week had been an exercise in tunnel vision. What began as a cursory scroll through various hookup apps quickly bordered on obsession. Liam spent every free minute—during lectures, at stoplights, in the bathroom at work—searching for the elusive Leo/Jonah profile. He narrowed his location search through every nook and cranny of the Greater Chicago Area until he was stopped short by a photo: the bare curve of a shoulder and a buzzed head, faced away from the camera. And underneath: *Leo, 19*.

The rest of the photos were equally clandestine, featuring the same faceless young man in various states of undress, but Liam knew it was him.

He was careful when he reached out. He kept his identity private and gave no indication that they had history, already suspicious that Jonah might not be the only one with access to the messages. The fresh bruises tonight only served to validate that theory.

Liam had been so consumed with the idea of finding him again, of having access to him long enough to check in, that he hadn't formulated much of a plan past that. Get him here, ask if he's okay, offer to get him help. That was the entire checklist, and he had already blown through two and struck out on the third. He supposed the only thing left to do was to offer the same thing he had last time: a safe place to sleep and a hot meal.

A good idea in theory, but he couldn't help but notice that the food in Jonah's lap was mostly untouched. It was a stark contrast from the way he had devoured every bite Liam put in front of him last week. He had been picking at the same piece of chicken for the last several minutes, peeling off small pieces of breading and dropping them onto the plate.

It was obvious he was on edge. There was a certain apprehension in the way Jonah looked at him. Perhaps *watched* was a better word for it, as if he was trying to calculate the exact moment when the rug would be pulled out from under him.

Hesitantly, Liam let his gaze slip over to him, hoping that Jonah wouldn't choose that moment to glance over and catch him gawking. But he barely seemed to notice Liam was there at all. Heavy, half-lidded eyes blinked twice in slow motion as he traced a fingertip idly along the edge of his plate.

Liam cleared his throat. "Is the food okay?"

Jonah blinked again, his head turning slowly, almost mechanically, in Liam's direction. "Hm?"

"Is it. . . Does it taste okay?"

Jonah looked down again, as if only then noticing the shreds of chicken. "It's good," he said, picking off another small piece and placing it in his mouth. "You didn't have to get me anything."

Yes, Liam thought, *I did.*

"Don't worry about it," he dismissed with a wave, his hands feeling heavy and awkward on his wrists.

When it seemed like Jonah had eaten all he was going to, Liam collected their paper plates and boxed up the leftover food, taking extra care to make sure Jonah saw him put it in the mini fridge beneath the television, in case he got hungry later.

"In retrospect, I should have, like, brought something to do. I'm afraid I'm not very good entertainment on my own."

"You don't owe me entertainment."

Liam opened his mouth, then closed it, then opened it again. "Jonah?" he began, waiting until he had his eyes to continue. "Do you want me to leave?"

That seemed to catch him off guard.

"I mean that sincerely," Liam continued. "I won't be offended. I wanted to see you again, and I'm really glad I got the chance to, but I'm not going to force my company on you. If you want, I can give you the money and the room will be yours for the night. I promise not to bother you again. Just say the word."

Jonah stared at him long enough to have Liam shifting under the scrutiny. Finally, he said, "Do you want to leave?"

Liam thought about it. The immediate answer was *no*.

"It's not like I'm missing out on any big Friday night plans," he said, because it felt slightly less pathetic than saying *I'll just be alone if I leave now.*

"Things haven't improved with your friends?" Jonah asked, neatly avoiding the question.

"If we were hanging on by a thread before, last weekend was the snapping point."

"Because of me?"

"Because of them," Liam corrected.

There was a weighty pause. "I'm sorry," Jonah said.

"I told you, it's not your fault."

"No." He shook his head. "For earlier. I didn't mean to come off... I was just..."

"You don't have to explain." Liam sank onto the opposite bed, putting them closer to eye level.

Finally, Jonah said, "Your company isn't so terrible."

Liam laughed, a bright, relieved sound. "C-minus as far as compliments go, but I'll take it."

That got a small smile out of Jonah, which felt like a bigger victory than it should have. Eager to keep the mood light, Liam grabbed the remote and handed it to Jonah. "Should we put on a movie?"

Jonah turned it over in his hands, quiet and considering. "Actually," he said, "can I take a shower again?"

"Oh!" Liam stood, his memory catching up with him. "That reminds me." He crossed to the duffel bag he had tossed in the corner chair and rifled through it until he found what he was looking for. "I meant to offer earlier, but I—" *got distracted by the bruises on your face* "—forgot."

He turned back and presented Jonah with a bundle of clothes: a pair of old, gray sweatpants and a maroon crew-neck sweatshirt.

"I noticed you got chilly last time," he explained when Jonah met him with a carefully blank expression. "And no one should ever have to sleep in jeans."

Jonah shuffled to the edge of the bed, bringing his feet down to touch the floor. He was looking at the pajama set like he was waiting for it to bite him.

"You brought those for me?"

A sudden trickle of heat crept up the back of Liam's neck, filling in the tips of his ears. "Well, I–Yes. You don't have to wear them if you don't want to, I just thought. . ."

"Thank you." Jonah stood and took the clothes from him.

"You're welcome."

Jonah studied him for a few moments longer, holding the clothes to his chest, then made his way to the bathroom.

Liam watched as he disappeared, clicking the door shut behind him.

He woke to the red glow of the alarm clock, glaring back at him with some ungodly hour. Liam rolled onto his side. It took a minute to get his bearings. He squinted into the darkness, narrowing in on the–*shit.* On the very empty bed across from him.

Liam propped up on his elbow, groping blindly at the nightstand for another note left in Jonah's wake. It was past two in the morning; surely he hadn't ventured out on his own at this hour, and if he had, Liam didn't even want to think about the possible implications behind that or what he was doing or–

"Liam?"

His heart jolted a second time. He spun around to find Jonah perched in the oversized windowsill, the curtains pushed back to allow a spill of moonlight. Splayed open on his lap was what appeared to be the standard hotel copy of the Bible.

Relief deflated Liam's chest. "Hi," he said, his voice thick with sleep.

"Sorry. Is the light too much?" Jonah closed the book in his lap. "I can close the curtain." He was already reaching for it when Liam raised a hand to stop him.

"No, no, leave it." He yawned as he pushed himself up to sit against the headboard. "What are you doing up?"

"Couldn't sleep," he said, then hesitated, adding, "I didn't want to risk waking you again. After last time."

It took Liam a moment to connect the dots, and when he did, he hated the shame that he saw in Jonah's reaction. It occurred to him that they hadn't had a chance to talk about what happened.

"Do they happen often?" Liam asked. "The nightmares? Or whatever that was last time?"

"Often enough," he said with a shrug, ever the man of few words.

Liam chewed his lip. "You should try to get some sleep," he said. "It's not a big deal if you end up waking me." *And it's not your fault*, he wanted to add.

Jonah shook his head. "I'm okay. I slept in late today, anyway."

Briefly, Liam thought about trying to push the issue, since he was beginning to think Jonah didn't get much sleep outside of this room, but it occurred to him that maybe the fear of waking Liam wasn't the only thing keeping him up. Who was he to try and force Jonah back into whatever awaited him behind closed eyelids? He wouldn't pry, but that didn't mean he had to leave him alone to suffer, either.

Liam cleared his throat. "You know, I used to have really bad nightmares, too," he said, drawing Jonah's gaze back to him. "Mostly when I was younger. They've gotten a little better with time, but. . . Trust me, this isn't my first midnight rodeo. And I don't know about you—" he swung his leg decisively over the bed "—but if we're in this for the long haul, I'm going to need some caffeine."

"'We?'" Jonah echoed.

Liam flipped on the lamp and padded over to the cheap, plastic coffee maker on top of the dresser. "You want some?" he asked, tearing open the first packet of grounds with his teeth. He conveniently left out the detail that this was almost entirely for Jonah's benefit, as Liam himself detested the taste.

When no answer came, Liam turned back and found him staring at Liam, as if he had offered him his kidney instead of a paper cup of what was sure to be the worst coffee he's ever had.

"Um, sure," Jonah said, blinking back to himself. "Thank you."

"Cream and sugar?"

"Black is fine."

Liam made a face out of his view and went about making the drinks in comfortable silence; one black, and one with as many sugar packets as Liam could discreetly dump into a cup without judgment or permanent organ damage.

When he carried them back to the window, Jonah took his gratefully, cupping it between his palms with another sincere "thank you."

"Mind if I join you?" Liam asked.

Jonah pulled his knees a little tighter to himself in invitation, even though there was plenty of room. Liam settled into his place across from him, resting his back against the opposite side of the window frame. He stared out, following Jonah's gaze. It wasn't as nice as the view from the hotel Nathan's dad had paid for, but there was a smattering of buildings with windows glowing against the night, and a sliver of the crescent moon was visible between two of them, so it wasn't a total bust. He tilted his head, a smile tugging at the corner of his mouth.

"Some light reading?" he asked, gesturing to the book in his lap. "Jonah and the whale, right?"

Jonah ducked his head. "It's been a while since I've read it," he said, fanning through the pages with his thumb.

"The whole thing?" Liam asked. "Like front to back?"

He nodded. "It was a requirement."

"At your church?"

"In my home."

With every crumb of information that he was given about Jonah's life, another chasm of questions opened up. Liam found himself wanting to know everything but afraid to push him too hard, considering the last issue he'd pushed had almost resulted in Jonah bolting from the room before the night could begin.

"Did you grow up around here?" he asked, settling for something more neutral.

Jonah shook his head. "What about you?" he asked instead of elaborating.

"Kind of," Liam said. "Everyone who grew up in the northern suburbs of Illinois likes to claim they're from

Chicago. It sounds way cooler than saying you're from Naperville."

He expected the conversation to lapse into another silence, which would have been fair, considering rural Illinois was hardly a jumping-off place for riveting conversation, but Jonah seemed genuinely interested.

"Did you like it?" he asked. "Or, do you still, I guess?"

Liam rested his head against the window. "It could have been worse. I'm close enough to the city to be on the fringe of having a life. I can commute in every once in a while to audit an art class, or see exhibits when they pop up."

Jonah perked up. "You're an artist?"

"That might be overstating things." Liam chuckled, suddenly self-conscious. "I mess around with a few things. I mostly draw. I paint sometimes, but I need to get better. I take what few art electives my college offers."

"College?"

"Community college," he said, unable to hear the words without the elitist sneer of Nathan and his parents when they'd found out about Liam's plans after high school. "I'd like to save up enough to transfer somewhere with a good art program. New York is the dream, but that is probably all it will ever be."

"Why?"

It didn't escape him that Jonah was keeping all of the attention on Liam with his questions, but he humored him with a sardonic smile.

"The good ones are expensive," he said. "The diner I work at pays decent, but not *that* decent. And my parents aren't willing to shell out money for an art degree, but they make too much for me to qualify for much financial aid. It's. . ." The words died on his tongue as he glanced up at Jonah and realized, horrified, how privileged he must sound. Complaining about going to community college and whining about how his parents made too much money.

Several iterations of an uncomfortable apology tangled in his mouth, but Jonah spoke before he could get any of them out.

"Will you draw me something?"

Liam blinked at him. Personal experience and a lifetime of poor self-esteem made him assume Jonah was joking. He gave an obliging smile, but when Jonah didn't laugh it off, Liam asked, "You really want me to?"

"Only if you want."

He glanced at his duffle. "I didn't bring my stuff," he said, still half-certain it was a joke. "I usually have my sketchbook with me."

Jonah looked around, tapping his fingers where they rested on his knees, then slid off the window. He returned a moment later with the small hotel-branded notepad and a pen. "Your canvas," he said, presenting it.

Liam's smile relaxed into something genuine. "Okay," he agreed.

Satisfied, Jonah climbed back into his post, taking a sip of his coffee while Liam got to work on his masterpiece.

"What are you drawing me?" he asked.

"It's a surprise."

He began with hesitant pen strokes, as he did almost every time he tried to create something with a specific audience in mind. But once the idea took shape, Liam fell into a familiar rhythm, only glancing up every so often for reference.

Maybe it was the lack of direct attention now that Liam had a task at hand, but something in Jonah's demeanor seemed to loosen as the night went on. Slowly, he began to talk. It was nothing groundbreaking; he was still careful about what he revealed, but Liam pocketed every shared tidbit like something precious. He learned that Jonah liked to run, and that he had played soccer and ran track in school. He learned that he grew up somewhere in the Midwest, though he did not specify where, and Liam didn't ask. He started to tell Liam about a childhood cat he'd grown up with, but there was a somber shift in his tone that made him retreat quickly. Liam was happy to change the subject with a timely drop of his pen.

"Done," he announced.

Jonah sat up straighter, visibly thankful for the distraction. "Let's see it."

Strangely nervous, Liam tore off the top page of the notepad and handed it over.

Jonah stared down at it for a full three seconds. "It's Jonah and the whale," he said, nearly a whisper, then looked up at Liam. "You drew me."

"And a whale," Liam added, shifting under the attention.

"*On top* of a whale," Jonah amended, turning the paper over to display the cartoonish depiction of Jonah saddled on a whale's back, complete with a cowboy hat and lasso. "Have you read the book, Liam? I'm pretty sure this story is about him getting *swallowed* by the whale."

"No," Liam said. "The story is about him getting *out*."

Jonah looked at him and Liam looked quickly away. They were quiet for a few long seconds. Finally, Jonah smiled and shook his head.

"I definitely missed the part where he rides the whale into the sunset afterward."

"It's all there." Liam shrugged. "In the subtext."

The first thing Liam did when his eyes opened to a sliver of daybreak peeking through the curtains was check to make sure Jonah was still there. A breath of relief rushed out of him when he saw him, already awake and propped against the headboard.

"Good morning," Liam croaked, pulling his arms up into a stretch. Jonah blinked, waking from whatever trance he was in to smile back at him.

"Morning."

At the foot of the bed, the borrowed pajamas were folded into a pile again. Thankfully, not accompanied by a cryptic goodbye note this time. Still, Liam's heart sank a bit.

"I have to leave soon," Jonah confirmed. There was a heaviness behind the words.

"Can I get you breakfast before you go?" Liam asked. "The hotel doesn't offer it, but I think there was a diner close by."

Jonah shook his head. "I can't."

Liam wanted to press for answers. He didn't.

"I wanted to wait until you were awake so I could say goodbye," Jonah said. Then, with a rueful smile, added, "This time."

Liam pushed himself up, swinging his legs off the bed. "Can I see you again?" he asked, emboldened by the idea of Jonah walking out of this hotel room and back to the person who gave him that bruise.

Jonah stood and paced away from the bed, suddenly interested in a loose thread at the hem of his shirt. "You can message me to set something up."

"I meant. . ." Liam tracked him with his eyes, treading carefully. "Maybe somewhere outside of a hotel room?"

"I don't really have nights off."

"What about the daytime?" Liam didn't care that he sounded desperate. "I can be flexible on time."

Jonah still wouldn't look at him. He had his lip pulled between his teeth, grinding it back and forth with enough force to look painful. "It's not really that simple," he said. "Look, it's not that I don't want to."

"I can pay for another night," Liam blurted, and Jonah looked up, eyes wide. "Not tonight, I mean. I'll have to wait until I get paid again, but. . . I could swing it again next week. Same day?"

Jonah opened his mouth and closed it a few times, looking genuinely lost. "That's a lot of money," he said eventually. "You're not even getting anything out of it."

"That's not true. Just because I'm not. . ." He cleared his throat, pretending like he couldn't feel himself turning red. "I like spending time with you." He paused, deliberating how much he wanted to say out loud about the feelings he still couldn't pin down himself. "I don't know how permanent of an arrangement we can make this, but for now, I'd like to see you again. I wouldn't have offered if I didn't think it was feasible." Which wasn't precisely true, but the sentiment remained.

Jonah shook his head. "You're too nice to me," he finally said.

"I think you're overstating my generosity," Liam said. "Or underestimating my selfishness."

Jonah looked away, and Liam's grin faded.

"Do you want to?" Liam asked after a moment. "If you really don't, I won't press. I promise."

A nervous energy buzzed in the air while he waited for his reply.

"I want to," Jonah said. "I just don't think it's fair to you."

"Let me decide that."

"I need to get going," Jonah said again, gesturing toward the door.

Liam stood as well. "Can I at least drive you somewhere?"

He brought a hand up to scratch at the back of his neck, getting shifty in the way he did when Liam asked too many questions.

"I have a ride," he said. "He'll be outside soon. I shouldn't make him wait."

Liam walked him to the door in a desperate attempt to hold onto him for just a few more moments. The two of them hesitated as he reached for the handle. Maybe Liam wasn't the only one trying to hold off the inevitable.

"See you Friday?" Liam said.

Jonah nodded. "Message me to set it up," he repeated.

"It isn't you, is it?" Liam asked before he could stop himself. Jonah froze, his back turned to him. "The person on the other end of those messages? Making the arrangements? It isn't you."

Jonah was preternaturally still, like a machine whose kill switch had just been activated. Liam waited, half expecting for him to call the whole thing off, to walk out of there and demand that Liam never contact him again. Instead, he turned over his shoulder before he opened the door and said, "See you Friday."

In the lingering silence of his departure, Liam was pretty sure he had his answer.

CHAPTER 7
Jonah

The water in the showers never got warmer than room temperature, to say nothing of what happened during the colder months. Jonah braced himself for the sting but still flinched at the first spray against his chest.

The house didn't have private bathrooms. Instead, there were six shower stalls and three toilets in a single room on the second floor. Privacy, in general, was a forbidden luxury for most of the residents. Too risky, given their histories.

On the day Jonah moved in, Ross Shepard had explained the rules in black and white: No locked doors, no broken curfews, you fulfill your community shifts, you do as you're told, and your papers get signed. You break the rules, you get a one-way ticket to a cell. It was a privilege to be trusted with a second chance, and the residents of Shepard's Fold were expected to act accordingly.

This wasn't freedom, he had drilled into their heads from day one. It was the chance to prove you've earned it.

Most of the residents were recent parolees, juvenile age-outs, and guys with minor drug charges. No violent offenders permitted. A select few, like Jonah, were here as a court-mandated alternative to serving time. They took a community-service-based approach to rehabilitation, requiring all residents to complete daily shifts at the local soup kitchen, hand out coats in the winter, clean up litter from highway roadsides. Their goal wasn't to punish, but to reform.

Ross Shepard was the house supervisor. He had the posture of a military commander and wore the silver tags around his neck to match, he smelled perpetually of cigarette smoke and stale coffee, and he had taken an interest in Jonah right away.

For a while, he had kept a close eye. Jonah watched him watching him, but he credited the attention to his newcomer status. It made sense, he supposed, that he would want to know if the new kid was going to be a problem. Jonah had no intention of being one. His plan was to lay low and avoid interactions of any kind, which was made all the simpler by having his own room. It was secluded from the rest, situated in the downstairs hallway, the only resident dorm on the ground floor. He had thought that was a good thing, once. Then he'd learned that the isolation was an intentional move.

Jonah had only been in the house for a week when Shepard came into his room with a threat disguised as an offer. He must have possessed the predator instinct for scoping out the perfect opportunity, catching Jonah at his lowest and weakest. Never before had he found himself in such a perilous position, desperate and terrified, with no one in his corner. Ross Shepard had known that. He smelled blood in the water, and he struck.

By the time Jonah had realized just how far beneath the surface he'd been pulled, he was too deep to swim out of it. It had only been a steady sink from there.

Jonah was accustomed to the lack of privacy, but he still stiffened at the sound of the bathroom door opening and closing behind him. The rest of the guys were out on a highway cleanup assignment—one that Jonah was conveniently excused from, for a meeting with a caseworker who didn't actually exist. It was in these windows of time where Shepard found ways to slip, undetected, into Jonah's space.

He tensed but refused to turn around. Feigning ignorance would only delay the inevitable, but if that was all Jonah had, he would cling to those few seconds.

Shepard came to a stop just outside his stall. Jonah felt his gaze on his back like jagged fingernails, scraping down, drawing blood.

"Another overnight request." His voice made Jonah jump despite himself. "Seems like someone has a happy customer."

Jonah pushed his face under the cold spray, hoping for the sharp bite to ground him, but his skin was nearly numb to it by then. All he got was a dull ache.

"Think it will be a regular thing?"

"I don't know," Jonah said honestly.

Shepard clicked his tongue. "Not very confident, are we?"

Jonah cut off the spray, dropping them into an echoey silence. When he reached for the towel hanging on the hook, Shepard snatched it away, holding it just out of reach. Jonah bit down on his cheek until he tasted blood.

"Come and get it," Shepard whispered.

Shivering and exposed, Jonah stood with his arms wrapped around him for a few endless moments, his eyes fixed on the grimy tile beneath his feet. As he forced himself to take a step forward, the bathroom door opened again. Both heads turned in the direction of the noise to find Shepard's hired muscle peeking in.

"What?" Shepard snapped.

"Traffic's backed up on 90," Marcus said. "We need to head out early."

"Right now?"

Marcus checked his watch. "ETA is already pushed twenty minutes."

Jonah curled his body toward the wall for some semblance of coverage. He expected Marcus to close the door and leave them to it, but he stood there long enough for Shepard to give in and take a step back.

"You heard the man." He threw the towel at Jonah, who scrambled to catch it before it hit the wet floor. "Get dressed."

He left, brushing past Marcus, who stood there a few seconds longer. He kept his eyes averted when he said, "I'll be in the car."

CHAPTER 8
Jonah

The thump of the bass was so heavy it reverberated through Jonah's ribcage, his heart beating in time with the music like he was a part of it. A red light pulsed from the ceiling, feeding him glimpses of the room; a sea of sweaty bodies through a hazy, neon glow, drinks raised and spilling over tangles of limbs. The borrowed shirt clung to him like a second skin, tight mesh cropped at the midriff. Jonah remembered feeling self-conscious when he put it on, but he couldn't remember why.

Around the room, eyes followed him, watched him, entranced by the movement of his body as he lost himself in the warmth of the alcohol and the safety of the low lighting. There was no one in particular who stood out, just a sea of blurred faces that churned with unified desire. Jonah had never been looked at like that before. Their attention, distant and anonymous, was intoxicating.

Hands found his waist from behind. Familiar chapped lips dragged over his neck. He let his head fall back against Dominic's shoulder, hips and legs and torsos moving together like one body. A laugh bubbled out of Jonah. It all just felt so good.

For the first time in his life, Jonah felt alive.

Sweat covered every inch of his body, hair clinging to his face in sticky, wet clumps, but Dominic didn't seem to mind, because he was just as hot and sticky in the most appealing way. Of everyone who looked at Jonah tonight like they wanted a taste, he only had eyes for one. Overtaken by a rush of desire and affection, Jonah pushed his hips back against him, rewarded with the graze of teeth over his neck.

"You feel so good," Dom murmured against his ear, making goosebumps erupt over his flesh. He spun Jonah so that they faced each other, capturing him in an eager kiss. Jonah wound his arms around Dominic's neck, only in part to steady his weight as the room spun around them.

"I feel good," Jonah echoed. He could almost make out the sound of Dom's laughter over the noise.

"I have something for you." He drew Jonah in closer and leaned forward to whisper it against his ear, making him shudder at the heightened sensation. Everything felt so much more like this, so much better, and he didn't ever want it to ever stop.

A finger tapped twice on his bottom lip and Jonah opened his eyes. There was a tiny pill pinched between Dom's fingers, presented inches from his face. Jonah had to blink a few times to bring it into focus.

"One for each of us," Dom said. He popped one into his mouth from his other hand and swallowed it dry, then gestured for Jonah to take the other. For the briefest moment, a sharp peck of clarity

tapped the foggy glass of Jonah's intoxication, some buried-deep instinct trying to call attention to a bad idea. An old, familiar guilt roiled in his stomach. Conviction, his pastor would have called it.

But that wasn't who Jonah was anymore. He had left that life behind, or it had left him behind. Either way, he wasn't bound by the laws that had dictated most of his life.

But if Jonah had already crossed about a thousand lines he never thought he would, this particular temptation felt like a line too far.

"I don't know," Jonah said, leaning in close so Dom could hear him.

He was already having fun. It was perfect. He would have liked to have stayed just how he was, but Dom was smiling so close to him, little kisses peppering his jaw, his neck, and it felt so nice. Dom was so nice.

He wouldn't do anything to bring Jonah harm. He had been the one to take him in. He had been the one to bring him home and clean him up, give him a place to sleep for a few nights that had turned into weeks. Dominic gave him clothes to wear and the first sense of trust he had been able to feel since climbing onto the night bus just outside of Indianapolis almost a month earlier.

Besides, Dom had taken the pill, too. It couldn't be that bad.

"Please?" Dom purred against his skin. Jonah could feel the vibration more than he could hear the word. "I don't want to come down yet. I want to feel like this with you for as long as I can."

Somehow, in the moment, Jonah couldn't argue. He opened his mouth.

A finger pushed gently between his lips, placing the pill on his tongue. Dom closed his mouth over Jonah's and kissed him, hard and deep, until he swallowed.

The night got harder to track after that.

Time was fragmented, jumping and skipping like a broken tape, moving in slow motion one moment and careening into freefall the next.

At some point, the scene changed around him. They were still at the club, the bass pounding in muffled staccato on the other side of a wall, but it was quieter. Emptier. He could tell, even without opening his eyes, that it was darker, too.

"They're looking at you." *It took a moment to realize the voice came from Dominic, who was pressed against his back. Jonah was sprawled on his lap, a sticky, vinyl sofa beneath them.*

"Who?" *The word slipped out of him, dazed and slow.*

"Everyone."

Jonah opened his eyes and saw that Dominic was right. Eyes peered at him from the darkness, a silent audience washed in the glow of a single strip of red light from above. The men from the dance floor—or were these different men? He couldn't tell.

"You could have anyone you wanted tonight," *Dominic told him.*

"I want you." *It came without thought, without reservation, but Dominic was laughing. The sound was easier to hear away from the crowd.*

"I get you for free," *he said.* "They're just easy money."

Jonah didn't understand. Not at first. The connection clicked when he remembered the sparse details of Dominic's past that he had shared. The way he had gotten by in the city when he was Jonah's age. He started to sit up, sobered slightly by the suggestion, but Dominic shushed him with a flat hand against his stomach, gently pulling him back.

"Shh, it's okay. You don't have to do anything you don't want to do," he said, and Jonah relaxed, mollified by the promise. "But you haven't had much luck with work, and you're good at this. I know from experience," he added with a kiss to his cheek.

Jonah laughed, heady and charmed. "I don't know," he said for the second time that night. *I don't know, I don't know, I don't know.* He was beginning to realize there was a lot he didn't know about the world.

"Isn't it illegal?" Jonah asked, feeling younger than he was.

Dominic smiled against his neck. "Do they look like cops to you?"

Jonah thought—but did not say—wouldn't that be the point? "Do you want me to?" he asked.

"I don't mind sharing."

"But do you *want* me to?"

He was quiet for a long time. Jonah began to drift again, but he was pulled back to earth when Dominic said, "It might be nice to have some help." Jonah twisted around so that he could look at him, his expression pinched. "With bills. Rent." Jonah's guilt must have shown on his face, because Dominic squeezed him around his middle. "You know I love having you. It would just help me out a little."

Jonah's stomach was splitting open. Maybe it was the pill. It had to be the pill. His body couldn't really be pulled apart at the middle by the gnawing feeling inside of him.

"I could try," he said quietly. Then, spurred by Dom's easy affection, repeated it. "I could try."

As if beckoned by his acquiescence, quiet as it was, another presence appeared at their side. His weight dipped the couch beside them, jostling Jonah's body.

"He your boyfriend?" the man asked, little more than a shadow silhouetted in red.

Dominic's hand came up to push away the sweat-damp hair from his forehead.

"Don't be shy, Jonah. Say hello."

"Hello."

Liam was smiling when he opened the door. Jonah let out a breath. A cynical part of him had been expecting anyone else, preparing for the possibility that Liam had come to his senses and decided to leave his brief encounters with Jonah in the past. But there he was.

"Hi," Jonah said.

Inside the room, the same stack of clothes Jonah had borrowed the week before were folded on the corner of the bed. On top of them were two paperback books, both worn and tattered at the edges. There was a takeout container on the dresser with a logo he didn't recognize on the side. The smell made his empty stomach roll with hunger.

"I came straight from work," Liam explained when he saw him looking. "We get a comped meal with every shift. I hope you like burgers."

"And these?" Jonah asked, gesturing to the books.

Liam flushed, his pale skin making the color stand out. "Don't feel obligated to read them," he said. "I thought you might get bored of just watching TV and blaspheming our former religions all the time. I brought a couple of my favorites from home."

Jonah picked up the thicker of the two novels, turning it over in his hands. He skimmed the synopsis on the back, thumbing over the glossy paperback. "Thank you," he said.

"No problem." There was a brief lapse before Liam cleared his throat. He turned, heaving a large backpack onto his designated bed. "I also wanted you to have something to do because I'm going to be pretty bogged down tonight." He unloaded two textbooks and a notebook onto the bed. "School stuff," he said, glancing up at him. "I have exams coming up, but I've been picking up so many extra shifts at the diner that I haven't done any of the prep for them."

A cold weight settled in Jonah's chest. Overnight calls weren't cheap, and the rooms couldn't be either, even the more modest ones they found themselves in. Jonah didn't know much about Liam's financial situation, or about his life in general beyond the walls of these weekly hotel rooms, but it seemed like a fair assumption that the 'extra shifts' were going toward his visits with Jonah.

If Liam noticed his mood drop, he didn't say anything. Instead, he settled into his bed and cracked open a textbook.

"I ate before I came, so feel free to dig in," he said. "Or you can shower first, if you want. I'll be here, suffering."

Jonah looked at the box of food, then to the pile of clothes, opting for the latter. Suddenly, he didn't have much of an appetite.

They had been working in silence for at least an hour—Jonah making headway on one of the novels and Liam scratching away at his notes—when a loud *thunk* startled him. He looked over to see Liam had thrown his head back against the wooden headboard, hands over his face.

Jonah closed the book, using a finger to keep his place. From behind his hands, Liam said, "I'm dropping out of school."

"Seems hasty," Jonah said. "What are you working on?"

"Math. A required credit. No one would take this of their own volition."

The ugly stab of jealousy snuck up on him before Jonah could quash it. It was easy enough, most of the time, to push away thoughts of what could have been. The image of an acceptance letter pinned to his fridge, his parents smiling. *What-ifs* were parasitic; they sucked your energy dry. Jonah had gotten good—better, at least—at rationing his mental energy and steering himself away from this kind of useless self-torment.

It was harder to do with Liam around.

At his age, Jonah should have been sleeping in a lofted dorm bed at whatever state school would take him, instead of bouncing between the prison of Shepard's house and a series of nondescript hotel rooms. He would have given anything to be drowning in homework, his largest concern an impending exam or a heavy course load. That was the way it was supposed to be. Those were the kind of stressors people his age were supposed to have.

But of the two people in the room, Liam was hardly the one at fault for that.

"What kind of math is it?" Jonah asked.

"Calculus," Liam said. "Sorry, I won't bore you with this. I was just complaining into the void. Don't let me keep you from your book."

"*Your* book," Jonah corrected, swinging his legs off the side of the bed. "Can I help?"

Liam raised an eyebrow, looking at him in a way that Jonah couldn't quite decipher. "Really?" He shrugged when Jonah nodded. "Sure, have at it." He plucked the worksheet closest to his bent knee from the pile, handing it across the gap between the beds.

Jonah leaned over and took it, bringing it closer to inspect. He scanned over the loopy scrawl of Liam's pencil marks, mentally trying to work through the problem. He couldn't help but smile at the sheer number of smudged eraser marks and scribbled out numbers that littered the page, as well as the distracted doodles he had done off in the margins. After a moment of deliberation, he looked up at Liam, whose hair was tousled and unruly from the stress.

"You kind of suck at this," Jonah said.

Liam's mouth popped open in feigned offense. "I was very transparent about my shortcomings. You don't have to rub it in."

"I'm mostly kidding," Jonah said with a smirk.

"*Mostly*," Liam echoed. He rubbed the heels of his palms over his eyes. "Honestly, maybe I should just bomb the exams. At the very least, it will serve as an 'I told you so' to my advisor, and maybe I'll be able to take my *Math for Idiots* class next semester as God intended."

"You're not an idiot," Jonah said. "You actually were close on a couple of these, you just missed a step, and it threw off the rest of your work. Here. Can I borrow your pencil?"

"Please," Liam insisted, clicking his mechanical pencil up a couple notches before handing it over.

Without thinking about it, Jonah sank down next to him on the bed, propping his leg up to supply a writing surface.

He scribbled his additions alongside Liam's work as he talked him through the equation, small, jagged streaks of graphite stark against the smooth, curvy penmanship. It was kind of amazing, even to him, that he was able to slip into the process like an old sweater after all this time, the feel of a rapidly scratching pencil as right as rain between his fingers.

Numbers had always made sense to him. He couldn't deny the tiny thrill he felt at the realization that this part of him hadn't withered completely with time, the way so many others had.

When he finished, after plugging in the answer to check his work, Jonah breathed a long exhale and circled the new number, flashing it toward Liam with a smile.

"See how I got that?"

"I absolutely did not."

Jonah's mouth quirked, and he got to work on the next problem.

Somehow, inexplicably, the distance between them shrank little by little over the course of an hour. By the end, they were side by side against the headboard, the knees of their pajama pants brushing just slightly as they balanced the notebook between them. At some point, Liam had retrieved the leftovers from Jonah's dinner from the mini fridge, rewarding himself with a cold fry every time he got a question right on his own.

That became a game within itself, as Liam, desperate for any short distraction from the math, challenged Jonah to try and toss them into his mouth. They usually missed, and one time he'd thrown it a bit too aggressively, resulting in a retching gag as the fry harpooned the back of Liam's throat, but that only made them laugh harder.

It was the most like his age Jonah had felt in a long time.

CHAPTER 9
Liam

"Hot date tonight?"

Liam was counting out his cash tips just outside the back entrance when Kim stepped out for her smoke break.

"What?" he said, folding the bills into a thick stack. It was busy, even by Friday standards, and a couple of big tippers had ensured a half-decent dinner for him and Jonah tonight. Maybe they could try someplace new. He found himself wishing, not for the first time, that he had some way of texting him directly.

"Don't *what* me," she said, shielding her lighter against the cold wind. "I see you're all dolled up."

He shot her a dry look. "We're wearing the same uniform."

"Mhm." She smiled around the cigarette between her teeth, giving him a once-over. "And the clean shave?"

"I don't like scruff."

"And the sudden interest in hair gel?"

"It's mousse," he shot back. "Aren't you the one who told me I should learn how to work with my natural curls?"

"Right," she said. "Well, since you're not busy tonight, a few of us are going to Stanley's after close. Come out with us for once."

"I didn't say I don't have plans," he said. "I'm going to see a friend in the city."

"Oh, a friend?"

"Yes, a *friend*."

"Good," she said. "You need to hang out with someone other than those twin behemoths you're always dragging around."

"I haven't spoken to them in weeks," he said. "So I can't imagine they'll be coming around any time soon."

"What did they do?"

Oh, you know. Took me to the city, abandoned me on my birthday, set me up with a prostitute who may or may not be being coerced, whom I am now meeting up with, platonically, on a weekly basis.

Liam shook his head. "I've just been busy."

Kim narrowed her eyes.

"What?" he asked.

"I know you've been busy," she said. "You've been picking up shifts left and right. You worked three doubles last week. You were here on Wednesday during breakfast, when I know for a fact you have class."

"It was canceled," he lied.

"As your manager," she said, ignoring him, "I appreciate the initiative. As your friend, I need to know you're not spiraling."

"I'm not spiraling," he promised.

"Liam. You've been here since you were sixteen. I know what it looks like when things are getting bad for you. Is that what's happening?"

He was shaking his head before she finished the sentence. "No," he insisted. He didn't want to talk about that. He didn't like the reminder that the people in his life held the teenage version of himself in their memory. If he could wipe it from his own, he would. "No, Kim. I'm fine. Just trying to save up."

She stubbed out her cigarette on the bottom of her shoe. "You know you can tell me if that changes, right?"

He nodded, eyes on the ground.

"Hey," she said, waiting for him to look at her before she continued. "Have fun tonight. You deserve it."

Liam's hands were nearly vibrating by the time he got behind the wheel, though he told himself it was in anticipation of the night ahead, and not a result of the conversation behind him. He tucked his tips away in his wallet, turned on the radio, and let the muscle memory pull him toward the city.

CHAPTER 10
Liam

FRIDAY, OCTOBER 25TH

Liam looked up at the sound of soft snoring coming from the bed next to him. He pushed his glasses up his nose, squinting away from the harsh light of the laptop.

Jonah had fallen asleep reading. His most recent borrowed book was propped open against his chest, his head tilted back against the headboard. Liam didn't dare put a name to the feeling in his chest at the sight of him, warm and comfortable enough to sleep in Liam's borrowed sweatshirt, when, only recently, it had been a challenge to convince Jonah to fall asleep in his presence at all.

Some selfish part of him thought, or maybe just hoped, that it was a sign of trust. That Jonah finally felt safe with him. Whatever the reason, Liam was glad for it.

He reached over and flicked off the small light that hung over Jonah's bed, watching the darkness fall over his sleeping face. Then he adjusted his laptop back into position on his legs, ready to buckle down again and crank out the rest of his

English Lit paper, but he found his eyes pulling almost magnetically back across the room.

After a moment of deliberation, Liam set his computer off to the side, his knees and ankles cracking as he unfolded them. Carefully, quietly, he crossed the gap between the beds, hesitating before gently pulling the book away from his chest. Slender fingers that just barely poked out of the sleeves of the sweatshirt fell lightly against his chest. Liam dog-eared the page he'd left off on, setting the book on the nightstand.

He considered him for a moment, standing back with his hands on his hips. Jonah's lips were parted just enough for a light whistle to escape with each steady exhale, the muscles in his face completely at ease for what had to have been the first time since Liam met him.

There wasn't much he could do to adjust his position without risking waking him, no matter how stiff his posture looked propped against the headboard, but he could try to make him as comfortable as possible. Watching for any signs of stirring, Liam pulled the edge of the thick white comforter up as far as it would go, laying it gently over the place where Jonah's fingers rested against his sternum. Liam's hands lingered for just an extra moment before he pulled back.

He crawled back into his own bed and propped the laptop back onto his knees, checking the word count at the bottom of the window. He was still a thousand words short on his essay, and he could feel his eyelids drooping, but there was something else pulling at him.

Between the burnout of work and school, it had been months since Liam felt inspired enough to start a new project. But something about that moment—about watching Jonah sleep in the half-light of the room—lit a spark.

Liam closed his laptop and tossed it aside, reaching instead for the sketchpad in his backpack. Grabbing the first pencil he could find, Liam began to draw.

CHAPTER 11
Jonah

His hands were shaking as the officer placed the receiver in his palm.

"What's the number?" the man asked. He wasn't the same one who had been in the motel room with Jonah. Jonah hadn't seen him since he put the handcuffs on and dropped him in the back of the police car.

He closed his eyes and tried to get a grip on the panic that was clawing up his chest, into his throat. This couldn't be happening. Dominic told him this wouldn't happen. It was a dream. The whole thing, everything that happened from the moment he'd stepped off the bus at Union Station was just some horrible nightmare.

"The number," the officer asked again, patience thinning. Jonah flinched.

For a wild, surreal moment, he considered calling his mom. The numbers were there at the tip of his tongue, the first he had ever memorized and knew by heart even still. It was only the thought of her rejection, the probability that she would hear his desperate voice on the end of the line and hang up the phone, that stopped him.

Instead, he asked the officer to check his phone for Dominic's phone number. It was the only one he had saved since Dom bought it for him a month earlier.

His sweaty fingers slipped over the plastic as a voice in his ear told him that this call was being monitored and recorded. It rang three times before Dominic picked up.

"Hello?" He sounded worried. The sound of his voice tamped down on some of the fear that tried to close Jonah's throat.

"I need your help," Jonah said.

Jonah was careful as he told him where he was and what had happened, mindful of whoever might be listening to this call. He left out any details that would have implicated Dominic for his part in it, omitting the part where Dominic had been the one to set up the meeting with the man who turned out to be an undercover cop.

Dominic was quiet for so long that Jonah thought he hung up. Then he said, "Okay. It's going to be okay." Nothing in his tone aligned with the words, but Jonah nodded, desperate for some hope to cling to. "Jonah, I know someone. Okay? I know a guy who can help you out. He can. . . I'll call him, and he can talk to your lawyer, and they can work it out."

"What guy?" Jonah shook his head. "I don't have a lawyer."

Dominic made a sound that was almost a sigh. "They have to give you a lawyer if you ask for one, Jonah. You need to ask for one."

There was still so much he didn't know.

"Who is this guy?" he asked again. "What can he do?"

"He's just. . ." Dominic paused. "He's someone I used to know. He runs a program here in the city. For young guys, your age.

Keeping them clean, off the streets, out of jail. They work with the legal system. They might be able to get you a deal."

"I can't go to prison." *Even the words, as they trembled out of him, sounded like something from a far-off nightmare.*

"I'll call him," Dominic promised. "Okay? He. . ." There was a long, crackling pause. "He helped me once before. Maybe he can help you, too."

Something in his voice told Jonah he might be the only one who could.

If he had been able to see through his panic in the moment, Jonah might have detected the note of regret in Dom's voice.

He wasn't expecting that phone call to be their last.

But when Jonah was released two days later, after a brief court hearing, into the supervision of Ross Shepard, the phone Dominic had given him had been deactivated. And he was nowhere to be found.

FRIDAY, NOVEMBER 1

"What happened to you?"

Liam's eyes dropped to Jonah's arms as soon as he opened the door, which he knew was going to happen. Jonah had been dreading it all day, knowing there was no way to hide the evidence or avoid the confrontation. In addition to its inadequacy against the brutal temperatures, his threadbare t-shirt betrayed a collage of bruises mottled along both arms, reaching a peak at the wrists.

He curled in on himself, but even the pressure of crossing his arms over his body triggered a flare of pain. For once, he wished he would have taken Liam up on his offer to keep his borrowed hoodie between visits. Jonah never wanted to risk it getting damaged or stolen at the shelter, and he could admit, if only to himself, that he didn't want it to lose its familiar, comforting scent. He didn't want it to stop smelling like Liam.

Just this once, though, it would have been nice to be able to cover up.

"I'm fine." He kept his gaze leveled on the carpet as he stepped into the room, kicking off his shoes in the corner. "Just had a bad night."

"'A bad...?' Jonah, you're covered in bruises." Liam closed the door behind them, following him into the room.

"It looks worse than it is," he lied.

"It looks like someone beat the shit out of you."

"Maybe someone did."

They both stopped moving. Jonah's eyes fell to the pile of clothes on the bed. The usual thick sweatpants and the maroon sweatshirt. Having them in such close proximity made him ache for their warmth. He usually waited until after he showered, wanting to rinse away the grime of his week before touching Liam's things, but tonight...

"Can I put them on?" he asked.

"What?" Liam said, then followed his line of sight to the clothes. His eyes, hard with worry, softened. "Of course," he said, picking up the pile and handing it over.

Jonah bit down on a groan as he lifted his arms over his head to pull the shirt into place. The flare of pain was worth enduring for the immediate comfort.

Liam wasn't ready to let it drop.

"Was this. . . ?" Liam swallowed audibly. "Did one of your. . . the guys you go to see. . . ?"

"Do you really want me to answer that?" Jonah asked with more heat than he'd intended.

Silence. Liam pulled his bottom lip in between his teeth, watching him.

"Jonah," he said. "I know you don't like to talk about it, but if you decide you want to go to the police to get help, the offer is always on the table. I'll go with you. You know I will."

"Liam," he warned.

"I know," he said quickly. "I know, I won't push, okay? I just hate seeing you like this. I hate knowing what you go back to when you leave here."

"It's not always like this."

"The fact that it's *sometimes* like this is bad enough."

Jonah was quiet in the face of that truth.

"Is there anything I can do to make it better?" Liam asked. When Jonah looked up to meet his gaze, there were tiny splotches of red forming at the corners of Liam's eyes. "Anything at all?"

He thought if Liam started crying right now—crying because of *him*—it might snap his last threads of composure. Jonah took a deep breath and exhaled through his nose.

"I'm okay," he promised, tamping down on the small voice inside him that wanted to cry out, *help me, help me, help me.* "I just don't want to think about it tonight. Please."

At length, Liam nodded, conceding. "Yeah," he said, blinking away the start of tears. "Okay. Whatever you need." He cleared his throat, reaching for his backpack beside the bed. "Lucky for you, I come bearing hours worth of distractions."

When he lifted his calculus textbook into view, Jonah smiled, ignoring the tug on his split lip.

"Making me understand mathematical concepts is a full-time job," Liam said, and they both ignored the watery shake to his voice. "I assure you, your mind will be fully consumed."

Jonah sank down on the edge of the bed, concealing a wince. "I'm up for the challenge."

CHAPTER 12
Liam

FRIDAY, NOVEMBER 8TH

Liam's eyes cracked open at the first sound of something distinctly not right. His sleep-sogged brain caught up to him at the sharp inhale of breath from the other side of the room. He pushed his head up and squinted into the darkness to see Jonah twisting against his sheets.

Another nightmare—or whatever it was that had seized him that first night Liam had spent with him. He flipped on the table lamp and, just like that night, approached Jonah's bed. The outward display of panic didn't seem to have escalated quite as much as last time, and Liam was determined to pull him out of it before he got to that point.

"Hey," he said, placing a palm against Jonah's shoulder. The movement stilled under his touch, just briefly, before he jerked again, a soft whimper escaping. "It's alright."

He raised his voice enough to hopefully puncture his unconsciousness.

"You're okay, Jonah, it's just a dream."

When his eyes shot open, wide and bloodshot, it was with a choked-off gasp, as if the air was caught in his throat. It evidently only served to exacerbate the panic, because Jonah's hand shot up to clasp Liam's wrist; not in an effort to push him away, but a desperate, silent plea for help.

"Breathe," Liam instructed, his own voice coming out mercifully more steady than he felt. "Try and take a deep breath for me."

Jonah nodded, the fingers around Liam's wrist clamping tighter.

"There you go." Liam nodded, rubbing his thumb over Jonah's shoulder. "Again."

This time he breathed with him, both of them filling their lungs together. The tension in Jonah's body visibly receded on the exhale, his grip on Liam's hand falling away. Liam followed suit, dropping his palm to the mattress. He let Jonah take a few more full breaths before attempting to speak.

"You okay?" he asked, finally.

There was only a moment of hesitation before Jonah nodded. Liam could read the transparent apology written all over his face, in his flushed cheeks and downcast gaze, and he thought he might physically lose his dinner if he had to hear that boy say he was sorry for what just happened.

Instead, he spoke up before Jonah could, letting the words fall from his mouth without much filter. "Do you want to sleep with me?"

His mouth popped open.

"Not, like. . . I just meant, did it make it better last time? Having someone next to you afterward?"

At least Jonah wasn't blushing alone now, but if he was at all perturbed by Liam's question, he did a great job of masking it. His eyes flitted back up to Liam's, shinier this time and even redder than they had been before.

"God, that's... That was a stupid thing to suggest. Just, never mind. Are you—?"

"Please."

Liam blinked. "Please?"

"It did help," Jonah admitted.

Liam was nodding before his brain could fully catch up. "Okay," he said. "Yeah, let's... yeah."

He stood from his crouch, ignoring the pop in his knee, and hovered uncertainly beside the bed. Jonah wriggled back a few inches, making room and pulling the sheet back with him. Liam pulled one long leg into the bed, then the other.

"Is this alright?" he asked softly, one hand hovering over the edge of the blanket. The tears that had gathered moments earlier were running silently down the side of Jonah's face, over the bridge of his nose and dripping onto the pillow. *Oh, Jonah.*

"Tell me what you need," he whispered.

Jonah pressed his lips together and stared back at him. "This is okay," he said. "This is good."

Liam settled into his own pillow, shifting around to try and get comfortable without knocking into him.

"Do you want the light on?" Liam thought to ask before reaching back for the switch.

He shook his head. "Go ahead."

Darkness draped over them at the flick of a switch and Liam settled back into his spot. There was quiet for a long moment, save for the whispers of fabric as one or both of them shifted, the soft groan of the spring mattress beneath them.

"Thank you." Jonah's voice pierced the quiet.

Liam's throat tightened. He couldn't even trust his own voice enough to manage a hum of acknowledgement, so instead he nodded against the pillow, hoping that even in the darkness Jonah could feel his response.

CHAPTER 13
Liam

FRIDAY, NOVEMBER 15TH

"So, there's a pool," was the first thing Liam said when Jonah closed the door behind him. "To be clear, I didn't choose this hotel with the express intention of partaking, but I thought you should know it's there, as an option." Before Jonah could respond, he added, "There's a solid chance it's overrun by tourists and unsupervised children and maybe full of pee, and I don't know if you even like swimming, but I thought. . . why not offer, you know?"

Jonah raised an eyebrow. "I didn't exactly come prepared with swim trunks."

Liam procured a pair of kelly-green shorts from his bag. "I brought extra, just in case," he said. "You'll probably be swimming in them—pun intended—but there's a drawstring, so I'm sure we can make them work."

Jonah accepted the offering, turning the material over in his hands. "Do *you* want to go to the pool?" he asked.

Truthfully, pools—or anywhere that encouraged putting your body on display—were not at the top of Liam's list. But it was there, and they had access to it, and Liam was constantly worried about boring Jonah with their uneventful routine. Jonah didn't seem like the type to judge him for his body, and, it was worth noting, he had already seen Liam shirtless under less appropriate circumstances. If it was just the two of them, he thought it might actually be fun.

"I'm game if you are," he said.

In the end, it was not, in fact, overrun by tourists or children, unsupervised or otherwise. The jury was still out on the pee. When Liam and Jonah keyed into the small, humid pool room, they were the only ones there. Liam chose to take that for the tiny miracle it was.

They placed their towels on a faded chair and walked to the edge of the pool. The smell of chlorine was almost strong enough to burn Liam's eyes.

"I haven't been swimming in a long time," Jonah said, looking down at the water. The drawstring on the borrowed shorts was pulled tight, the excess string tucked into the folded waistband. Liam was, very respectfully, keeping his eyes above shoulder level.

"You *can* swim, right?" Liam asked, suddenly nervous. "I promise it wasn't my intent to drown you tonight."

Jonah pointed out the black lettering in the tile beneath their toes. "It's only five feet deep," he said. "Worst case, I'll just stand up."

Then, to his surprise, Jonah leapt forward with his knees tucked to his chest and crashed through the surface of the water. Liam let out a startled laugh as the tidal wave splashed back on him. Jonah surfaced a few seconds later, water running off of his cropped hair and down his face. His first thought was: *his eyelashes look even longer wet.*

"It's warmer than I expected," Jonah said.

"Yeah, well," Liam said, sinking onto the ledge of the pool, "you know me. I spare no expense on the luxuries."

Jonah smiled at him, then sank back beneath the surface. Liam watched as he kicked off the wall and darted gracefully to the other side, surfacing a few feet away from him. "Aren't you getting in?" he asked.

He had been, before he got distracted by the carefree way Jonah moved around in the water. Wordlessly, Liam hoisted himself off the edge. Jonah was right: it was warm.

Liam couldn't exactly call what they did *swimming*. Well, Jonah swam, occasionally dipping beneath the surface to pop up somewhere else a few seconds later. But for the most part, the two of them sort of just. . . floated, idly bouncing between the walls, running their arms through the smooth texture of the water, bending their legs to keep themselves submerged to the chin.

As they talked, they began to move in a sort of unconscious orbit around each other. Something about the languid movement made it feel like a dance.

Eventually, they resorted to childhood challenges, like who could hold a handstand longer, or who could keep their eyes open underwater without blinking.

The world went quiet when Liam submerged his head. When he opened his eyes, Jonah was there, looking back at him. For a moment, just that moment, nothing outside the silence of that water existed. For a moment, they were just two boys, alone in a pool. Liam found he didn't want to surface.

Their fingers were pruned by the time a hotel employee knocked on the door to let them know the pool was closed, but he caught Jonah's reflection on the elevator ride to their room and saw he was smiling. Liam couldn't help but smile, too.

CHAPTER 14
Jonah

FRIDAY, NOVEMBER 22ND

Jonah lay on his side, a lazy string of limbs covered in someone else's too-big clothing. The bed was soft where it sank beneath his weight, enveloping his body in a welcome embrace. Liam was across from him, propped up on one elbow so that his head eclipsed the bedside lamp in just the right way, creating a crown of light in his curls. Jonah thought he could have looked at that picture forever.

They were sharing a bed this time.

Liam had been mortified when they showed up to the room to find the hotel had mistakenly booked him a single-bed room. His reaction might have been endearing, in the flustered way that Liam got sometimes, if he hadn't also been so sincerely apologetic about it. Jonah had assured him it was fine, but Liam still made a valiant effort by going down to the front desk to sort it out.

It didn't work. They were overbooked.

Not that he would admit to it out loud, but Jonah felt a little bit pleased by that. He had been thinking about it all week; how when he woke in the night with a scream trapped in his throat and phantom hands on his body, Liam's presence helped guide his descent back to earth. It wouldn't be the worst thing in the world to allow himself that reprieve.

They had abandoned all attempts at studying a while ago, finally throwing in the towel after hours of diligent focus (on Jonah's part) and countless attempts at distraction (on Liam's part). Some re-run of a 90s sitcom hummed softly in the background, cutting in with a laugh track every few minutes, but their focus was entirely on each other.

For hours, they just. . . talked.

Liam told him more about his job. How he had started working at the diner as a busboy at sixteen and slowly worked his way up to host, and then server, where he could finally take home decent tips. He told Jonah about his manager Kim, who was only five years older than he was and probably the closest thing he'd ever had to a big sister.

He talked about how there were whispers of bumping him up to assistant manager next year if he stuck around, but how he probably wouldn't take it if they offered, because something about accepting a full-time job in his hometown felt like signing the death certificate on his dreams.

He asked about Jonah's family and didn't press when he was reluctant to give too many details. Jonah told him he had a brother who looked just like him, and a little sister who was six years younger but somehow smarter than both of them put together. Jonah told him how he missed them so much, and wondered aloud if they ever thought about him. If they ever wondered where he was. He wondered if they missed him, too.

When Liam asked about his parents, the cellophane around his lungs shrank tighter. He closed up, unable to find the words.

"You don't have to talk about them," Liam told him, effortlessly reading the shift in his demeanor. Jonah resisted the urge, not for the first time, to pull him into a hug.

Liam didn't try to touch him, didn't try to kiss him or inch closer or turn the evening into anything more than it already was. He never did, which Jonah appreciated more than he could put into words, even though sometimes he got lost in the fleeting daydreams about what his hands might feel like in his hair, on his waist, his hips.

He hadn't wanted those things from anybody in a long time, and he didn't know what it said about him that he still could. There was a dull sense of shame, but maybe something like hope, too; maybe he wasn't as broken as he thought he was.

CHAPTER 15
Jonah

FRIDAY, NOVEMBER 29TH

There was a bottle of champagne and a six pack of beer on the nightstand when Jonah walked into the room. He looked at it, then to Liam, who smiled brightly back at him.

"We're celebrating," Liam announced. "Thanks to you, I'll never have to take another math class for as long as I live."

A smile split Jonah's face, entirely without effort. "I knew you had it in you."

Liam bent down to retrieve two glasses from the lower shelf of the nightstand, handing one to Jonah. He took it hesitantly and Liam must have sensed his apprehension, because he frowned. "What's wrong?"

"What?" Jonah said. "Nothing."

"You don't have to drink it if you don't want to," he assured him, looking suddenly hesitant about the celebration. "There's no pressure or anything. I just thought. . . I don't know. It might be fun."

Jonah swiftly reminded himself that Liam was not the other men who pushed bottles into his hand, and that losing a little bit of control tonight didn't have to be a bad thing. He took one look at Liam, who was watching him apprehensively, twisting the neck of the deep green champagne bottle in his hands, and knew he would be safe.

"No pressure necessary," Jonah said.

The cork gave way with a loud pop, rocketing across the room to land somewhere in the fold of curtains.

"We've earned this," Liam declared.

"*You* earned this," Jonah corrected, but Liam was having none of it.

"No," he said firmly. "I may have been the one physically taking the test, but you deserve at least seventy percent of that C+."

"I think seventy percent of a C+ might be a failing grade."

"Shhh, the point of this is that we're done with math now."

The champagne foamed to the top of Jonah's glass as Liam poured, and Jonah took the opportunity to observe the candid glimpse of Liam's happiness. The smile on his lips was genuine and soft, his eyes light, and Jonah had a real moment of gratitude that he was here with him. That whatever else the week held for him, he got to be here now, in this room.

And for a moment, looking at Liam's face, he could almost let himself believe that Liam was grateful, too.

The warmth had settled over them like a sunset, starting in their chests and bellies and spreading outward into their limbs, their toes, their noses and fingers. Two lazy heaps sinking into the mattress. They were side by side, close enough to touch, but just far enough away that they didn't.

Jonah lay with both arms strung up at his sides, bent at the elbow, open hands parallel with his head against the mattress. In the still quiet, Jonah could feel the slow, even movement of Liam's breathing from beside him. He closed his eyes, losing himself in the comforting rhythm.

"I have a confession to make." It was Liam's voice that broke the silence minutes later. Jonah opened his eyes, his head lolling lazily toward him, waiting.

"I hate coffee."

A laugh bubbled out of Jonah. "What?"

He felt light and dizzy in the best way as he rolled onto his side, propping himself up onto his elbow.

"Despise it," Liam returned the laugh, rolling up to mirror his position. "I don't understand how you drink it black."

Jonah pressed a fist to his mouth. "But you drink it every week! I've seen you. I—Why would you. . . ?"

Liam shrugged, shifting his gaze to the stretch of duvet between them. Jonah watched as he traced a line of stitching with his index finger. A delightful pinkness crept into his cheeks from more than the alcohol consumption. "I didn't want you to drink alone."

If Jonah's heart thudded a bit harder in his chest then, it was probably just a side effect of the alcohol. "Is that why you put like, seven sugars in it?"

Liam made an outraged sound. "*'Seven'* is a dramatic rewriting of history."

"Oh, am I the dramatic one now?"

"Are you implying that *I'm* dramatic?"

"You," Jonah replied around a hiccup, "are drunk."

They were quiet for a beat, and then Liam's answering hiccup sent them tumbling into a helpless fit of laughter.

"*You're* drunk," Liam slurred.

"I'm drunk," Jonah agreed in a whisper.

Liam snorted—a crass, uncensored sound that he definitely wouldn't have made sober—and swatted a haphazard hand in Jonah's direction. It landed with a thump on the bed, incidentally close enough to Jonah's that their pinky fingers overlapped. Warm skin twitched against cold at the contact, and when Liam turned his hand just slightly, his finger hooked around Jonah's instead of pulling away. Maybe it was an accident, or maybe he was too drunk to notice, but neither one of them made a move to separate.

Jonah was just starting to drift again when Liam spoke through a yawn. "Your turn," he said.

"For what?" Jonah yawned in return.

"I gave you a confession, now you have to give me one."

Jonah chuckled low in his throat, his eyebrows turning down. "I don't remember agreeing to those terms."

"Fair is fair," he declared.

"What do you want me to say?" Jonah asked.

"Anything. Whatever comes to mind. It doesn't have to be as embarrassing as mine."

Jonah didn't bother to mention he hadn't found Liam's to be embarrassing in the slightest. Instead, he let his mind wander, trying to find what he wanted to say. There were plenty of secrets he kept hidden, and there were some truths he had decided early on to keep from Liam. Unfortunately for him, the alcohol was one hell of a force for breaking down all inhibitions, and he felt his mouth forming the words before he could stop them.

"The night we met in that bathroom, I was at the bar to meet someone," he said. "A client, I mean."

He regretted it the second it left his mouth, because the air in the room seemed to freeze over at his words, Liam visibly stiffening next to him. In his periphery, Jonah saw him turn his head in his direction.

"Is that why you were crying?" he whispered. "Were they. . . ?"

Jonah squeezed his eyes shut. "Sorry," he said. "Sorry, I didn't—I shouldn't have said that. I didn't mean to drag down the mood."

"Jonah, if you want to talk about it. . ."

"I don't," Jonah said quickly. "Please, forget I said that."

Liam pulled in a deep breath, but eventually conceded with a nod. They fell back into a heavy silence, thicker this time than the comfortable, light one they had before, and

Jonah hated himself for ruining the moment. It had been so nice while it lasted.

"Can I choose a different confession?" Jonah dared to ask, his voice pinched tight. He was glad Liam was no longer looking at him.

"'Course. Go for it."

Jonah swallowed, pressing down the sudden swell of nervousness in his chest, because this needed to be said.

"You're the best friend I've ever had."

He didn't dare turn his head to see Liam's reaction. They both kept their eyes on the ceiling, even as Liam's pinky unlatched from his, just long enough to slide his palm fully over Jonah's, lacing all their fingers together. He gave a squeeze, and Jonah gave it right back.

"Yeah," Liam whispered. "You're mine, too."

CHAPTER 16
Liam

Jonah's breathing had leveled out some minutes ago, the near-constant crease that lived between his brows smoothed out in a rare show of peace.

Liam wasn't far behind. He could feel his own eyelids starting to sag, dipping into his vision with each slow, lethargic blink. Some rational part of his mind—growing quieter by the second—urged him to get up and pull Jonah's legs up onto the bed, to lift him into a proper position and cover him so they could both get a more restful sleep. He wanted to, but he was so, so, delightfully drunk, and his limbs felt so heavy and somehow, he was comfortable right where he was.

Mostly, the idea of letting go of Jonah's hand for any amount of time, for any reason, was an absolute deal breaker.

"I have another confession," he whispered into the silent room.

Liam let his eyes trail over the profile of Jonah's face; the long, sloped nose, the cupid's bow of his lip, the eyelashes that kissed the skin of his cheek with his eyes closed and a jawline that was just a little more pronounced than it should have been. Liam tightened his hand around Jonah's.

The alcohol was a sedative quickly pulling him under, but Liam knew, even then, that wasn't the reason for the warmth that flowered in his chest.

"I think I might accidentally love you."

CHAPTER 17
Jonah

The first sensation Jonah registered, as darkness began to split at the edges, was coarse fabric under his cheek.

The next was pain. First in his head, sharp and heavy and pulsing, then trickling down his body as he came to awareness. He hurt everywhere.

His eyelids were as heavy as the rest of him, but they were the only parts he could even think about moving. It took considerable effort to hold them open, blinking slowly as he scanned his surroundings. He couldn't see much. Somewhere above him, dim light painted a haze at the edge of his vision—sunlight breaking through a crack in the wood slats that covered a high-up window.

He was in a basement.

With that realization came the sudden awareness of the earthy, damp smell, like rotted wood and age. He tried to push himself up but flattened again at the sharp stab of pain through his core. The movement accompanied the familiar groan of bed springs. He dragged his fingers over the surface beneath him and realized it was a bare mattress.

Memory came in short, sporadic bursts.

Mr. Becker. His house. The blood.

Jonah held up his hand, trembling, to the faint stream of light: He had to blink once, twice, again to make sure they were real: the deep red stains on his skin.

Horror shuddered through him. He scrambled back into the darkness, wiping his hands against his shirt, the mattress, the wall, but he couldn't escape the blood. It was all over him.

He remembered now.

A muffled, metallic clunk drew his attention upward just as the door at the top of the staircase swung open. Jonah squinted against the sudden burst of light, pulling his body into a defensive curl.

Two sets of footsteps thundered down the wooden planks. The light clicked on with the tug of a string, a single bulb flickering overhead. Jonah looked up to Shepard standing over him. Marcus, always his trusted shadow, stood back with his arms crossed.

"It's taken care of," Shepard said.

Jonah uncurled himself, forcing his body to sit upright despite the pain. A glance up the stairs told him he was in the basement of the halfway house.

"What's taken care of?" His voice was just as broken as the rest of him. "Why am I down here?"

Shepard swiped the back of his arm across his forehead. There was an erratic tick to his movements that made him all the more volatile. "I couldn't let the others see you like this, could I?"

Jonah looked down at himself and felt bile rise in his throat. In the light, there was no mistaking the blood on him.

"I killed him," Jonah whispered before he could stop himself.

It was a statement, not a question, but Shepard bent down, hands on his knees to meet him at eye level. "Yeah. You did," he spat. "And you created a real fucking mess for me to clean up."

He hadn't meant to. He hadn't, he hadn't, he...

It was an accident.

Mr. Becker was—he was hurting him. He had both hands around his throat. He was going to kill him. All Jonah had meant to do was push him away, but the man was wasted, several shots in and high on whatever he had forced Jonah to snort off his coffee table, and then his head was cracking against the side of the nightstand. And then there was blood. So much blood.

He never meant to kill him. Jonah just wanted him to stop.

He couldn't keep the vomit down. Shepard and his hired muscle watched silently as he lost his meager stomach contents on the basement floor.

"I didn't mean to," he pleaded, as if somehow hoping for absolution from the monster in front of him.

Shepard dropped into a crouch beside him, reaching out to trace a palm over his face. Jonah was too stunned to even recoil from the touch.

"Do you think anyone's actually going to believe that?" he asked gently. "With your history?"

Jonah didn't know when he had started crying. "No," he whispered, an answer and a plea all at once.

"No," Shepard echoed sympathetically. "You're lucky I was there to clean up after you."

"What did you do?" Jonah's eyes flicked to Marcus, who stared back at him unchallenged.

Shepard turned his face back to him. "You don't need to know the details," he said. "But you owe me for this, kid. And I always get what I'm owed."

He stood, leaving Jonah shivering on the mattress at his feet. He waved a vague gesture to Marcus, who followed like a dog called to heel.

"Get him a bucket of water and a change of clothes," he ordered. "We need to burn these."

The bathroom was hazy by the time Jonah turned the handle, cutting off the spray of water. His body tingled in the immediate absence of the heat, tiny pin pricks over the surface of his skin. It was proof that the temperature of the water was probably higher than what was healthy, but Jonah didn't care. These showers were one of the parts of their Friday night routine he was most thankful for.

The rings on the curtain screeched along the rod as he pushed it aside, grabbing a towel from the shelf above the toilet. He pressed his face into it first, appreciating the softness, even at the lower end hotels. He dried himself off quickly, aware of the slight sting of friction across his irritated skin, and hung the towel on the hook on the back of the door.

Liam's pajamas were folded in their usual stack on the counter. He brought the sweatshirt to his chest—the same as always, maroon and over-long and tattered from years of wear—and dropped his head to inhale the comforting scent. He had yet to put a name to this feeling, the one he was slowly losing himself in beyond all control, but it was getting harder to stave off.

Perhaps because there was a much larger part of him that desperately did not want to.

The distinct smell of Friday nights encompassed him as he pulled the shirt over his head. He paused, then wiped his palm over the mirror to clear away some of the heavy condensation.

Through the steam, the reflection that stared back at him looked like it could have belonged to someone else. He wished he could be someone else, too.

There were parts of him now that were nearly unrecognizable to the person he used to be. The legs that stretched out beneath the hem of the sweatshirt were pale and thin, all the tan, wiry muscle from years of track and soccer diminished from months of malnutrition. He'd lost some weight around his stomach, his arms, his face—places where he hadn't really had much to lose to begin with. Now he just looked kind of sickly.

He forced his eyes away.

He was reaching for the pajama bottoms when Liam's voice, muffled and pitched up in a way he didn't often hear, pulled his attention from the other side of the door.

"... know it's expensive. Yes, I know. It was just a... Mom, it was just an informational packet. I haven't even applied yet."

Jonah busied himself with redressing, folding his own dirty clothes into a neat pile, but it was impossible not to overhear his conversation through the thin walls.

"We don't know that for sure. There's always financial aid and scholarships and... Yeah, I know it seems like I'm working a lot, but it's not that bad. My coworkers are nice, and it's... it's just a few double shifts."

Oh, there were those seeds of guilt again. They seemed to have bloomed into full-grown weeds.

It wasn't the first time he had heard Liam mention picking up hours at work, and certainly not the first time he had managed to work himself up over the idea that he was a direct cause of whatever financial distress Liam was facing. Somehow, though, it hadn't really occurred to him until now that these weekly financial setbacks could be seriously hindering Liam's future plans.

"I am still focusing on school. I can do both at once. I would have to do it in New York, too, you know. A lot of people my age work full time in school."

Full time? Had Jonah known that? He knew he worked a lot, but... no wonder he was always so tired.

Guilt won out, or maybe he just selfishly couldn't listen to any more of the problems he had inadvertently caused, and Jonah flipped the faucet on the sink, letting the running water drown out the rest of the conversation.

When silence fell outside the door, he cut the water and turned off the lights.

Liam was on the bed, his hair messy in the distinct way it got when he'd been running his fingers through it. Jonah was used to seeing that look after a particularly gruesome math problem, but the visual was much less appealing when he knew that the stress came from somewhere deeper.

"Hey," Liam greeted him with a smile.

Jonah sank down on the edge of the opposite bed, his back turned to him. He fiddled with the socks in his lap, unfolding them to put on, mostly as a distraction from looking directly at his friend.

"Pizza should be here in ten," Liam said.

"Okay."

"Hey, you okay?" Liam asked.

"Fine," Jonah tried.

He heard the familiar chime of the keychains on Liam's backpack as he set it on the ground.

"What's wrong?" Liam made no move to crowd his space, which Jonah appreciated as always, but he could practically feel the burn of his gaze searing through his back. The sting behind his eyes was building to an intensity he wouldn't be able to contain much longer. He had several responses queued up and ready to fire back at him with perfect composure; a thousand different ways to say *'I'm fine'* that he had mastered for the sake of survival. But none of them could get past the lump in his throat.

"Jonah?"

None of them but the truth.

"I don't think we should do this anymore."

If perfect stillness had a sound, like water freezing into ice, it would have been the silence that followed his words.

"What do you mean?" Liam asked, carefully calm.

"I. . . appreciate what you've been trying to do," Jonah spoke slowly and deliberately. "But we both knew this was never a permanent arrangement, right?"

He was still facing away from Liam, his eyes flat and detached in the direction of the wall, but he could hear him shifting uneasily behind him. He could practically feel him fighting the urge to come closer.

"Maybe not permanent, but. . ." Liam paused, something like genuine hurt in his voice. "Did I do something?"

His eyes slipped shut. Of course Liam's first instinct was to put his own head on the chopping block.

Jonah raged with the urge to retaliate against the absurd suggestion. He wanted so desperately to take it all back, to pretend he'd never said anything at all, because he knew, he *knew*, he was setting himself up for one hell of a fall.

But he could deal with it, he would, if it meant shielding Liam from all of this; from himself and the money problems and the constant periphery of danger that followed everywhere Jonah went.

"This isn't good for us." Jonah set his jaw.

There was another gap of silence, and then—

"No."

The firmness in Liam's voice was enough to shock Jonah into turning to face him.

Liam stood with his arms crossed over his chest, his feet set apart in defiance. "I'm not going to just cut you off, Jonah. After all this time? How could you expect me to do that?"

The muscles in Jonah's face twitched as he struggled to uphold his resolve. The perfect response, the one he knew would hit right where he needed it to, was coiled and poised on his tongue, ready to strike.

"Liam," he began. Beneath his borrowed sweatshirt, his heartbeat pounded against his ribcage.

"No," Liam cut in. "I'm not going to *drop* you like you're nothing."

"I guess I don't get a say in it, do I?" He forced himself to look up into Liam's eyes as he spoke, watching the horrified flash of recognition land on him. "It's really your choice," he pushed forward, hating himself with every syllable. "You make the arrangement, and I show up. That's how this works."

It was low, and he knew it, and maybe he was low for going there with Liam and knowing it would work. For a moment, he really thought it had, until Liam surprised him for a second time.

"What is this really about?" He took a step closer to the bed where Jonah sat, sinking down onto the corner across from him without making contact. "You know I wouldn't do that. You know I wouldn't... *force* you to be here if you didn't want to be. You do know that, right?"

Jonah turned his head back toward the wall. He closed his eyes. "I know."

"So, tell me what you're trying to do here."

"I'm trying to do the right thing," Jonah said.

"For *who?*"

He was grateful to have chosen then to turn away, because there was no stopping the tears that spilled over. He could have kept up the fight, and probably should have, for Liam's sake, but Jonah was so tired.

"I heard you," he confessed. "On the phone, just now."

Liam blew out a puff of air. "Okay," he breathed. "Well, that makes more sense. What exactly did you hear?"

"Enough," Jonah answered, wiping his eyes with the back of his—well, *Liam's*—sleeve. "Enough to know that you're struggling because of what we're doing here."

"Jonah, what you heard was..." He shook his head. "It was one of many battles in a years-long war. One that I was fighting long before I met you."

"You're throwing away hundreds of dollars every week, and for what?" Jonah argued, unsure of how to fight a battle he desperately didn't want to win. "Money that could be going toward New York and college and everything you want. You could actually have it, and instead you're here with me."

"I'm not throwing anything away, Jonah. Not my dreams, and not you either. You're not disposable. After all this time?" There was a genuine twinge of hurt in his voice. "You really think that's how I feel about you?"

"I just. . ." Jonah pinched his eyes shut. "I don't want you sticking around out of some misplaced guilt. You don't owe me anything, Liam, and you've given me so much already. We met by chance, and you were kind to me. That could be the end of it."

"You were kind to me first," Liam said, surprising him.

"Soliciting you for sex you didn't want wasn't kindness."

Liam shook his head. "Before that. The night of my birthday, in the bathroom at the bar. You could have told me to fuck off, but you asked if I was okay. You let me talk your ear off about my problems even though you were clearly the one having a worse night."

That was dangerous territory, and not something Jonah wanted to approach now, of all times.

"I wasn't the one washing my shirt in the dirtiest sink in Chicago," Jonah deflected weakly. It was enough to pull a small smile onto Liam's face, but it fell again quickly.

"Maybe at one point, this could have been something I walked away from," Liam said. "But it's not anymore. Not for me."

In Jonah's periphery, Liam's hand nudged slightly closer to his on the bed, landing inches away in an unspoken invitation. He watched it, remembering vividly the feeling of Liam's fingers brushing against his in their blissfully drunken haze the week before; a burn on his skin he hadn't stopped feeling since.

Suddenly the air in the room felt thicker, the silence weightier than before. Jonah's own fingers twitched at the memory, or perhaps the anticipation, of the touch. Like some invisible, magnetic force pulling him, he wanted nothing more than to reach out and hold the thing that felt so forbidden to him. The person he couldn't have without hindering him. The person he didn't deserve, but who was here anyway, fighting to keep him around with a hand outstretched like an olive branch Jonah so desperately wanted to take.

He was close, so close, to breaking out of his own head and just going for it when the shrill ring of the hotel phone split the bubble of tension down the middle. Both of their hands jerked back at the same time.

"I'll get it," Liam said. Unnecessary, as he was already halfway across the room. "Hello?" he picked up. "Yeah. Oh. Right, yeah, that's me. Okay, thanks. I'll be down."

He hung up and, with what looked to be a considerable conscious effort, brought his eyes up to meet Jonah's.

"The pizza's down in the lobby," he said, his voice far more strained than such an announcement required. "I'll go grab it, just. . . shit. Okay. We're gonna talk some more when I get back, alright? We'll talk about this."

Jonah only nodded, his heart still hammering in his chest. Liam grabbed his shoes and his key card, then stopped halfway to the door, turning back to him as if something had just occurred to him.

"You're not gonna run off on me, are you?"

The look on his face was so genuinely concerned, and once again, if the circumstances hadn't been so heavy, Jonah might have laughed. Instead, he offered a weak smile and shook his head. "No," he said. "I'll be here."

Liam nodded. Then he was gone.

Suffocated by the sudden silence of an empty room, Jonah let his face fall into his hands and sobbed, one broken, strangled sound that led to another until he was weeping openly without really knowing why. Perhaps it was the lingering guilt that remained despite Liam's assurances. Maybe they were tears of relief, wrought with inexplicable gratitude that his attempts to push Liam away hadn't worked. He had refused to take the easy out that Jonah had gifted him, and decided instead to push back. To fight for him in a way no one had ever bothered to do.

He sat up when he heard the faint beep of the key card at the door, greeting Liam with bloodshot eyes. Liam placed the pizza box on the dresser and paused there for a moment, his back turned to Jonah.

They were quiet. Jonah watched his shoulders move with each breath, waiting to hear what he had to say. Finally, Liam turned around, shifting his weight back against the wooden frame.

"I. . ." He swallowed, then started again. "I know how you feel about this, so don't get mad, okay? But I've been doing some reading. Research, I guess. About resources, shelters, ways to get help for. . . For people who are stuck in situations like yours."

Situations like his. "Liam, please."

"If you're afraid of getting hurt, the police will protect you."

He didn't bother holding back his laugh, though he hated the bitterness in the sound. "The police," he echoed. If only Liam knew.

"But if someone is... is coercing you or something, it's not your fault."

"What if it's not that simple?" Jonah dug the heels of his palms against his eyes. Something was building and unraveling all at once, slipping further from his control with every soft plea, every kind word. It was rising to the surface, burning like lava through him, over him, enveloping him. He felt all of it, all at once; all the pain and the secrets and the lies he kept locked behind dull eyes and the lifeless smile of a boy called Leo. He wanted to tell somebody. He wanted to tell *Liam.* He wanted it out, out, *out.*

"Jonah?"

"I killed someone," he heard the words tumble out in his own voice before he could stop them.

The answering silence rang through him like a bell. Jonah couldn't pull his hands away from his face. He was sure that if he looked at Liam right now, the world would crumble around him.

"It was an accident," he whispered. Would he ever be able to say those words without sounding like he was trying to convince himself? "I wasn't trying to kill him, I was only trying to..." He pressed his knuckles into his eyelids until it hurt. "He had his hands around my throat. He was... hurting me. I thought he was going to kill me, so I pushed him." The last two words broke off entirely. His voice was shaking too much to keep going.

Liam cleared his throat. Jonah tensed, bracing for whatever came next. He knew it would be what he deserved.

"So," Liam said, slow and tentative. "It was self-defense?"

Jonah's hands dropped from his eyes, disbelief momentarily surpassing his fear. He looked at Liam, who was looking back with undue equanimity. "Liam, I just told you that I *killed* someone."

"And I'm not trying to diminish that," he said, raising his palms. "But you also told me he was choking you. You had every right to defend yourself. Anyone could see that."

"The circumstances didn't exactly lean in my favor."

"What circumstances would make the police look past someone trying to murder you?"

"He was paying me to be there," Jonah pushed himself off the bed and paced away, crawling out of his skin with the memories. "And it wasn't the first time."

"That's not an excuse," Liam said, but Jonah was already shaking his head, because Liam didn't *understand*. How could he?

Jonah scratched lines down his arms, trying to hold himself together. He was getting all mixed up. Everything was spilling out of order, when he hadn't meant to spill anything at all. In one moment of weakness, he was going to shatter the fragile lens through which Liam viewed him as someone worth defending. And still, the deeper he dug his grave, the more he felt the need to explain himself.

"He was a regular," he said. "There were always drugs involved, and he was always. . . violent, but never as bad as it was that night."

"Okay," Liam said with a level of calm that had to be an affectation for Jonah's benefit. "So at one point you were. . . you know, doing this of your own free will?" Jonah's flush of shame must have been visible, because he quickly followed up with, "There's nothing wrong with that, if you were! I promise, I'm just trying to understand."

Jonah rubbed the back of his neck. "It's complicated."

"Try me?"

He dared a look at him over his shoulder and saw, in fact, that there was no judgment in Liam's eyes. "There was a time when I did, yes," he said. "It was quick money when I was desperate for it. But it wasn't like that then. Not with him."

"What was it like, then?"

It was like coercion.

It was like blackmail.

It was like Ross Shepard coming into Jonah's room at the end of his first week and telling him he knew all about his history, and that he needed to earn his place in the house.

It was his signature on Jonah's court papers, and Jonah's desperation to keep himself afloat.

It was a series of *favors* that got out of control—first for Shepard, then his friends, and eventually for strangers—and

Jonah seeing less and less of the money each time. Until he stopped seeing any at all.

It was a growing well of debt that Jonah had no chance of climbing out of, and leverage he could never wriggle out from under. It was a slow spiral into freefall.

And then there was a body, and Jonah knew that he might as well have been the one to die. Because there was no slipping out from under Shepard with a secret like that hanging over him. *"I can make sure they put you away for life. You don't want to find out how a princess like you gets by in prison."*

Jonah turned to face him. Liam looked so innocent, so out of his depth, sitting there on the bed. But to his credit, he wasn't flinching away, and he wasn't backing down. Jonah couldn't tell him everything. He wouldn't dare put Liam at risk by bringing him into the fold. But he needed him to understand.

"The person who sent me there that night, when I killed that man," he began. "The person who sends me *here*. . . he could do a lot of damage."

He already is, he could practically see the response burning in Liam's eyes, but he kept quiet and let Jonah explain.

"I could go to prison," he continued. "And sometimes I think, if it was only that, then. . ." He broke off, shaking his head. "But it's not just that anymore. He knows things about my family, my siblings. He's violent, and he's unpredictable, and he hides it well from the people who matter. The police love him. They think he's a local saint. If it ever came down to my word against his, I don't stand a chance, and we both know it."

Liam was quiet a moment, as if letting Jonah decide he was finished. "What am I supposed to do with that?" he said finally. "How am I supposed to know this is happening to you and just sit back and let it?"

"Because you'll only make it worse by doing anything else," Jonah insisted, nearly a plea.

"Jonah."

"It won't—" Jonah bit down on his cheek. "It can't last forever. At some point, he'll lose interest, or he'll get sloppy and get caught, and I'll get out of there. I'm just doing what I need to do to survive in the meantime."

"Do you really believe that?" Liam whispered.

"I have to."

Suddenly the room felt like a battleground after the white flag was raised, and they were standing alone in the rubble as the dust settled around them. Liam ran a hand through his hair, curls fraying apart under his fingers and falling limply back against his forehead.

"I don't know what to say," Liam whispered.

"You don't have to say anything," he said. "But I need you to understand why I shut you down when you suggest trying to get me out of this."

No matter how badly I want it, too.

Liam looked from the box of pizza on the dresser back to Jonah. There was a second in which it looked like Liam wanted desperately to find a loophole, to push just a little bit further, but he stayed quiet. Finally, he nodded.

"You should eat something," he suggested.

Jonah let out a long breath. He was starving, but every nerve in his body felt like they'd just been scrubbed raw. He could only imagine the food would taste like sawdust in his mouth. Regardless, he didn't have it in him to argue. He easily accepted a slice of pizza when Liam held the box out to him.

"Are you alright?" Liam asked after Jonah managed to keep down a few bites.

Jonah swallowed. "I'm okay."

"Okay," Liam replied, not sounding all that convinced. "Can I just. . . can I say one more thing about it, then I'll let it go?"

Jonah eyed him warily.

"I'm not going to pressure you, okay? Never again. But I want you to know," Liam said, "If the time ever does come when you change your mind, or if circumstances change enough so that you can do something, I'll do whatever I can to help you."

He didn't know what to say to that, so he took another bite of pizza, hoping that at least would appease him. Liam watched him for another moment before he was struck by some idea, leaping to his feet to retrieve the hotel-branded notepad and pen from the nightstand drawer.

"What are you doing?" Jonah asked as Liam scribbled something just out of his line of sight.

The perforated edge of the stationery tore seamlessly as Liam pulled it away and handed it across the bed. Jonah took it, and when he looked down, he saw a familiar, loopy handwriting across the page:

Dear Jonah,
Call me.
Your friend,
Liam

Below was his phone number.

Jonah looked up at him.

"I know you don't have access to a phone, so maybe this is stupid." Liam shrugged, setting the pad and pen off to the side. "But maybe, somehow. . . I don't know. It'll just make me feel better, knowing you might be able to reach me somehow. If you ever need to. If you ever can."

Jonah set his napkin-plate on the bed beside him and took extra care to fold the paper neatly into fourths. Wordlessly, he crossed the room to where his jeans were folded on a chair and stuffed the note inside the front pocket.

When he sat back down, Liam turned to him.

"Please, don't do that again," he said.

Jonah froze. "What?"

"That selfless-martyr-thing you tried to pull before," Liam clarified. "Trying to end things like that." Jonah resisted the urge to correct him, to say that if there was any hero to be named in this story, it certainly wasn't him. "Next time, just. . . talk to me first, before you go mapping out your exit strategy, okay?"

Liam's voice was light and accented by the tug of a kind smile at his lips, but Jonah's brain was stuck on the 'next time.' The implication that Liam still wanted this thing between them—whatever it was—to continue, even after everything he'd just learned.

"None of that changes my concern for how this is affecting you," Jonah pointed out.

"I told you, I wouldn't be doing this if I didn't think it was feasible."

"Feasible, maybe," Jonah allowed. "But for how long? At what cost to you?"

Liam fell quiet. It lasted long enough for Jonah's stomach to drop, regret clouding the clarity that had made him fight so hard to prove his point. What if Liam listened to him? What if this was the end?

"What if we cut out the hotel cost for a little while?" Liam said suddenly.

Jonah turned to him, blinking. "Where would we go?"

"Anywhere." There was a gleam of something adventurous in Liam's eyes. "Even if we have to hang out in my car for a night. I can't promise it would be the most exciting night of your life, but at least I would know you're safe. Is that allowed?"

"I need an address to stay overnight," he said, choosing his words carefully. "A pickup and drop-off point."

Liam got that look that he did when he wanted to ask more than he should. Jonah watched him bite his tongue, grateful when he didn't push. "Well," Liam began slowly, "we should be able to fake that. It's not like he—*whoever*—walks you to the door, right?"

Jonah shifted uneasily. "Not typically, no."

"So, we could just meet at a hotel, hide out in the lobby or something until the coast is clear, and then sneak out to my car. We can go wherever we want and get you back by morning. That could work, right?"

The immediate response, the conditioned one, was no. Because Jonah's life didn't work like that. Luck didn't sway in his favor. He was the one who always got caught, and he was the one who had to pay the consequences, no matter what anyone else seemed to get away with.

As he sat with the idea, though, a thread of hope began to form, sprouting from some place inside himself he didn't know still existed. From the last scraps of Jonah Prince that lay behind the broken mask of Leo.

He looked at Liam, who was watching him back, and saw the same hope reflected there. Jonah's heartbeat was thick and heavy in his throat, rivaling the voice in his head that told him he could never keep someone like Liam for himself. The reality was almost as cold and unforgiving as the indulgent fantasy was warm and inviting; fire and ice under his skin that flared whenever he was close enough to touch.

"Whatever we have to do," Liam said. "Anything, if it means getting another week."

Fire. Ice. A heartbeat in his throat. A voice that tried to drown it all out.

And a single spark of rebellion that hadn't yet been extinguished.

CHAPTER 18
Liam

Was this a bad idea? It was starting to feel like a bad idea.

Jonah was a few minutes late, and it was probably Liam's imagination, but he was beginning to think that the front desk staff were getting suspicious of him.

He'd strutted in a few minutes before nine, as planned, with all the false confidence of an honest-to-God patron. The original plan had been to walk past the desk without acknowledgement, but halfway through the execution, his Midwestern-bred manners kicked in and he shot the girl a panicked smile that definitely looked completely natural and not at all guilty or constipated.

Fortunately, the bored-looking young woman at the counter didn't appear to give a single shit where Liam was going, as long as he wasn't making excessive noise or dripping pool water all over the lobby.

He had been standing in the first-floor vending machine room where they had agreed to meet for a solid fifteen minutes. He leaned against the ice machine, the steady mechanical hum sending vibrations through his back. Liam's lifetime record of general rule-following was making itself known in the anxious tap of his fingers on every surface he could touch.

Sneaking around wasn't really in Liam's repertoire. For that matter, neither was commuting to the city every weekend to live out some fucked up Pretty Woman fan fiction, but hey. Life comes at you fast.

Liam was anxious by nature, but it was only exacerbated by this particular set of circumstances, including the fact that he had no way of contacting Jonah to see what was going on.

Thankfully, he didn't have much longer to ponder all the possibilities, because the sound of footsteps in the hall was ample distraction. Part of him expected to see an annoyed hotel manager, who had been watching him hover like a freak in the snack room for fifteen full minutes on the security cameras. But relief melted over him when a familiar buzzed head rounded the corner, peeking through the rectangular panel of glass in the door.

Liam pushed off the ice machine and crossed the room in three steps. He flung the door open and, before he could stop himself, pulled Jonah into a hug.

There was a half second of hesitation, maybe less, before Jonah was returning the gesture. "Hey," he greeted him, the vibration of his throat against Liam's shoulder.

"Hey, you." He pulled back after only a couple seconds, taking a step back to give Jonah space. "It's good to see you."

"I hope you weren't waiting long," Jonah said.

"I wasn't," Liam lied, then immediately realized he didn't want to lie. "Well, fifteen minutes. Not that I was counting. I mean—it's fine. I was just. . ." he swallowed, gesturing around at the closet-like room, wondering why he couldn't shut the hell up. "Um. Hanging out."

Jonah raised an eyebrow, concealing the smallest of smiles. "Are you alright?" he asked. "You seem nervous."

"Nervous? Nah." Again with the honesty. "Maybe a little? It feels like we're sneaking around."

"We are."

Liam bubbled out a nervous laugh at his deadpan rebuttal. "That explains the nerves, I guess."

"Do you know where you want to go?" Jonah asked.

"Actually," Liam said. "I did have an idea I wanted to run by you. And just to preface, you can absolutely say no." He took a breath. "I wondered if you might be interested in coming home with me? Not. . . I mean, you don't have to come back to my actual house if you don't want to, and we don't have to stay all night. It's a little over an hour away, so I just thought, since we have the whole night, there's plenty of time to get there and back. Does that. . . ? How does that sound?"

In the quiet of Jonah's answering stare, Liam felt the wind leave his sails. The selfishness of the suggestion was suddenly so obvious, in the way that it could only be once it'd already left his mouth.

"You'd really want to bring me there with you?" Jonah asked.

"Only if you want to," Liam reiterated. "It could be a change of scenery. I thought maybe I could show you around? Give a little tour of the world's most boring suburban life? I don't know."

"Yes," Jonah said, nearly cutting him off with the immediacy of his response. "Let's do it."

Liam deflated with relief. "Really?"

"Yes, really."

"Okay." Liam couldn't keep the smile off his face. "Oh, here. Before I forget." He crouched down to his backpack on the floor and pulled out Jonah's usual sweatshirt, along with an old winter coat and a knitted hat. "It's freezing out. I didn't think a sweatshirt would cut it tonight."

Jonah accepted the clothes with the same heartbreaking gratitude he afforded to every small kindness Liam offered.

They waited a few minutes, wanting to be sure that whoever dropped Jonah off was gone before they left the hotel. When they stepped outside, passing the bored desk attendant, Jonah pulled the hood of his coat over his head for reasons, Liam assumed, that had nothing to do with the cold. He kept vigilant watch, sneaking glances over his shoulder every few seconds until they ducked into the train station.

CHAPTER 19
Jonah

They took the commuter train toward Naperville out of Union Station. Liam paid for both tickets.

Jonah assumed he had opted for public transportation to save money on fuel, but Liam told him he just preferred the train. He said that it made him feel like he was part of the city instead of just someone who happened to live in the margins of one. Though, he assured Jonah he would be driving him back to Chicago at the end of the night. He didn't want to risk a faulty train schedule making him late.

Liam brought the most recent of Jonah's borrowed books for the journey, the post-it note still poking out from where he had left off the week before. Jonah held it in his lap, unopened, watching out the window as the city fell away behind them.

He wasn't running away, he had to remind himself with each breath that the distance allowed him. This wasn't freedom. Not beyond the scope of a single night.

Liam seemed just as entranced by the sights, though surely it was a route he was familiar with to the point of boredom by now. They sat across from each other, in seats that faced inward. With Liam distracted, Jonah allowed himself to stare. He watched Liam, the way he leaned his head against the window, the way he seemed comfortable in this space in a way he so rarely did.

Unbidden, he imagined Liam in a few years' time, riding the subway in New York. What would he look like then? The same? Would he have grown out the bronze scruff stubbled along his jaw? Would there be a stronger sense of self-assurance in his eyes, in the way he carried himself? Would he, by then, no longer hold himself like he was taking up too much space in the world?

Jonah thought the answer was yes. That someone as fundamentally good as Liam only needed time to see it for himself.

The image made him smile, but there was a trickle of melancholy that snuck in behind it. The idea of Liam existing in a future that Jonah had no part of sat heavy in his chest. He always knew that was the plan, that it would be naive to expect anything different, but it was harder thinking about it in such concrete terms. Liam getting into art school. Liam saving up the money to move. Liam moving on, forging a future and leaving Jonah stagnant and stale, a distant memory in the past. Just part of his story; a series of Friday nights strung together during one strange autumn, and the boy he left there in the end.

Where would Jonah be then, at that point in the not-so-far-off future?

He decided he didn't want to know.

"Hey." The toe of Liam's shoe knocked against his, bringing him back to the moment. "You okay?"

Jonah nodded, soothed by his concern and only a little unnerved by his ability to read him. For now, it was a reminder that they were both still here, together, and that they still had time. However much of it was left.

The ride wasn't long, an hour and fifteen minutes from station to station, but Jonah found himself mourning the loss as they stepped out onto the platform. Liam was right: the train was nice.

Liam had parked his car near the station, so it was waiting for them when they arrived.

Predictably, his top priority was making sure Jonah was fed. They stopped at a drive-in restaurant, where servers on roller skates brought burgers and fries directly to the car. Liam kept the heat running while they ate, the radio providing them with the backdrop of soft Christmas music that played on every station.

They drove around for a while after that, aimless and relaxed. Liam pointed out landmarks from his life along the way: the fence that he'd crashed his car into a month after getting his license, the movie theater where he'd kissed a girl for the first (and last) time, the mall where he had learned, loudly and publicly, that Santa was just a man in a fake beard. Jonah hung on every word, endlessly charmed by his ability to tell a story.

Liam was a good driver. It was almost too true to character, in the most endearing way, how he followed the rules to a T.

"What?" he asked when Jonah's laugh slipped out.

"Nothing." Jonah was inexplicably unable to keep the smile off his face. "You're just very. . . you."

"Oh, great."

"That's far from a bad thing," Jonah said.

Liam shot him a sidelong glance, as if searching for a punchline that wasn't coming. "Thanks," he finally said, looking back toward the road.

They pulled to a stop outside of a children's playground. Even in the dark, Jonah could see the pristine condition in which everything was kept. Fresh, shiny coats of paint covered every piece of equipment. He had understood from the moment the train pulled into town that Liam's hometown was a wealthy one, but this was a stark reminder of their differences in upbringings.

"When I was seventeen," Liam began, pointing to a white fence along the back wall of the playground, "I won an art contest through the city, and I was selected to paint a mural there. I was so excited. I mean, at the time, it was the best thing that had ever happened to me. I never really talked much about my art, outside of the few classes I had in school, so I thought. . . This is my chance. Finally, people will see that I'm not just the weird kid who follows Ben Baker and Nathan Scott around like a puppy. That I can actually do stuff, too.

"It was summer break. I spent every single day on it, staying past dark with a portable light I brought from home. The city supplied the paint, but I went out and spent my allowance on special brushes so I could make it just how I wanted it to look. I mean, if it was going to be a permanent fixture in the neighborhood, I had to make it good. I put everything I had into that mural."

He paused, and Jonah felt a tight knot forming in his stomach.

"On the last day," Liam continued, "I showed up to add the finishing touches, and the whole thing had been covered. Dried, splattered eggs. Buckets of paint that had just been thrown over it. And, because teenagers can never be creative, a few predictable words spray painted on. It wasn't the first time I'd been on the receiving end of that kind of insult, but it was certainly the most public."

"Liam. . ."

"Obviously, as you can see, they had to scrap the whole project; they hired people to paint over it the next day." He gestured weakly to the white fence with a laugh. "They offered me the chance to start over if I wanted to, but I knew it would just happen again. I figured I'd save everyone the trouble. I didn't realize how much it would affect me, but after that I sort of. . ." Liam shrugged, reaching up to rub at the back of his neck. "I just kind of lost all motivation. For anything. It was bad timing, because it was my junior year, when I was supposed to be putting together a portfolio for art school and getting a head start on applications and college tours, but I just... couldn't. I couldn't bring myself to look at any of it. I started missing shifts at work and skipping school to just lie in bed all day. My parents were angry, but I think, more than that, they were worried. And honestly, they had every right to be. I had all but given up."

Jonah didn't know what to say. He only knew that he wanted to erase that look from Liam's face and never see it there again.

"Anyway," Liam said after a moment. "That's how I got where I am. I might have been in New York by now, actually doing something with my life, but instead I let a rough patch at seventeen throw my whole life off track."

On that point, at least, Jonah could relate.

"Those kids are going to regret that," Jonah said with conviction. "When you're a big-shot artist in New York City, and they're still just the losers who never left."

Liam quirked a smile. "You have a lot of faith in this uphill battle of mine."

"That's a faith I can get behind," he said. Then, "I'm sorry. I'm sure your mural was beautiful."

Liam stared at the fence, as if he could still see the remnants of the art. "You know," he said after a moment. "It was."

Jonah followed his gaze, then let it slide over to the swing set, chewing on the idea that had occurred to him when they first pulled up. Desperate to ease the weight that had settled over Liam, he said, "Do you want to swing?"

He turned back to Jonah, blinking. "It's cold."

"We have coats," Jonah pointed out. For a moment he thought Liam would turn him down, but then he killed the ignition, reaching for the door handle.

"Fuck it. Let's swing."

Liam wasn't wrong about it being cold. The chains on the swings were like blocks of ice under their palms, but they tugged their coat sleeves down and made it work. Jonah couldn't bring himself to care about the temperatures, not when there was the promise of a warm car after, and a smile back on Liam's face.

They settled into a mutual silence, falling in and out of sync as they swung. Only when the wind from his own momentum pulled cold tears from the corners of his eyes did Jonah kick to a stop. Liam followed his cue, but they didn't leave. They floated for a while, bumping side to side on their swings with their toes planted on the rubber asphalt.

"I know what it's like," Jonah said, breaking the silence. "Feeling like an outsider in the place you grew up. Not exactly the same circumstances, but I know these places aren't always kind to people like us. It was the same for me in Indiana."

Liam's eyes fell on him. "Indiana," he repeated. "Is that where you're from?"

Jonah nodded. "It was a little different for me. I wasn't out for most of my life there. Not. . ." He pressed his lips together, grinding his teeth. "Not until the end. I knew how it would be received."

Liam was careful with his approach, as if sensing how precarious a line he was walking. "You don't say much about your home life," he said.

"My parents," Jonah began, then had to stop to swallow around a lump in his throat. "It's not easy to talk about."

"You don't have to," Liam said softly.

Jonah knew that. Liam had made it clear countless times before, never pushing, never pressuring, always letting things drop when Jonah clammed up. He thought that was exactly why he felt the resistance falling away now.

"They caught me with a boy from my soccer team," he said, laying the words bare before he could second-guess them. "It was my senior year, months away from graduation. And it was... It was just a kiss." He swallowed, breaking off into a whisper. "We were just kissing."

He closed his eyes, and he could picture it so clearly: the back of his father's hand across his cheek, his mother's streaked mascara, a folded brochure slid across the table to him. *It's a really great program, Jonah. These people can really help you. Don't worry about the cost, it's already taken care of. No, Jonah, it isn't up for debate.*

"My father never shied away from corporal punishment," he said. "'Spare the rod, spoil the child,' and all that. But when he hit me that time, I felt the difference. I knew it was personal. He wasn't hitting me to correct my behavior; he hit me because he hated the person I had just shown him that I was."

Jonah glanced up to find Liam watching him with such intense horror that he had to look away.

"They didn't even look at me for a week," he continued. "They didn't speak to me. My mom cried all the time. I could tell my siblings were scared. I don't think they understood what was going on. I felt like I had destroyed my whole family.

"They came to me a couple weeks later with an ultimatum. Our pastor was sitting at the kitchen table with some packet about a camp for *boys like me*. The church was willing to help foot the bill. I was turning eighteen in a few weeks. I told them they couldn't force me to go." He swallowed. "They told me it was that or nothing. It was the condition I had to meet to live under their roof, to have access to any of my college savings. But I couldn't. . ."

Jonah resented the burn of oncoming tears. He had promised himself a long time ago he wouldn't shed any more tears for his parents.

"Do you know how many times I've wondered what would have happened if I'd just stayed and stuck it out?" Jonah asked, turning back to Liam, who seemed to be holding back tears of his own. "A few months of enduring their bullshit camp, and I could have built a different life. I could have lied, I could have been smart about it. But they had me cornered, and I was so angry, and I was so sure I was doing the right thing by running away. I had a couple thousand saved up from summer jobs, and I thought it would be enough... I didn't know..."

"How could you have known?" Liam whispered.

"I couldn't have," Jonah agreed. "I was just some sheltered kid from the country, out on the streets with no one to turn to. Of course I fell blindly to the first person who showed me sympathy."

Liam went still beside him. "Was that—? I mean, the man who...?"

"No," Jonah said. "There was someone else, before." His bravery withered as he approached this gap in his history, but he pushed forward. "His name was Dominic. I had only been in Chicago a couple of months when we met. I thought..." He took a deep breath and watched it mist around him on the exhale. "He was the first person I ever thought I loved."

"How did you meet?" He could tell Liam wanted to ask more but was choosing wisely.

"He was on a smoke break at the time I happened to be getting mugged." Jonah offered him a wry smile. "I'd already blown through my savings by that point and was sleeping on the streets when I couldn't get a bed at a shelter. He found me that night and took me in. It was just supposed to be long enough to get me cleaned up, but it turned into weeks. He kept asking me to stay, and I did."

Sometimes it was hard to believe that time in his life existed at all, that it wasn't some strange dream. Looking back, the details were already fickle in his memory. Had it been four roommates or five? What color were the sheets on

Dominic's mattress on the floor? Was it cigarette smoke or marijuana that always left the shared bathroom slightly hazy? Had he ever really loved Jonah at all?

"Things got intense between us," Jonah continued. "I had never had that kind of freedom before. I was still so angry at everything behind me, and he was so nice to me when he didn't have to be, so I gave everything to that relationship. It was all I had. If he offered me a drink, I took it. Drugs, whatever. I wanted him to keep wanting me." He squeezed the swing's chains, letting the rigid metal bite into his palms. "When he told me I could have sex for money, it wasn't something I had ever really thought about. But it was hard to say no when he had done so much for me, and I had no way of paying him back. So I did it. And kept doing it."

"Was he taking the money?" Liam asked.

"No," Jonah said quickly, too defensive. "It wasn't like that. Most of the money went toward rent and food, which was fair since I was staying with him. I got caught, though," Jonah said. "I wasn't being careful enough, I guess, because I was arrested. I don't. . ." He stopped and looked up at Liam. "I still don't want to get into the details. It's not that I don't trust you. I just—"

"Jonah, it's okay." Almost hesitantly, Liam uncurled one hand from his swing and held it out between them. Jonah took it, squeezing tightly.

"Dominic is the one who introduced me to the person I work for now," he said before he could back down. "It got me out of a bad situation and put me in a worse one, but I have to believe that Dominic thought he was doing the right thing at the time. I guess I'll never know for sure." At Liam's questioning look, he said, "By the time I was released, he was gone. His phone was deactivated. His room at the apartment was cleared out. It was as if he'd never existed."

"It sounds like a guilty conscience," Liam said with more heat than Jonah expected.

"I know," Jonah said. "But I still want to believe some part of it was real for him."

Liam nodded again, though not without some hesitation that time. "It makes more sense, now," he said after another lapse in silence. "Having the context of why you're so against going to the police. I'm sorry."

"You didn't know," Jonah said.

"You know this doesn't make me feel differently about you, right? The knowing?" Liam said.

Jonah pushed his toes into the asphalt, knocking his swing against Liam's. "I think that speaks more to your character than mine."

Liam grabbed Jonah's chain before he could swing away, keeping him close. "No," he said. There was an intensity in his gaze that Jonah couldn't look away from. "What you did in the past does not make you deserving of what's happening to you now. You were only trying to survive."

Jonah was unmoored by the sudden closeness, their foggy breath mixing in the scant distance between them. It would have made him retreat if it were anyone but Liam, but it wasn't anyone else. It was him, and Jonah didn't want to pull away.

"Maybe you're too forgiving of me," Jonah said.

"There's nothing to forgive."

I could kiss him right now. The thought landed soft and sure, like a snowflake on the tip of his tongue, melting into him on contact. *I want to kiss him.*

But he was frozen in place, too afraid of closing the gap, and Liam, because he was Liam, took that hesitation at face value. He was the first to back away, releasing his hold on Jonah's swing.

"It's cold," he said. "Your nose is turning red."

He didn't point out that every inch of Liam's exposed skin was wind-bitten pink. "Where should we go?" Jonah asked.

"I have somewhere in mind."

The diner where Liam worked was open twenty-four hours. It was just after one in the morning when they arrived.

It was mostly dead at the late hour, so they didn't have to feel bad about taking up residence to warm up with refills of coffee (for Jonah) and hot chocolate (for Liam).

Jonah had spent so much time wondering what Liam's life looked like outside the confines of their isolated Friday nights. He had wondered about this place in particular, after enjoying the takeout boxes Liam brought with him, smelling the remnants of fried food that clung to his skin and his hair, and catching glimpses of his uniform poking out from his backpack. It was almost surreal to be inside of it now, like he had been transported into a world from a book he'd once read.

The place was quaint, with checkered floors and vinyl booths. Music floated in from an actual, functioning jukebox in the corner. It was the kind of vintage that wasn't engineered to fit a trend; it was just *old*, as evidenced by the cracks in the tile, the wood-paneled walls, and a waitress who looked like she had been built into the place with the beams. Liam called her Darla, and she ruffled his hair like she was genuinely happy to see him there on his night off. Jonah liked her immediately.

The Christmas decorations, which surely hadn't seen an update since the 1980s, added to the idyllic charm. Strings of rainbow lights stretched around the interior perimeter, accented with gaudy ropes of red and green tinsel.

Under the table, their shoes knocked against each other every few minutes, a byproduct of Liam's long legs, which he apologized for repeatedly. Jonah should have told him there was a comfort in the small moments of contact, but he kept that to himself.

There was a dreamlike quality to the scene. Jonah couldn't shake the thought that he had been shrunken down and transported into a snow-globe, encased behind glass as a picture-perfect snapshot, far from the realities outside. He never wanted to leave. He knew the night would end, that the glass would crack when morning came and send him spilling out into the world, but he wouldn't think of that now.

Jonah had switched to decaf after his first cup, and his eyelids were starting to feel heavy.

"Tired?" Liam asked, catching him mid-yawn.

Jonah shook his head. "I'm fine."

Liam smiled, seeing right through it. "It's okay if you are. It's been a long day, and it's late."

A glance at the clock told him it was past two in the morning. The tables around them had steadily cleared out over the course of an hour. The only people who filed in this point were the post-bar crowd, stumbling in after last call in search of something greasy.

"I was wondering," Liam started, his hands fidgeting on the table, "if you might want to go back to my place? Just to get a few hours of sleep," he added quickly.

Jonah blinked at him. "You. . . want to take me to your house?"

"Technically, it's my parents' house," he said. "And not that they would mind if I brought a friend over anyway, but they'll be dead asleep by now." He must have read Jonah's silence as a rejection, because he followed up with, "We don't have to, if that makes you uncomfortable. We can always catch a few hours in the car instead."

"It's not that," Jonah was quick to assure him. But then, what was it? The fear that this excursion into Liam's personal life was an invasion, leaving tainted footprints in his wake? The guilt of leaving his mark on his world, when Jonah couldn't really be a part of it? That was hardly something to bring up over coffee. "Are you sure?" he asked.

Liam tilted his head, as if it never occurred to him to be anything but. "Of course. I even cleaned in anticipation of company."

Of course he had.

"Okay," Jonah agreed.

The bell on the diner's front door, accompanied by the commotion of drunken chatter, signified the entry of a new group, fresh from the bars. Liam and Jonah were in a corner booth, secluded enough to reduce them to background noise, but when Liam glanced over Jonah's shoulder, he went rigid.

"Shit," he hissed.

Jonah had his back to the door. When he tried to turn to find the source of Liam's distress, a hand tapped frantically against his. "No, no, don't look," Liam whispered, ducking his head low. His agitation put Jonah on edge.

"Who is it?" Jonah asked. "What's wrong?"

"We should go." He was already pulling a twenty-dollar bill out of his wallet, tucking the corner beneath his empty mug.

"Is everything okay?" Jonah asked, sliding out of the booth at his cue.

"Yeah, sorry. Just... a confrontation I'm really not looking to have tonight."

They made it to the exit just after the hostess led the group to their table. Jonah kept his head down, resisting the urge to seek out whatever threat had Liam so shaken.

They were one foot out the door when a voice called out from behind them.

"Hey, Cassidy!"

They stopped. Liam cursed under his breath, and Jonah suddenly understood why.

Because he recognized that voice, too.

CHAPTER 20
Liam

Nathan caught up with them in the parking lot, apparently determined enough to harass Liam that he left his friends at the table.

"Cassidy," he said again, undeterred as Liam ducked out from under the hand on his shoulder. "You can't still be avoiding me."

I really, really can.

"We were just leaving." He double-tapped the key fob in his coat pocket, his car lighting up down the row.

"Who's your friend?"

Jonah, who hadn't said a word since they stepped outside, kept his head down. Liam placed his hand gently on his elbow and kept them moving toward the car.

Nathan stepped directly into their path, then went still. "Wait." He ducked to get a look at Jonah's face, and his eyes went wide. "No shit." He rocked back on his heels, glancing from Jonah to Liam. "Seriously, Cassie? Is *this* why we haven't seen you in weeks?"

Liam cringed at the nickname. "I've been working," he defended.

Nathan turned back to Jonah. "I guess you both have."

Jonah's eyes hadn't left the ground. His jaw was a hard line of tension, agitated twitches of muscle under his skin. A surge of protection ripped through Liam.

"Watch it," he warned.

"It's a joke," Nathan said, in the familiar tone of all the *jokes* he had hurled at Liam over the years. "He can take a joke, right? Hey, you should be thanking me. I didn't realize I was playing matchmaker, but it looks like everything worked out."

His face warmed despite the cold wind, but he didn't know if it was from embarrassment or rage. "Jonah is just my friend."

Nathan blinked, cutting his eyes to him. "'*Jonah?*'" he echoed.

He felt Jonah stiffen beside him. Liam wanted to run himself over with his own car. It had been so long since he thought of him as Leo, and he was frankly surprised Nathan remembered him by any name at all, but still—it was a careless mistake.

"Don't let us keep you from your friends," Liam said, desperately swerving away from the subject.

"Right," Nathan said, glancing between them again. His eyes lingered on Jonah a few seconds longer. "Are you coming to dinner next weekend? Or will you still be avoiding me then?"

Liam had already been dreading seeing Nathan and Ben at their families' yearly pre-Christmas dinner. Now he wanted to withdraw from it entirely. He could only imagine the ways that Nathan would dangle this story over him in front of everyone. In front of Liam's parents.

"I'll be there," he said, short and clipped.

"Great." Nate smiled, a wolfish grin. Before he left, he turned to Jonah one more time. "Good seeing you again, *Jonah*."

Liam waited until they were back inside the car before he pressed his palms against his face. "I'm so sorry," he said miserably.

"For what?"

"For using your real name, for one. And for the fact that you had to interact with him at all." Liam dropped his hands. "Believe me when I say he was the last person I wanted to run into tonight."

"It's fine." Jonah glanced his way long enough for a quick smile. Liam watched as he fidgeted with his sleeves, visibly on edge.

"Are you okay?" Liam asked.

As if catching his own tell, Jonah stilled his hands, flattening them against his lap. "I'm good," he said. "I'm having a really good time. Don't let him ruin it for you."

Liam shook his head, forcing a cleansing breath. "You're right. Sorry."

As expected, the house was dark when they arrived. Liam took Jonah to the back door, since it was a more direct route to his room.

Jonah crouched to unlace his shoes as soon as they stepped inside, but Liam waved him off. The last thing he needed was his parents finding a pair of unfamiliar men's shoes on the way to the bathroom and jumping to the most obvious conclusion.

"On your left," he whispered, pointing toward his room. Jonah moved with eerie silence behind him, his footfalls barely registering on the carpet.

They slipped in undetected. Once the door shut behind them, Liam turned to find Jonah smiling at him. "What?" he asked.

"Nothing," Jonah said. "That just seemed very practiced. You have a lot of experience sneaking guys in?"

Liam snorted. "You know me. A real Casanova."

"You got *me* here, didn't you?"

There was still that curl of a smile at the corner of his mouth, and for a moment Liam couldn't find the line between the truth and a joke. Jonah seemed to have the realization at the same time, turning away to instead examine the inside of Liam's room for the first time.

It was surreal to see him there, outside of a bland hotel room and transported into Liam's most intimate space, like a dream come to life.

Jonah toed off his shoes in the corner and walked the perimeter, fingertips drawing lightly over the collage of Liam's sketches plastered to the wall.

"You did all of these?" he asked.

Liam hadn't accounted for the attention this visit would bring him. He shoved his hands in his pockets, putting on his best impersonation of someone who was very, completely cool about his work being observed. "Yeah," he said, then added quickly, "Some of them are years old." He pointed to the one Jonah had stopped in front of. "I drew that when I was fourteen. Not my best work."

"Fourteen?" Jonah looked back at him. "Liam, that's amazing."

He was pretty certain all the blood in his body had pooled in his face.

Jonah continued his tour, and Liam watched with sudden horror as he stumbled on the most embarrassing piece on the wall. "Oh, that's. . . God, don't look at that. I can't believe I still have it hanging up." In truth, he had almost torn it down a number of times, most recently after his twenty-first birthday. But every time, some pathetic part of him held him back from throwing it out.

"Is that. . . ?" Jonah crouched to get a better look: three young boys with their arms around each other, as depicted by a ten-year-old Liam.

Jonah looked up at him. Liam stared at the picture, if only to avoid Jonah's eyes. "Believe it or not, there was a time when things were good." Back before they had been old enough to notice the differences between them, or to care about them even if they did. "I guess some part of me clung onto the hope that things could be good again. What does that say about me?"

Jonah stood to his full height and turned to face him. "That you're a good friend," he said. "They don't deserve you."

An edge of real anger laced his words.

Liam watched his expression, the encounter from the diner parking lot still close to the surface. "I never did ask you," he began cautiously. "I mean, I assume you had to spend some time with them the night we met? Nathan and Ben. Were they. . . ?" He cleared his throat. "I know how they can be."

Jonah turned back toward the wall. "It wasn't a long walk back to the hotel."

That. . . decidedly didn't feel like a real answer, but he could feel Jonah closing up on him, and he didn't want to push. Nathan and Ben had no place here tonight.

"You know," Liam said, sinking down onto the side of his bed, "I probably have a lot to apologize for from that night. I was so awkward. I–" He broke off into a startled laugh at the memory. "I mean, shirtless and rambling in the bathroom was not a stellar first impression, but then I really doubled down in the hotel room. Could I have handled that any worse?"

"You could have." Jonah turned back to him, an easy smile back in place. He walked over to the bed and sat next to Liam. "I got the impression you didn't make a regular habit of hiring rent boys."

"I don't know where you got that idea." Liam leaned sideways to bump shoulders. The brush of contact felt more charged than usual inside this room. He pulled back. "I don't have anything against making money from it, you know. When it's safe and consensual and. . ." He stopped himself before he could venture too far down that path. "It was purely a *me* thing. I'm. . . I've never. . ."

"Paid for it?"

Why had he brought this up? "Anything," Liam said, face heating. "All of it. I'm. . ."

"A virgin?"

Liam covered his face. "Does the energy just radiate from my pores?"

"They may have mentioned it," Jonah said. "When they set me up with you."

Liam wanted to melt into his bedsheets. "Of course they did," he said. "Why *wouldn't* they find a way to make the whole thing even more humiliating."

"It's nothing to be ashamed of," Jonah said.

Liam brought his head up to look at him. "I'm twenty-one."

"You were also raised religious," Jonah pointed out. "And even if you weren't, so what? Even if you never wanted to, it's nobody's business. Definitely not theirs."

"I do," Liam said, a little more quickly than he intended. "Want to, I mean. Eventually, with the right person or whatever. It's not like I'm waiting for marriage or anything. I may be a hopeless romantic, but I'm hardly a traditionalist."

"Have you ever kissed a guy?"

Liam was busy twisting a loose thread from his pillowcase around his finger when Jonah asked the question. It snapped free, the blood flow rushing back to his fingertip. He looked up at Jonah, who was looking back at him, his whole body angled in Liam's direction.

"You haven't, have you?"

Liam swallowed. "No," he admitted.

Jonah placed his hand on the mattress between them, inching toward Liam without making contact. "Do you want to?"

He couldn't put words to the shift that happened then, the buzz in the air that seemed to intensify from his words. He couldn't say who leaned in first, but they were definitely closer than they had been moments before. Jonah's eyes were the first to twitch downward to his lips, and Liam felt a bolt of electricity thrum from his scalp to his fingertips.

"Jonah," Liam whispered. "I'm not. . . I didn't bring you here with any expectation of. . ."

Jonah inched back, watching him carefully. "Is that a no?"

Liam was shaking his head before he could even finish processing the question. "It's not a no," he said. He reached down and covered Jonah's hand, turning it over to fold their fingers together. "I'm just very aware of. . . I never want you to feel obligated."

"It's not like that," he promised. "Not with you."

They were close enough now that he could feel Jonah's breath against his lips. Jonah raised a hand to cup Liam's cheek, rough fingertips sliding over the stubble on his jaw. Liam closed his eyes.

"Ask me," Jonah whispered.

Liam's swallow was loud enough to puncture the quiet. "Can I kiss you?"

Jonah answered by pushing forward to close the distance. The first graze of their lips was so subtle he almost thought he'd imagined it. It wouldn't have been the first time.

The second kiss, though, was unmistakable.

CHAPTER 21
Liam

"*Liam.*"

He woke to the sound of his name in Jonah's mouth. Liam hummed, rolling his face into the pillow—his own, he realized, and not the generic fluff from a hotel. Recognition trickled in, warming him with memories of the preceding hours: Jonah in his bed, the taste of his mouth and the warmth from his hands as they soaked up his last few moments of freedom—

"Liam, *please.*"

His eyes sprang open, alertness chasing away the last remnants of sleep. Liam's stomach bottomed out at the sunlight reflected off the wall.

They had overslept.

No. *No.*

He sat up, searching out Jonah, who stood from a crouch by the bed.

"Your phone died." Jonah scraped his fingers over his arms, leaving pink tracks in their wake. "It must have gotten unplugged somehow. I don't know, but it died, and the alarm didn't go off, and I-*Fuck*. I have to go. I need to get back *right now*."

"Shit." Liam kicked off the blankets, rolling ungracefully to his feet. "Shit, Jonah, I-I'm so sorry."

Jonah pressed his fist against his mouth, as if containing a scream. He shook his head. Liam risked a glance at the clock on the wall. Jonah was supposed to be outside of the hotel in Chicago seven minutes ago.

"Fuck," he breathed, trying to get a hold on his panic. "Okay. Okay. I'll get you back, okay?" He knew that wasn't enough, but he couldn't help repeating, "I'll get you back there."

He scrambled to pull himself together in record time, grabbing for the first pair of shoes he laid eyes on, forgoing socks and a jacket entirely.

Jonah stood against the wall, out of the way, chewing his fingernails. Liam got the sense that he was suppressing the urge to ask him to hurry. There was a caginess to him that Liam hadn't seen since their earliest days together, his body shrunken in on itself as if he wanted to disappear. Still draped in Liam's oversized sweatshirt, it looked like he might do just that.

"Come on," Liam said, grabbing his car keys off the dresser. "We can sneak out the back."

Their only mercy was that they were able to get out and lock up without crossing paths with Liam's parents. If there was ever a time to avoid introductions, it was now.

His hands were shaking when they got to the car. He fumbled the keys twice, then went several rounds of hitting the automatic locks at the same time Jonah tried to open the door. Liam wanted to bash his own head against the window.

He slapped the radio switch as they peeled out of the driveway, killing the cheerful hum of Christmas music that had provided such a calming backdrop the night before.

Liam felt like he had woken to a nightmare.

They were silent for most of the drive. He could feel Jonah's gaze flicking back to the GPS tracker every few seconds, willing Liam to go faster. Liam kept vigilant watch on the rearview mirror, half expecting a flare of police lights to sneak up behind them at any moment, but still he pushed the acceleration.

The tension was like a tangible fume in the air, thick and unstable. He was sure that if he were to light a match, they would have been blown to pieces.

Jonah curled himself against the passenger door, one arm wound tightly over his stomach while the other supported his head on the window. Liam felt every inch of his restlessness, his fear. It was particularly disquieting after seeing such a vastly different side of Jonah the night before.

For nearly an hour, Liam had the privilege of watching Jonah open up to him, watching the tension he always carried in his body melt away bit by bit, cheeks flushed and smiling and loose as he held Liam close and let himself be held in return.

And now, this.

Surely Jonah would hate him now, and Liam would deserve it. He had asked a lot of him, trusting Liam to come away from the city and into his home, and he had let him down. More importantly, Jonah would be in trouble when he got back—whatever that might entail—and Liam was the one responsible.

The city came into view like a tsunami on the horizon, tall and threatening. Panic seized Liam's chest as he took the appropriate lane. What would happen from here? Would Jonah show up to their next visit sporting new bruises, as he had before? Would it be worse this time?

Would he even want to see Liam again?

Would he be allowed to?

The closer they got to their hotel, the more daunting the possibilities grew in his head. He was spiraling out of control, keenly aware with each passing second that his time was running out. In just a few minutes, he would have to watch Jonah climb out of his car and walk back into the arms of his abuser, knowing that, intentionally or not, he had set him up to be hurt.

"Don't go back today." The words tumbled out of him before he could stop himself.

Jonah looked over at him for the first time since they got in the car. "What?"

"Don't go back to him." Liam's voice was on the edge of hysteria. "Stay with me, let me drive you somewhere. Anywhere. We can tell someone. We can do something. Anything. Please, just don't make me take you back to him."

"Liam." His voice was unexpectedly hard, but Liam pushed onward, undeterred.

"Jonah, look at you." He waved his hand in a wild gesture toward where he was shaking apart in the passenger seat. "How can I let you out of my car right now knowing what you're going back to?"

"'*Let me?*'"

Liam winced. "You know what I mean."

Jonah was quiet for a moment, and Liam experienced a wild surge of hope that maybe he was considering his words. When he spoke again, the rawness in his voice shattered that dream on impact.

"Did you listen to a word I told you last night?" Jonah asked. "I thought you understood now. I trusted you to understand. I can't run from this."

They were only blocks away from the hotel now.

"There has to be some way," he pleaded.

There was an agitated rustle of movement in the passenger seat. "Let me out here," Jonah said. "I can walk. I don't want him to see you."

"Jonah, please."

"Liam, let me out!"

He hit the brakes, cars honking past him as he swerved into an empty fire lane. There was a fleeting moment of dead silence.

"I'm so sorry," Liam whispered. He was surprised to feel a hand on his wrist a moment later, squeezing tight.

"It's not your fault," Jonah said, then, when Liam couldn't immediately meet his eyes, he squeezed harder, just approaching the edge of pain. "Hey. Look at me." Liam did, his tears spilling over. "This was not your fault."

The words sounded too much like *goodbye* to be of any comfort.

"Will you—" Liam broke off in a panic when Jonah released his arm. "Jonah, will you be okay?"

There was no hesitation. "I'll be fine."

"Will I see you again?"

Jonah pulled his sweatshirt—the one Liam had become so accustomed to seeing on him—over his head, dropping it on the console between them. He opened his mouth to reply, then reached for the door instead.

"I have to go," he said, climbing out onto the sidewalk. "I'm sorry."

The door slammed shut before Liam could say another word.

For a few stunned moments, it was all he could do to watch as Jonah made his way down the block, hands swiping furiously at his exposed arms. Liam reached over and touched the sweatshirt, still warm from Jonah's skin. When he picked it up, bringing the fabric close to his chest, a papery rustle drew his eyes to the passenger seat. There, having fallen from the pocket, was a crumpled wad of cash.

Jonah's money.

Liam nearly ripped the phone charger out of its port in his haste to get out of the car, breaking into a run. "Jonah!" he called, but he was too far ahead to hear him. He picked up the pace.

He was just catching up as Jonah turned a corner, disappearing from view. "Jonah," he repeated as he rounded after him, but he skidded to a stop as soon as he cleared the corner.

Jonah had stopped, too, just a few feet in front of a tall man in a leather jacket, who was halfway out of his car. He towered over them both as he stood, looking down at Jonah with dark eyes and a mean, flat line of a mouth.

Liam's body went numb, plastering him to the sidewalk.

So this was him, he thought.

They both wheeled on Liam at the same time. It was Jonah's widened eyes that made him realize his mistake, and his rage hardened to ice-cold dread.

He'd used the wrong name.

Again.

Liam took a step closer, but as he did, the man took hold of Jonah's arm and yanked him toward the car.

"Do we have a problem, kid?" the man said to Liam. They were close enough now that he kept his voice low. The streets were relatively empty this early on a Saturday morning, so there was no one around to see the flash of black metal tucked into his waistband as he drew back the hem of his jacket.

Liam froze. His eyes moved to Jonah, who was silently pleading with him from behind the man's shoulder. There was already a patch of red blossoming on his upper arm from the way he had been handled. Liam wanted to scream.

"It's my fault he was late," he whispered. "Completely my fault."

The man stared at him, unmoving. Behind him, Jonah shook his head, and Liam wasn't sure if it was in disagreement with his assertion of fault or if he was begging Liam to stop making things worse.

"Leo, get in the car," the man said without looking away from Liam. Jonah didn't hesitate to comply, closing himself into the backseat without so much as a glance back at Liam. The man stepped into Liam's space. "There a reason you're following him?"

"I—" Liam began, but the man snapped his fingers in front of his face.

"Don't look at him. Look at me. I asked you a question."

Liam's eyes snapped back to his. He couldn't see Jonah through the tinted window of the backseat anyway. "I didn't— I wasn't..." It was hard to speak in the face of someone he both hated and feared in equal measure. "I forgot to give him this." He held out the wad of cash, crushed and damp with sweat from where he was squeezing it tightly in his palm.

The man snatched the money from his hand, making him flinch, and then making him hate himself for flinching. He counted out the bills in front of Liam and tucked them into his jacket. When he reached for something else in his pocket, Liam froze, sure that he was going for the gun, but he pulled out his phone instead. A second later, he flashed a headless photo of Liam at him—the picture from his profile.

"This is you?" he asked.

Unsure if that was rhetorical, Liam nodded. Then he watched in horror as he tapped the red button at the bottom of the screen, effectively blocking Liam's only line of access to Jonah.

"I don't know what you think this is," he said. "But it's over. Don't try to contact him again."

Before Liam could begin to muster a response, an objection, a plea, the man turned away from him and rounded to the driver's side door. He could do nothing but watch as the car pulled away, leaving Liam standing in the cold.

CHAPTER 22
Jonah

The absence of Liam's sweatshirt was a cool burn over his skin as the car carried him toward the outskirts of the city. Jonah dug his fingers into his sides as he tried to focus on breathing.

The crash from the whirlwind of a morning was landing hard. The fear of whatever repercussions awaited him almost paled in comparison to the guilt of how he'd left things with Liam. The image of him standing there on the sidewalk with desperate, pleading eyes was seared into Jonah's memory. Even after an hour of Jonah at his worst—impatient and snappy and scared out of his mind—Liam still looked at him like he was someone worth saving. And Jonah had left him there, alone.

It stung to realize that this was the natural consequence of his actions. Jonah had been playing with fire for too long, inching closer and closer to the warmth of the flame he had been kindling with Liam, and he had finally been burned.

He only wished he could have spared Liam the trauma of the fallout.

They were minutes away from the house, the dilapidated landmarks of the neighborhood coming into view, when Marcus spoke up from the front seat.

"You want to tell me what that was about?"

Jonah winced. What could he say? Telling him anything about Liam was out of the question, but Marcus had seen too much to buy him playing dumb.

"You were late." Marcus met his eyes in the rearview mirror, impatient for an answer.

"I overslept." Jonah's voice cracked. "It was an accident."

"That wasn't the direction of the hotel you were coming from."

His ribs were going to bruise from how hard he was digging his fingertips in.

"He called you Jonah," Marcus accused.

He squeezed his eyes shut. There was nothing he could say to that. Nothing he said would ever dig him out of the hole he had dug for himself.

"I went up to the room number," Marcus continued, "after thirty minutes with no word. Imagine my surprise when a woman came to the door, looking nothing like the guy from the profile. Said she didn't know any *Leo*."

A lash of anger whipped out of Jonah before he could stop it. "Why does it matter where I go as long as I'm getting the money?"

"You're sneaking around, careless with your curfew, and giving out your name to clients," Marcus fired back. "What do you think you're doing?"

"I'm not hurting anyone."

"He'll kill you, you know." The words came bluntly, as casually as if they were discussing the weather. "If Shepard thinks you're running your mouth to people? He'll put a needle in your arm and make it look like an accident. Is that what you want? Are you trying to get yourself killed?"

Hot, prickly fear crackled under his skin. The threat was nothing new, one of the many Shepard wielded over him. It wasn't the first time he'd pondered that question, either. *Was he trying to get himself killed?* Not actively, he didn't think, but there were traces of evidence—the dark, empty wall ahead of him when he tried to picture a future outside of his current circumstances, the rare moments of resistance when he wondered just how far he could push Shepard to provoke him to the kind of violence from which he could never come back.

Marcus seemed to know better than to expect an answer. "You're done seeing him," he said flatly. "Whoever that was, whatever it was. . . it's over."

Jonah watched the past few months slip away from him like a dying light. He'd always known this was temporary, but it was evident by the crash landing just how far he'd let himself get caught up in the hope.

"I go where I'm told," Jonah said. "I don't really get much say in that."

"It's taken care of."

His stomach bottomed out. "Leave him out of this," Jonah begged. "He didn't do anything wrong. He always gives me the money."

Their eyes met, just briefly, in the rearview mirror. "I'm not going to hurt him, if that's what you're implying. You think Shepard would extend the same courtesy, if he found out about your little boyfriend?"

"Please don't tell him."

There was a long, terrifying pause.

"He's still asleep, as far as I know," Marcus said. "I haven't heard from him all morning. He doesn't need to know you were late."

Nausea rolled thick in the pit of Jonah's stomach. He closed his eyes. "What do you want?" He hated how it came out as little more than a broken whisper.

Marcus had never tried anything with him before. Somehow, Jonah felt like it would be worse with him, the quiet, brooding man who toted him from bed to bed and watched him in the rearview with a scrutiny that made him squirm. He could live with it, though, if that was what he needed to do to protect Liam from Shepard's attentions. He could already feel his nerves steeling, his mind closing him off from whatever awaited him.

The eyes in the mirror narrowed in what could have been mistaken for a wince. "That's not what I'm after," he said firmly.

"Then what?"

Marcus sighed. "You keep your mouth shut and your head down, you stay out of trouble from now on, and you save us both a headache. Can you do that?"

He kept his eyes on Jonah long enough to catch his nod of agreement, then looked back toward the road, putting a stop to the conversation.

Jonah leaned his head against the window for the remaining few minutes of the drive, grieving for the boy he lost, the boy he had been inside the safety of their bubble, and the goodbye he'd never get to say.

CHAPTER 23
Liam

At some point, Liam found himself parked in front of his house. He blinked up at it, trying to remember at what point he had decided to walk back to his car, climb into the driver's seat, and drive home.

His arms shook from his iron grip on the steering wheel. He forced himself to let go, watching his hands unclasp as if they belonged to someone else, blood rushing back into his fingers. He glanced at the clock. What was normally an hour trip out of the city had taken him nearly two. The spells he'd spent pulled over on the shoulder, gasping for air through fits of panic, had slowed him down and left him wrung out, exhausted, and numb. Not numb enough, however, to dull the knife-twist in his chest.

His parents would be up by now. Never before had he resented living at home so deeply. The idea of having to force himself through human interaction, having to pretend it was just another Saturday morning, felt insurmountable. It was a jarring step into a reality so separate, so sheltered, from the one he lived in now. All these Friday nights tucked away with Jonah had slowly drawn Liam out of the mundane life he was so desperate to escape, but in an instant, the castle they had built above the rest of the world had crumbled.

All his life, Liam had been sheltered from the monsters that only existed in stories and headlines—the parents who put their children out on the street for the crime of existing, and the people who exploited that vulnerability for their own gain. The world was different now that he could put a face to the darkness he had only ever known about in the abstract.

Liam, in his suburban home, in his wealthy neighborhood, with his perfectly upper-middle-class parents, could have gone his whole life without ever knowing about the things that happened right under his nose. But then he'd met Jonah, and everything had changed.

Except nothing had. These things hadn't just popped into existence once Liam had deigned to see them. The world had always been this way. *Jonah's* world had been this way for so long. And now he was back to facing it alone.

Eventually, Liam managed to make it from his car to the front door. The house was quiet when he walked in, save for the soft melody of worship music playing from the radio in the kitchen. He hoped it would be enough to keep him undetected on the way to his bedroom.

"Liam?" He was almost in the clear when the music turned down.

His eyes fell shut. "Hi, Mom," he said. He spared a glance in the hallway mirror before he turned the corner, deciding there was little he could do about his disheveled appearance.

"Long night?" his mother said, looking up at him from the bowl of eggs she was whisking on the countertop.

Liam tried to crack a smile and quickly realized the attempt was probably more harrowing than his flat expression and gave it up. "Yeah," he said.

"I used to hate working third shift." She shook her head in commiseration. "Are you sure picking up all these extra nights is worth it, honey?"

Worth every second, he didn't say. "It's only temporary."

"Well, I'll have breakfast ready soon, if you're hungry."

The idea of eating curdled his stomach.

"Thanks," he said. "I'll probably try to catch a couple hours of sleep, actually."

"Okay." She smiled, laying down her whisk to step around the counter. Liam half-leaned into her embrace, ducking down to accept a kiss on his temple. "You sure you're alright, kiddo?"

I'm not.

I'm so out of my depth.

Help me. I don't know what to do.

"Just tired," he said.

He didn't make it past the bedroom doorway before he broke. The moment he laid eyes on his bed, memories from the night before rushed to the surface: The first kiss. The second. The third and fourth and fifth melting into a liquid pool of desire and affection and longing and something else that Liam feared putting a name to. Jonah's cheeks flushed red, his body soft and warm and eager under Liam's unsteady hands.

And then the ice-cold plunge of the morning.

Liam knew if he took a step closer, he would catch the scent of Jonah still lingering on the sheets, proof that he had been here only hours ago, before the world collapsed out from under them.

As soon as the lock clicked into place, Liam's legs gave out from under him. He fell back against the door and slid to the carpet, burying his face in his hands.

"*It's over.*" The man's words rang over and over in his head.

Liam had checked the moment he got back to his car; sure enough, Jonah's profile had been erased from his inbox. The only link between them, severed.

He didn't know where Jonah lived, or the name of the man who controlled him, or where he went outside of his endless string of hotel rooms across the city. Liam's IP had been blocked from setting up another meeting, but even if he were to find a workaround—a faceless profile, a borrowed phone, anything—what risk would he pose to Jonah by trying? What risk would he pose to himself?

For weeks, they had been climbing higher and higher, every accidental brush of skin, every smile, every laugh, every secret bolstering the wind beneath their wax wings until they had flown too close to the sun. The view from the ground was unforgiving.

Liam had gotten so swept up in the comfort and familiarity of their arrangement that he had blinded himself to the framework that had always been there at the edges, and now Jonah, surely, would pay for his mistake.

The thought that haunted him to sleep that night was the likelihood that Jonah might mistake Liam's fear for abandonment. That, in Jonah's history, Liam would become nothing more than one more person who left him behind.

CHAPTER 24
Jonah

Days passed in a kaleidoscope of gray.

It had been a week since Jonah's derailed rebellion—a week since Liam had cradled his face between his hands like something precious, and kissed him—and he was sure there was a part of him that had never returned to the city, that stayed dead and buried somewhere in the walls of Liam's childhood bedroom.

Before the break of daylight had stolen it from them, that night in Liam's home had been one of the warmest moments of Jonah's life. Touching Liam, being touched by him with hands just as gentle as the rest of him, had changed something in his chemistry.

He had torn himself open as he had done for no one else, ripped his chest right down the middle and exposed all his soft, vulnerable parts. Then, he had been taken away before he could stitch himself back together.

Jonah was forced back into cruel reality with his heart open and bleeding. It was harder to block out the feeling of strangers' hands, harder to ignore the whispers of false affection, now that he knew what it felt like to be kissed by someone who cared.

If normalcy in Jonah's world had been bleak before, now it was utterly void. The vivid color Liam had brought to his life over the course of a few months had been washed out in the course of a single night. Without the promise of reprieve at the end of the week, the days became unbearably long. Had time always dragged so slowly before? He wasn't sure.

As far as he could tell, Marcus kept his word about not telling Shepard what happened on Saturday morning. He didn't know why, though his darker instincts warned him that there had to be an ulterior motive. Marcus had turned down Jonah's attempt to barter for silence that day in the car, but maybe he was only drawing it out, waiting for the right time to hold it over his head. The constant guesswork and anticipation wore on his nerves, which were already shredded thin.

Jonah was a bowstring, stretched taut and quivering, by the time the following Friday arrived; his first in months without Liam.

When Shepard came to him that evening with a client in the city, Jonah had to fight to smother the tiny spark of hope in his chest. He didn't know how Marcus planned to enforce his ban, but letting his expectations get away from him would only set him up for a crash landing. And Jonah wasn't sure how many more blows he could take.

Long, wispy strings of light blurred past the car window as they made their way into the city. Any residual hope Jonah had fostered of a chance of seeing Liam tonight waned the closer they got to the heart of it; the client had to be a wealthy one to secure a room on Michigan Avenue the week before Christmas.

Nicer hotels sometimes made for harder nights. The sideways glances from lobby attendants were bad enough, making Jonah want to shrink away inside his ratty t-shirt and jeans. But it was what happened behind closed doors that made Jonah dread nights like tonight.

The dynamic that came with the wider-than-usual wealth disparity was sometimes difficult to navigate. The guys with deep pockets saw Jonah as something they were entitled to. For some of them, there was no boundary they couldn't throw money at and make it go away. Sometimes, they were men who knew Shepard personally, and Jonah had to wonder just how much they knew about Jonah's choice in the matter at all.

Jonah made it all of four steps past the check-in counter before an older woman in a blazer and a nametag stopped him.

"Sir, the restroom is for guests only," she said, already pointing back toward the door. "I'm afraid you'll need to find somewhere else."

Jonah avoided her eyes, wrapping his arms around himself. "I'm here to see a friend," he said quietly. In his periphery, he could feel the curious stares of nearby patrons. He was too tired to be angry, so embarrassment won out instead.

"A friend," she repeated. "What's the room number?"

Jonah tried to be discreet as he glanced at the digits scribbled on his palm. "814."

"You won't mind if I ring up, then?" She was already picking up the phone, indifferent to Jonah's answer. He stared at the wall over her shoulder as she waited for someone to pick up. "Hello, is this— Yes, I'm so sorry to bother you, but I have a young man here in the lobby claiming he's here to see you. His name is. . ." She raised her eyebrows pointedly at him.

"Leo," he whispered.

She repeated it into the phone, and Jonah watched as the expression on her face melted into a different sort of judgment. "Okay. Thank you," she said, the cheer in her voice becoming a little more forced. "I'll send him up." The phone came down a little harder than necessary. "Elevators are in the second hall to the left." Her smile was cold and sharp. "Across from the business center."

Jonah ducked away from the desk, eager to escape the exposure of the crowded lobby.

The elevators were where she promised they would be, three sets of golden doors that were just smooth enough to reflect a fuzzy outline of himself. Even the featureless silhouette couldn't quite pass for someone who belonged here. Jonah looked away and pressed the call button.

He stood alone in the elevator bay as he waited, swaying on his feet. Hotel patrons in sleek black suits and evening gowns passed by in the adjacent main hall, their voices low and bubbling with laughter. Their movement drew his eyes to the left, and when the small crowd dispersed, he was left staring at the room across the hall. The business center.

Most of the room appeared to extend behind a wall, but the entryway was encased in glass, revealing the edge of a desktop computer, a black leather office chair, a printer. . .

And a phone.

Ding.

Jonah blinked at the arrival of the elevator, stepping back to make way for the group of guests that spilled out around him. He was left standing there when the doors closed again.

There was an analog clock embedded in the marble wall, which told him he had six minutes until the arranged meeting time. His legs were already moving in the direction of the small glass room. He looked both ways as he crossed the wide hallway, wary of. . . what? He wasn't sure. Paranoia clung to him like static, sure that every eye was watching him, that someone would come and rip the opportunity away.

No one even glanced in his direction. Emboldened by his invisibility, Jonah wrapped his palm around the door handle and pushed inside.

He swiped at his eyes one last time as the elevator opened onto his client's floor.

The number on his palm was smudged into a shapeless blot by this point, but he remembered. He walked to the end of the hall—a corner suite, he thought absently—and stopped in front of the door, pressing a hand to the flat of his stomach. He closed his eyes.

He didn't want to do this. He really didn't want to do this. Still, he raised a fist to knock.

The door swung open before he could make contact, and Jonah took an involuntary step back. For a few seconds, all he could do was blink up at the man on the other side of the threshold.

"Get lost on the way up?" Nathan greeted him, leaning casually to one side with a hand braced against the door frame.

Jonah's reaction, whatever it might have looked like from Nathan's point of view, must have been the one he was hoping for, because Nathan's smile quirked to one side. His appraisal made Jonah feel like he was wearing much less than the t-shirt and jeans he had on.

He had, of course, worn less in front of Nathan before.

"Come in," Nathan said, stepping back.

Stunned, Jonah stepped through the narrow margin between Nathan's body and the door frame. The proximity was just on the wrong side of subtle, giving Jonah no choice but to brush against him as he passed.

When the door clicked shut, Jonah realized he was shaking. He jumped at Nathan's sudden presence behind him when he stopped at the mouth of the short entryway, but Nathan only lingered long enough to scoot around him.

"Jumpy," he noted with a smirk.

Jonah was very aware that he had yet to utter a word. He backed himself against the wall as subtly as he could, watching Nathan's every movement.

"Want a drink?" Nathan crossed to the dresser beside the window, picking up a glass of amber liquid. Beside it was a bottle with nearly a third of its contents already drained.

Jonah shook his head.

"Not very chatty tonight." Nathan laughed. He took a long swig, barely making a face at the burn. "Cassidy probably does enough talking for both of you when you're together. Do you charge extra for the 'boyfriend experience?' I should have guessed that dinner and hometown visits would be more his taste."

Something in Jonah rose to the defensive at the way he talked about Liam, but he forced it down. "Did he ask you to come here?" he couldn't help asking. "To talk to me?"

Nathan paused with the glass halfway to his mouth, eyes narrowed. "Why wouldn't he come see you himself?"

Jonah swallowed, suddenly feeling like he had revealed more than he should.

"I don't know." He blinked, trying to recover, but fear was filling in all the blank spaces in his mind like cold water flooding a sinking ship. "I just thought—"

His words were cut off by a swallow as Nathan took a step toward him. He laughed again, raising his palms in a placating gesture, even as he continued his saunter toward him.

"Relax, Leo. Or, sorry, is it *Jonah?*" He took another step forward. "What have you told him about us?"

Jonah cringed at the word choice, biting back the impulse to tell Nathan that there was no *us* in their arrangement, and there never had been. Nathan had only ever been another forgettable face in a sea of plenty, notable only for a repeat string of visits over the summer while he was interning in the city.

Jonah hadn't seen him for months after that. Not until the night in October when Jonah had been called to the bar for a particularly aggressive hookup in a bathroom stall. It had only made sense later, why Nathan had been so adamant about bolting the bathroom door. Liam would have only missed walking in on them by minutes.

"I haven't told him anything," Jonah said honestly.

"Nothing? Really?" The corners of his smile were dangerously sharp as he moved closer. "You didn't mention me at all?"

"No."

"No?"

Jonah regretted backing himself into a wall, because there was no more room to shrink away when Nathan raised a hand, grazing the back of his knuckles down Jonah's cheek.

"So, you're not going to tell him about *this?*"

Any lingering threads of hope that Nathan was here under nobler intentions were snapped the second he pressed forward, covering Jonah's mouth with his own.

His faint noise of protest was swallowed up like it was nothing. Jonah's hands curled into fists at his sides, survival instinct telling him not to raise them, not to push him away, not to fight back.

But this was different. This was Liam's *friend*.

Keeping Nathan's secret from Liam all these months out of some misguided ethical code had weighed on him enough, but the idea of going along with what Nathan wanted tonight felt like too big a betrayal. Jonah couldn't do it.

"Stop." He jerked his head back hard enough to smack into the wall. His hands came up to push against Nathan's chest, but he quickly found himself flattened, pinned by a knee between his legs, fingers digging into his hips.

"What do you think you're here for?" Nathan sounded angry now.

It was the anger that faltered Jonah's resistance. He stared over Nathan's shoulder, his vision beginning to slip in and out of focus. His instincts warred with each other, screaming at him to stay still, to endure, and simultaneously begging him to resist. He felt his hands come up again with the intent of pushing Nathan away, but instead, he ended up clutching the larger man's shoulders in an attempt to steady himself.

He had direct experience with Nathan's physical strength, and knew he didn't have a good chance in a fight.

"Please," he tried. "Liam wouldn't. . . He won't—"

"Liam doesn't have to know." Nathan ground his hips forward and Jonah felt himself start to slip. Into his head. Into *Leo*. Into the body of someone who had survived this before, could survive this again.

Fingers curled around the back of his neck and applied pressure. His body folded obediently, eyes going blank as his knees hit the carpet. He turned away at the sound of a zipper.

"I didn't come all the way out here to *talk*," Nathan said.

A fog descended over Jonah, his body a disjointed composite of shallow breathing and closed eyes and tingling limbs. For an indeterminate amount of time, Jonah was rendered helpless, watching from a distance as his body was handled with no regard for the person trapped inside it.

At some point he became vaguely aware that Nathan was saying something to him. "Hey." A palm tapped his cheek. "*Hey.*" Jonah flinched. "You're not going to say a fucking word to him."

Jonah's mind went blank, a few seconds of blinding whiteout, like staring directly into a camera flash. When it dissipated, it was white-hot rage that rushed to the surface.

His hands came up to push at Nathan's thighs, sending him stumbling back. Nathan tripped on the jeans around his ankles and crashed to the ground. For a moment, Jonah was trapped between past and present: he saw Nathan hit the carpet, but it was Mr. Becker staring back at him, his head split open and bloodied.

The image froze him long enough for Nathan to get his bearings. Jonah scrambled away but only made it as far as the desk. Nathan snatched him by the shirt as he pulled himself to his feet, tearing the neckline. A sharp crack of knuckles across his face stunned Jonah to stillness long enough for Nathan to get the advantage.

Jonah cried out again as his arm was twisted painfully behind him, his body pinned across the surface of the desk. The tray of pre-packaged coffee grounds and cups clattered to the floor, two crystal glasses shattering.

Jonah kicked out behind him, trying to catch any part of Nathan's body. "Get off me!" he shouted, hoping for someone, anyone to hear and intervene. Nathan plastered a hand over his mouth, muffling the sound.

With one of Nathan's hands occupied, Jonah lashed out with the elbow that wasn't pinned down, knocking Nathan back just long enough to worm out of his hold. He collapsed to the ground and started crawling toward the door, but Nathan's weight was on him in an instant, crushing him against the carpet. For a horrifying moment, Jonah thought that was it. Then he opened his eyes.

Across from him, several feet away on the carpet, he caught a glint of light reflecting off a shard of glass. He had no time to hesitate, no time to think his plan through. When Nathan focused his attention on yanking down the waistband of Jonah's jeans, Jonah threw his arm out and clamped down on the broken glass. The sting against his own palm didn't even register. Praying for the best, he thrust his arm behind him with as much power as he could leverage.

"Fuck!" Nathan cried out as he made contact, and Jonah didn't waste the narrow window of opportunity to wriggle himself onto his back.

Face to face, he saw that the glass had struck Nathan's arm, a long gash of red bleeding down to the crease of his elbow. Jonah threw another slash, this time toward Nathan's face.

Nathan made a sound like a wounded animal. Both hands left Jonah's body to cover the weeping gash on his cheek. Jonah bucked his hips as hard as he could, brought both knees up, and kicked. The second he dislodged the weight on top of him enough to move, he pushed himself up and stumbled into a run. This time, Nathan didn't pursue him.

He couldn't risk stopping to look back at the person he'd left bleeding on the hotel floor. It wasn't until he reached the door that he realized he was still clutching his makeshift weapon. He stopped just long enough to uncurl his fist, cringing at the deep line of blood that cut across his palm.

He couldn't think about that now. Every thought, every nerve ending and instinct in his body was screaming the same thing at him, all at once: run.

He dropped the glass shard, and he did.

Rubber soles smacked against the thin carpet of the hallway, then even louder down the concrete stairwell—all eight flights. The cold wind smacked him in the face the moment he was out the door, but he didn't stop running.

Marcus was parked two blocks down, as arranged, waiting for the two hours to be up. Jonah slowed as he approached, his stomach churning as realization set in: he was coming back empty-handed.

Maybe at some point in his fight, he had made the decision that getting out of that room was more important than avoiding the consequences, but now he wasn't so sure. Either way, his bed was made.

Jonah tapped his knuckles twice against the back window and heard the lock click open. Wordlessly, he slid inside, tucking himself against the far door. A beat of silence passed, undercut with the soft rumble of the idling engine. Jonah kept his eyes unfocused in the direction of the tinted window, waiting to feel the car move. Instead, he felt Marcus's eyes narrow in on him in the rearview mirror.

"That was barely fifteen minutes," he said, words laced with warning.

Jonah swallowed, gagging around the taste of blood. "He didn't waste any time."

Another beat of silence followed, and Jonah really hoped he would drop it. The burn of his injuries was starting to seep past the wall of adrenaline. He cradled his hand in his lap, squeezing around his wrist to slow the blood flow.

"Where is the money?"

"I don't have it."

There was a nearly tangible shift in the air inside the car. He heard the creak of leather on leather as Marcus turned back to look at him.

"I don't have it," Jonah repeated, louder, before he could ask again. When he opened his eyes, Marcus was staring at him with that same indiscernible expression Jonah knew so well.

Jonah braced for shouting, for violence, but Marcus just sighed and turned back around. He heard him rummaging for something in the glove compartment, and there was a wild, unmoored moment of thinking Marcus might be reaching for his gun. Instead, he grabbed something and extended it behind him for Jonah to take. In the dark, it took a moment to see it was a handful of fast-food napkins.

Jonah blinked at the offering, then up at the mirror where Marcus was pointedly avoiding his eyes.

"Take them." He shook the napkins in Jonah's direction. "Try not to bleed out on the seats."

Unwilling to provoke him, Jonah reached out with his uninjured hand and took the offering, pressing one softly to his bottom lip and the other to his bloody palm.

As the car rolled out from the lot and onto the main streets, Jonah watched the lights from the city slowly taper off into darkness, the high-rises giving way to short brick buildings until those turned to withering houses along old back streets. Every mile, every inch that brought him closer to the house pulled Jonah further and further away from the certainty, the clarity, he'd had back at the hotel. Under the threat of what was to come when he walked through the door, he started to question whether he had made the right choice after all.

He could have kept his head down like he'd planned, could have gone through the motions he'd done a hundred times before. Maybe it would have been over by now. Maybe Nathan was right, and Liam never would have needed to find out. Maybe Jonah could have found a way to live with that secret the same way he learned to live with everything else—tucked away in the corner of his memory where the light didn't reach.

The thing about regret, though, was that it didn't do a thing to erase the past. Whether he stood by his decision now or he didn't, the damage was already done, left in a pile of bloody glass on the other side of the city.

Anxiety thrummed in his veins as they turned onto the street he knew too well. His pockets were empty of the money he was owed, but Jonah, undoubtedly, would pay.

CHAPTER 25
Liam

The week leading up to Christmas was one of the worst of Liam's life.

Not a minute went by where Jonah did not consume his thoughts, both sleeping and awake.

Twice, he had called in sick for his shifts at the diner in favor of staying under his covers. He couldn't fathom the idea of walking into that restaurant and laying eyes on the corner booth where he'd spent an evening bumping shoes under the table with Jonah.

When he got his credit card statement, however, he remembered he couldn't really afford to skip any paydays, debilitating depression be damned.

His behavior raised an eyebrow from his mother, who had watched him pick up hours relentlessly for the past several months, and who knew well what Liam looked like when he was spiraling. She was worried about him, and he felt bad for it, but every time she tried to nudge him toward a conversation, he pulled a little further into himself.

The isolation weighed on him. He felt like he was living a double life, and to some extent, he was. He was navigating this dark underbelly of a world that, a few months earlier, he hadn't even known existed, and there was no one there to share the burden of his knowledge. Of his *guilt*. Even his mother, whom he trusted more than almost anyone else in the world, couldn't know about this. If he told her everything that had happened, beyond being appalled at the danger her son had gotten involved in, she would undoubtedly tell him to go to the police.

Maybe that was exactly what Liam needed to do.

The temptation was there. Every day, he came a little bit closer to breaking. He would stand with his trembling hand on the doorknob of his bedroom, listening to the sound of utensils scraping in the kitchen, telling himself that she was right there, that he could walk out there and break the dam, let everything that beat against the walls of his chest pour out of him like it so badly wanted to. Because Liam couldn't stand it. For as long as he lived, he would never, ever forgive himself if his negligence, his *cowardice* ended up being the reason Jonah. . .

There was still some part of him that believed there was a way out. Even after everything Jonah told him.

"*I killed someone.*" He could still hear the way Jonah expelled the words, like they were an illness his body was trying to rebuke. It wasn't the confession of a cold-blooded killer.

There was no world in which Jonah should be held prisoner by an act of desperation he had committed while fighting for his life. Nothing he had ever done justified being blackmailed and abused. What was this man's role in Jonah's life that he could wield so much power? Make him so afraid that he wasn't even willing to try and speak a word against him? Liam didn't know. There were still so many unanswered questions, and even more unasked. He had tried to respect Jonah's wishes, and in doing so, he was afraid that he'd wasted any chance of helping him. Now he was stuck in this miserable in-between, constantly pulled in two directions and fraying at both ends.

His performance was suffering at work, which he might have given a shit about if it was anything more pressing than delivering plates to tables, but getting screamed at by customers over a side of ranch dressing was doing no favors for his mental health.

"I want this meal taken off the bill," a gruff middle-aged man barked at him on Friday evening, ten hours into a double shift. By that time, Liam could practically feel his eye twitching.

"Sorry," he gritted out, long past the pleasantries of a forced smile. "I can bring you a new side."

"No, I said I want it comped," the man replied, speaking slowly as if Liam was too dense to comprehend it the first time. "My food will be cold by the time you get back."

It's a salad, dipshit, it was served cold, Liam wanted to—but very bravely did not—say.

"I'll get my manager," he said, then turned on his heel toward the kitchen, not before the customer could make a poorly whispered remark about incompetent waitstaff.

The stainless steel counter rattled as he slammed down an industrial-sized tub of Hidden Valley, popping off the lid. His phone buzzed in the front pocket of his apron, but he didn't bother reaching for it. It was probably his mom calling to check up on him, as she was doing with increasing frequency as he slipped deeper into his depression. He couldn't handle lying to her right now.

As he poured a dollop of dressing into the side cup, he made a mental note to shoot her a text on his break.

"Kim," he made his way to the corner of the kitchen where she was helping one of the new hires roll silverware. "Table thirty wants a free meal. Says the food is cold."

She turned to glance out the square panel of glass on the kitchen door without pausing in her work. "It's a salad," she deadpanned.

"I'm aware."

Letting out a sigh so put-upon that it could only have come from someone with years of customer service experience, she placed down the roll of silverware in her hand and turned to him. "Take your fifteen, kid."

"I already did."

"Take another one." She raised an eyebrow when he started to object. "We're dead out there, and you look like you're halfway there yourself. Go. I'll close out your table and grab your tip."

Between his aching back and Kim's unmoving stare, there wasn't much room to argue.

"Don't worry," Liam said, already untying his apron. "There won't be one."

The air outside was too cold to be hanging around in short sleeves, but he needed a quiet space more than he needed warmth right now.

Liam sank down onto the overturned bucket the smokers used on their breaks. His lumbar throbbed as he relaxed his muscles for the first time in hours. He let his head thud back against the dirty brick wall, eyes slipping shut.

This was why he had objected to taking a second break. The exhaustion collided with him the moment he was finally able to rest, bearing down on his shoulders all at once. He probably could have fallen asleep just like that, sitting on a bucket behind the diner in the freezing cold. He might have, if not for his phone buzzing in his pocket again.

Peeling his eyes open took more effort than it should have, but the notification on his phone was unexpected enough to nudge him back to awareness.

One missed call, followed by a voicemail, both from the Marriott in Chicago.

He did a mental recount of all the hotels he and Jonah had stayed at over the past couple of months, but it was a pointless exercise. They had been confined to a strict budget, and the Marriott was firmly outside of it. Liam tapped a cold thumb on the screen, opening the voicemail.

The moment he pressed the phone to his ear, his body went numb.

"Hi, Liam. It's me. Jonah."

His voice was the only thing in the world. The scene around him fell away, leaving Liam anchored to the earth only by the tinny words coming through the phone.

"I know you're probably working or. . . I don't know. I'm sorry. I don't have much time. I just. . . It's Friday," he said. *"And I wish it was you waiting for me upstairs."*

Liam was going to shatter apart.

"Listen, I. . . I don't know when–if–I'll have another chance to say what I want to say to you, so I just. . . I saw the phone and I needed to call you and say I'm sorry that things ended the way they did. I never wanted you to get anywhere near all of that. Any of it. I hate that you did. I hate that I was selfish enough to let you."

A pause.

"I only have another minute, but I need to tell you that I meant what I said the first night we met: that I don't understand how you could possibly have a hard time making friends, because you are the best one I've ever had. And even if that last night I spent with you, at the park, and in your car, and in your room, I. . . shit. Sorry. I'm sorry." There was a pause and a rustle of movement. *"I don't want you to ever think I regret a second of it. Because I don't.*

"I told you, once, that I didn't want to leave without saying goodbye, like I did the first night. So I'm keeping that promise now."

"No," Liam whispered.

"I have to go now. Okay? But not before I had the chance to thank you. For everything, Liam. Goodbye."

CHAPTER 26
Jonah

The basement was worse in the wintertime.

The last time Jonah had been locked down here, it had been in the dead of summer. At the time, he'd thought nothing could be worse than the heat—the inescapability of it inside the small space, the way it seemed to take up volume of its own, bearing down on him like a physical weight. That was before he realized just how deep the cold could bury itself in his bones.

The cell—because that was what it was, a claustrophobic box intended to imprison—offered little shelter from the elements. It was a dank, windowless abyss.

If the building itself was old, the foundation was ancient, lined with stone blocks and wooden beams slatted along the low ceiling. A singular lightbulb was all Jonah had for light, but even that had been switched off before Shepard locked the door.

The hours passed differently with no way to track them. He didn't know how long he'd been down here, and more to the point, he didn't know how long Shepard intended to *keep* him down there. He couldn't afford to think about it if he wanted to retain his sanity, but he couldn't fool himself, either. Shepard was furious, and this time it was entirely Jonah's fault.

Maybe if it had only been the money.

Maybe if it had only been the bloody knuckles and the client he'd left in a wailing heap on the hotel floor.

But Jonah's mistakes hadn't ended there.

Shepard had found Liam's note.

It had slipped out of his pocket in the struggle—Shepard's twisted way of 'recouping' a night of lost earnings. Maybe his punishment would have started and ended with the assault if not for the evidence of the other offense written in ink.

Dear Jonah, Call me, the note said.

He should have known his decision to keep it would come back to bite him, but it had felt more important to hold onto that last thread of connection. Each week, when he'd seen Liam, some part of him was always braced for the possibility that it would be the last time. Now that day had come and gone, and in the end, he hadn't gotten to keep the Liam anyway.

It didn't help that it was the second time in a matter of months that the use of Jonah's real name had gotten back to him. Jonah had never seen Ross Shepard so angry.

A SERIES OF ROOMS

The rest of the house had been asleep upstairs, so he had dragged Jonah into the cellar to dole out his punishment. Jonah hadn't expected to be left down there afterward, but Shepard's fury bordered on something like hysteria. It was unsettling in a way that made every one of his survival instincts stand on edge, watching Shepard's cool, arrogant demeanor slip so quickly. Jonah was no stranger to his fits of anger and violence, but this had been different.

Jonah hadn't been able to convince him that he hadn't spilled the truth about Shepard's operation to someone. He wouldn't hear it. Before he locked him in, Shepard had left him with the vague warning that he needed to *"figure out what to do with him."*

Jonah didn't know what that meant, but he knew it wouldn't land in his favor.

When he was a child, Jonah had been taught that God's will would come to pass, no matter what. The things that happened in life—good or bad—happened because they were supposed to. Maybe this chain of events was, if not strictly what Jonah deserved, at least what he needed; a reminder that stringing hope along would only prolong the pain.

Someone like Liam was never meant to be in his life forever. Maybe it was better that there had been a clean cut, one that absolved either of them from the burden of being the one to end things.

Now, on the small mattress in the corner of the room, Jonah rolled onto his back, staring up into the darkness. It was the only position that didn't irritate the full bloom of bruises across his face, but it left him even more vulnerable to the cold. He curled his toes in his shoes, trying to see if he had any feeling left in them. He squeezed his hands into fists to do the same, but immediately released them when the cut on his palm flared bright with pain. He let out a breath, knowing he would have seen a cloud of vapor if he could have seen anything at all.

As he lay there, waiting for numbness to claim him, the story from Sunday school that had returned to him time and time again took root like a weed in his brain.

Jonah had become his own namesake.

If he squinted up at the ceiling, he could almost convince his eyes of vague shapes taking form in the blackness. His memory filled in the blanks of rotted beams slotted one after the other, like the ivory arches of a ribcage. The messy threads of dangling wires woven like capillaries. The cold, wet walls like a prison of flesh.

This was it, he thought. He had found himself in the belly of the whale.

CHAPTER 27
Liam

The Baker residence was, as expected, devoured by Christmas decor from the inside out: all warm-white string lights, scented pinecones, and chemical snow powdered over the garland lining the grand staircase. Nothing could have suited Liam's mood less.

"Look who's here!" Their hostess greeted them in the doorway, still in her kitchen apron. The fabric was spotless, and Liam spared half a cynical thought to wondering if she'd put on this piece of *fifties housewife* cosplay just for their entrance.

She hugged his mother and greeted his father with an air kiss on each cheek before turning to Liam. "Look at you!" she exclaimed, as if it had been years rather than months since they had last seen each other in passing. "Even taller than Benny now."

"Cassidy isn't taller than me," came Ben's objection from the next room.

Liam plastered on a smile he had no faith in. "Hi, Mrs. Baker. The house looks great."

She smiled. "I always hoped some of that politeness would have rubbed off on Benjamin after all these years."

"I *am* polite," Ben's voice came again, though the fact that the words were garbled around a mouthful of food sort of negated his point.

The coffee table was lined with veggie trays and Christmas-themed finger foods, along with a spread of assorted wines and the obligatory bottle of sparkling grape juice for the Cassidys. Ever the good Christians. Personally, Liam would have liked to snatch a bottle of red off the table and save their hostess the trouble of washing an extra glass tonight.

Ben's father was stationed in his recliner with a glass of whisky, eyes glued to whatever sporting event was on their flatscreen. He greeted them with a raise of his glass, barely looking away from the television, and, as if by the pull of some invisible straight man magnet, Liam's father found his way to the second chair.

"The Scotts are running a little behind. As per," Mrs. Baker added with a co-conspiratorial smirk. "But dinner is ready whenever they are. Help yourself to some appetizers in the meantime. God knows Ben has."

Liam sank down on the couch next to Ben.

"Hey," Ben said, eyes on his phone.

"Hi."

That was fine. Liam wasn't in the mood for conversation anyway.

He sat back, watching the scene unfold around him like an interactive Hallmark movie. The graying fathers watching sports and talking about their corporate jobs, the mothers clad in cashmere sweaters and polka-dotted aprons, not a hair out of place. This was the only life that Liam had ever known. This was the warmth of his privilege, to be so secure in his comfort that he could resent it.

He ached for Jonah, in that moment, as much as he ached with the absence of him. It was too easy to picture Jonah against this familiar backdrop, seated next to him on the plush cushions, warm and safe. Fed and strong and unbruised. Liam wanted that for him. More than he had ever wanted anything, he wanted Jonah to be safe. If there was a god watching over this universe—something Liam became less and less inclined to believe the longer he knew Jonah—there would come a day where that boy got to spend a holiday with people who loved him.

The rattle of bells against the front door signaled the arrival of Nathan's family. Mrs. Scott entered the room in a flurry of beige fleece, shrugging out of her coat while balancing a glass casserole dish on her arm. "Sorry we're late. Couldn't peel this one away from the game long enough to bear the five-minute car ride over."

Trailing behind her, Mr. Scott wore a sheepish grin. Behind him was Nathan, who—

"What the hell happened to your face?" Ben voiced the thoughts of everyone in the room, finally looking up from his phone.

A jagged line of raised pink flesh tore across Nathan's cheek, stretching from just below his eye to the corner of his mouth.

Liam was sure he wasn't imagining the brief glint of irritation before Nathan masked it with a smile. "You should see the other guy," he said.

"Was the other guy a bear?" Ben asked. "You look like you got mauled, dude."

"I think we've held dinner up long enough for everyone," Mr. Scott interrupted, putting a terse end to the questioning.

Maybe Liam wasn't the only one who sensed the tension in the room, because there was a brief, uncomfortable pause before Mrs. Baker stood, untied her apron from around her waist and shepherded everyone into the dining room.

The boys were the last to follow. Ben wandered off after a lingering glance at the scar, vowing to get the story out of him later. But Liam couldn't look away.

Even if everything else had just been in Liam's imagination, there was no mistaking the loathing glare Nathan shot him before he turned and left Liam standing alone in the living room.

The scrape of silverware on ceramic murmured over the dining room table.

As luck would have it, Liam found himself planted in the chair directly across from Nathan, where he could feel the ugly burn of his sneer like a heat lamp too close to the skin. Liam kept his eyes down, watching the piece of roasted potato he was pushing around on his plate. He was already expending all his mental energy just by being here tonight. He didn't know what was happening—with Nathan's new beauty mark or the silent warfare that seemed to be waging between the two of them—but he was far too tired for it.

Liam hadn't seen Nathan since the run-in outside the diner last Friday. So much had happened in the short time since, he'd all but forgotten about it. It was only now, under this new, indiscernible tension, that he remembered the strangeness of Nathan's behavior that night. Jonah had brushed it off when he brought it up later, but Liam knew what he had seen: that Jonah had been just as shaken by the encounter.

He nearly choked on a bite of dry chicken at the reminder of what Nathan could do with that information, here, of all places. There were any number of ways he could weaponize his out-of-context knowledge of Liam spending time with the sex worker Nathan had once hired for him, none of which would go over well at a dining room table full of his family friends.

"Liam." Mrs. Baker's voice pulled him to attention from the opposite end of the table. "Do you have any plans for the fall? You were planning to transfer out of your two-year program, right?"

Liam bit his cheek to keep the scowl off his face. He could hear the implicit comment between her words: *"You'll be going to a real college after this, right?"*

"Nothing solid yet," he responded as politely as he could manage. "I've applied to a few places. My top choices." He paused, sparing a sideways glance at his parents. His future plans were a point of contention between the three of them, and he would rather not have that conversation here. "But, you know, I'm aiming a little high. I probably won't get in."

"You've been so busy these days."

Everyone turned to face Nathan, who spoke for the first time since they sat down for dinner.

"Must be putting in a lot of work on those applications."

The edge of the fork dug painfully into Liam's skin. "I've been working a lot," he said without looking at him.

"That's an understatement," Liam's mom chimed in. "Poor Liam has been working himself to the bone at that diner. He's even started picking up graveyard shifts."

Liam didn't like the trajectory of this conversation, but he was struggling to find his voice.

Nathan, apparently, found his first. "I wonder where all that money is going," he said. Liam looked up at him, and into the fire burning behind his eyes. "Your college fund must be stacked by now. Unless you're spending it somewhere else."

There was no way the rest of the family wasn't feeling the heat of whatever was simmering beneath the surface. Liam never thought he would be grateful for the Midwestern Art of Forced Polite Conversation, but he could finally breathe again once Mrs. Baker stepped in to steer the conversation back to safer territory.

"Well," she declared loudly, raising her wine glass in Liam's direction. "I think it's great that you're working toward your goal. Nobody your age seems to want to work for anything anymore."

"Mom," Ben groaned.

Even as the idle chatter moved on around them, breaking off into sub-conversations, the silent exchange between him and Nathan only seemed to grow hotter, nearing a boiling point that Liam didn't know how to predict.

He kept quiet, unwilling to provoke a confrontation when Nathan was so clearly looking for one. Dinner was almost finished, and he had almost survived the whole ordeal with nothing more than a mental scratch, when Ben decided to upend the whole evening through another mouthful of food.

"Okay, for real," he said, pointing his fork toward the gash on Nathan's cheek. "Are you just not gonna tell us what happened?"

Nathan's spine drew up, his shoulders rolling back. "It's really not as exciting as you want to think it is," Nathan replied.

A *lie,* Liam clocked easily. Nathan never was any good at that.

"That's really not what I asked," Ben pushed.

Liam watched Nathan's jaw twitch again. "Wasn't a big deal. I went into the city with some of Becca's friends from school. We rented a hotel room. Things got out of hand."

From the end of the table, Nathan's father barked out a laugh. "'A *little out of hand?*'" he repeated. "Is that what you call waking up to a three-hundred-dollar damage charge from the Marriott on my credit card?"

The sound of silverware clattering on ceramic had every eye turned in Liam's direction.

The Marriott.

The pieces fell into place, one after another.

The tense conversation in the diner parking lot.

The caller ID from Jonah's voicemail.

Nathan's injury.

A *defensive wound.*

"What the fuck did you do?" The words were cold and flat, escaping in a whisper before he could stop them.

"Liam," his mother snapped from beside him, but he didn't look away from Nathan, who was staring back at him with eyes narrowed in confusion.

"What the fuck did you do?" He was suddenly yelling, and standing, through no active decision-making of his own.

"What are you talking about?" Nathan's cool reply only fed the monster of rage inside him.

Something in the finality of the realization, the unblinking reality of what Nathan had presumably done to Jonah, severed Liam's last thread of restraint. He had always known that the person pretending to be his friend since childhood was a lot of things, most of them unpleasant, but he had never taken him for a predator.

The world around him went red and messy.

The noises he registered blended together as one: Mrs. Baker's startled shriek, the shattering of ceramic against a hardwood floor, the crunch of Nathan's nose under his fist. Again. And again. And again. And ag—

"Liam! Liam— Okay, stop, that's enough." The arms around his chest might have belonged to Ben, but he couldn't see, and he didn't care. He swung out wildly, trying to escape, trying to catch another blow to Nathan's bleeding face, but he was yanked backwards, out of reach.

Liam went momentarily slack in Ben's grip. He only had a moment to register the tears on his face before Nathan was propelling himself off the ground, making a lunge for him. Liam was ready for it. He yanked against the restraining hands, eager to get his hands on Nathan again, but Mr. Scott swooped in behind Nathan and dragged him back.

"That's enough!" His commanding voice stopped them, both of them breathing heavily from opposite sides of the table. "Benjamin, take him outside. Nathan, upstairs. Now. Let's go."

Liam didn't have much of a choice, being the obvious weaker of the two and semi-paralyzed from the adrenaline crash. He let himself be pulled into the attached garage off the Bakers' kitchen. Ben's hands dropped heavily onto his shoulders when they came to a stop.

"Holy shit, dude." To his surprise, Ben was almost smiling, looking at him with a look of bewildered—if not a little concerned—amusement. "What was that about?"

Liam was supremely not in the mood for this. He jerked backwards out of Ben's reach, swiping at both his eyes. Sensation was slowly returning, a low throb of pain building in his wrists and his knuckles.

"Leave me alone," he snapped, fingers digging into his scalp.

"Okay, but I don't know if I should—"

"Just go!"

"It's okay, Ben." Liam's mother appeared in the doorway of the garage. "I've got him."

Ben straightened up, taking a step back. "I'll, uh. I'll be in the kitchen if you need me."

Liam's hands slipped down from his hair to cover his face. Quiet footsteps drew closer across the garage floor, but he didn't look up at his mother's approach. Something inside of him was hurtling toward a breaking point. He could feel it in his bones, like the vibration of a glass just before the shatter.

"Listen, I don't know what's going on with you, but—*oof.*"

Whatever chastisement he had coming was abruptly cut off by the weight of Liam's body collapsing against his mother. He threw his arms around her waist, buried his head in her shoulder, and the dam broke. She reciprocated without question, though he was sure she had plenty, pulling him in close.

"Liam?"

A sob tore free from his throat, and he squeezed her tighter. All the weight he'd been carrying inside him was spilling out, desperate for escape.

"Mom." His voice cracked around the word.

"Tell me what's going on," she said.

The invitation split him down the middle, throwing open the gates of secrecy and pain, and letting it all rush out of him in a long, wordless wail. *I'm sorry, Jonah. I'm sorry I'm sorry I'm sorry.*

That I can't keep your promise.

That I didn't break it sooner.

"Mom, I need your help."

CHAPTER 28
Jonah

He didn't realize he had fallen asleep until the sound of footsteps on the stairs woke him. Shepard's silhouette blocked most of the light from the upstairs hallway, but the sudden flicker of the basement bulb made Jonah wince. After so long in the dark, even the dimmest light was hard to take.

"Have a good nap, princess?"

Notably, he had come alone; no Marcus to shadow three steps behind him.

Jonah tracked his approach with wary eyes, the only part of his body capable of movement. Even as the distance closed between them, Jonah couldn't find the will to retreat. There was nowhere to go, anyway.

"Oh, are you not talking to me? Is that what's happening?" Shepard dropped into a slow, predatory crouch beside the mattress. "You're lucky, you know," he continued. "I could have left you down here to rot, but you've been requested for a job tonight. Big spender, friend of a friend. I thought it might be worth giving you a chance at redemption."

Dread solidified in Jonah's chest, like cooling magma. Anyone Shepard would risk sending him to, considering the evidence of a beating this bad still painted over his skin, clearly didn't have Jonah's best interest in mind.

"Nothing?" Shepard tilted his head. "No gratitude at all?"

He could feel the rise in tension as Jonah refused to look at him, refused to speak or move or otherwise acknowledge his presence. The throbbing in his face—a constant reminder of the price of his resistance—should have been motivation enough, but numbness settled over him, dulling his senses.

For a moment, he entertained the idea of going limp. Playing dead and accepting the consequences, whatever they might be. What would happen?

Would Shepard simply drag him upstairs, into the shower, and into a car by force? But then if Jonah still refused? After that? What would he do? Would he hit him? Rape him? He had done all that a hundred times before. What more was there left to fear from the devil he knew?

Maybe this would be the final straw. Would that really be all it took? Could ending this be as simple as lying flat on the basement floor and waiting?

Jonah closed his eyes. There was no order to his thoughts, if they were even complete thoughts at all. There wasn't even any particularly strong feeling behind them. It was just a rush of numbness so sudden and intense that it rendered him a statue. He couldn't obey even if he wanted to. He was no longer at the helm in his own body.

(How long had it been since he was?)

"Okay, then," Shepard said, a frightening chill in his voice. "Let's skip the pleasantries. I have something else I wanted to show you."

Jonah wasn't interested. What more could Shepard possibly have had on him? As if the threat of breaking his court order, the threat of turning him in for murder, and the constant threat of violence to him and his family wasn't enough. What was there left to take from someone who had nothing?

That was what he had thought, anyway.

The moment Shepard pulled out his phone and showed Jonah what he had pulled up on the screen, he knew he had underestimated him.

"It's amazing," Shepard said with a smile, "how much information you can trace from a simple phone number."

From the brightness of the screen, Liam's green eyes stared back at him in a photo that looked only a few months old. He was wearing an apron and smiling, his arm around a woman with long, beaded braids. Jonah was going to be sick.

"Liam Cassidy," Shepard said, the name sounding poisonous and wrong on his tongue. "Twenty-one years old, a student at the College of DuPage. Works at Lenny's Diner in Naperville, Illinois. That's not too far from here, Jonah. I could have someone there within the hour, if I wanted."

"He hasn't done anything." Jonah's voice was broken from disuse when he spoke.

"Oh, there he is." Shepard grinned, clicking the phone off and pocketing it once again. "I don't know if that's true. He seems to know a lot more than he should."

"He doesn't know about you," Jonah promised. "I never told him the truth."

"How can I believe you? You've proven to me over and over again how much of a liar you are. No. On second thought, I think I'm done giving second chances."

Jonah's heart was beating out of his chest.

"You, my friend, are going to follow through on this job tonight. You are going to be a good boy and make me back the money you tried to steal from me yesterday. And then you can come back here, and we can discuss how things are going to work going forward." He leaned down, dangerously close. "Because if you step one toe out of line from now on, little Liam is going to get a bullet in the head. Is that what you want? Two bodies on your conscience?"

He watched as Shepard stood to his full height.

It was never going to end. The realization spread over him like a physical chill.

If one threat ever weakened with time, there would always be one more thing to hold over him.

There was no expiration date on Shepard's plan to run Jonah's life into the ground, short of finding someone new to target, and Jonah didn't want that either. He didn't think he would last long enough to see it happen.

Shepard could do what he wanted to him as retribution; Jonah wouldn't allow him to wield Liam's life as a threat. He didn't dare show him that it would work.

He felt the moment the final thread snapped. The rest was freefall.

"You can go fuck yourself," he heard himself say.

An eerie stillness fell over Shepard. His eyes trained on him like a heat-seeking missile. "What was that?"

With all the strength left in his body, Jonah forced himself up and onto his knees, swaying slightly on the mattress. He braced one hand against the stone wall and looked Shepard in the eyes. "Go," he said slowly, "*fuck* yourself."

He was weak enough already that the first backhand flattened him, but it didn't matter. He had coaxed Shepard back into his space, and Jonah would fight like a cornered animal to kill him before he could ever lay a hand on Liam.

He barely recognized the fingers as his own as they scraped bloody lines down Shepard's face. A scream—a year's worth of anger and fear and bottled-up misery—erupted from his throat. He swung out wildly, never knowing if the hits landed before he threw the next. It all became too much to follow, just a storm-rocked ship of blood and pain and rage.

He didn't see the kick coming until it crashed into his side.

Jonah fell flat off the mattress, a ragdoll against hard cement, and he didn't get back up.

Still, the assault didn't end.

He closed his eyes and saw himself on the ground outside a park bathroom, parting with his last three dollars. He saw himself at the kitchen table with his parents and his pastor in his childhood home. He saw himself on a supercut of hotel mattresses, and he thought: Was this death? Was this the only way out he was brave enough to pursue?

When Shepard grabbed him by the shoulders, turning him onto his back, Jonah drove the nail into his own coffin.

He looked the monster in the eyes and spit in his face.

Hands closed around his throat. The crush of fingers cut off his air immediately. Jonah scrambled and scratched, but the hold was unyielding. Black spots danced in his vision, growing and growing until he could barely see the glaring eyes looking down at him.

A sickening realization settled into place—that those eyes would be the last thing he ever saw.

Jonah's death would be a silent one, confined within the walls of the same basement that had hosted his original descent into hell. It would likely be covered up, buried along with him, another disappearing statistic. A hapless ending to a tragic story that would never be told.

He hoped his mother and father might think of him again, someday, and regret what they had done. He hoped Liam might remember him and smile.

Everything went black. The only sound in the room became a ringing in his ears.

He was dying.

He was dead.

And then.

And then.

A blast so powerful he would have recoiled from the sound if his body had any life left inside of it. He could breathe again—just long enough for one desperate pull for oxygen—and then he couldn't, as a heavy, immovable, weight dropped onto his chest.

The weight was gone as soon as it came, and suddenly everything felt lighter. Fuzzier. There was something wet and sticky on his skin. He still couldn't open his eyes.

The noise faded out again, the ringing even stronger than before, and when it trickled back in, there was somebody else there with him.

"Jonah."

A voice. One he recognized. There was a smell, too—faint, but present—of cigarette smoke and coffee. A smell that felt like leather upholstery and the rumble of tires on the freeway.

The voice called him by his name, telling him to "*wake up, come on kid, open your eyes."*

Marcus, he thought. But the puzzle piece didn't fit. It couldn't have been him, because the hands on his neck, on his face, were gentle. Because the voice spoke like it wanted him to live. Because the voice introduced itself to someone as, "Agent Ellis. . . need a bus to the house. . . dead. . ."

Was he talking about Jonah? Was Jonah dead?

That didn't make sense. He was still in too much pain to be dead. Trying to piece the fragments together was too taxing, and Jonah didn't see the point anymore. He felt himself slipping further underwater, the world around him growing more and more muffled until—

A bright flare of light shone directly into his eye. Jonah tried to make a noise of protest, but the effort lit flames down his throat. A woman with blue gloves hovered over him, just past the light. *"Don't try to speak,"* she said from somewhere a million miles away. When his eye snapped shut again, he realized she must have been the one holding it open.

"Is he going to be okay?"

"Sir, please take a step back."

Jonah slipped under again.

In his next lucid moment, Jonah was somewhere else entirely. The air around him was cold like the basement, but the light on the other side of his eyelids was bright enough to make his head pound. The concrete beneath him had gone soft. He was. . . moving.

"Male, age nineteen. Significant trauma to the head and abdomen." Another voice carried somewhere far above him. *"BP is seventy over forty. . . pupils are responsive but delayed. . . Patient lost flow of oxygen for an unknown period of time."* Then, softer, *"Hon, can you tell us your name?"*

Even now, Jonah knew the rules. Be good. Lie. Don't tell anyone your real name.

"Leo," he tried to say.

"His name is Jonah Prince."

"Are you his father?"

My father doesn't care about me, Jonah tried to tell them, but there was something over his mouth and nose, trapping all of his words.

"No, I— No, I'm not his father."

"I'm going to ask you to wait out here, sir."

"Please, just. . . Please, don't let him die."

"We're going to do everything we can."

This time, when the current dragged him under, Jonah wondered if it would take.

CHAPTER 29
Jonah

A harsh flood of daylight rang through his skull the moment he tried to open his eyes. Jonah retreated into the darkness behind his eyelids but the pain remained; a steady throb that brought the rest of his senses into focus one at a time.

The surface beneath him was soft. A bed. The air smelled clean and cold. And the pain. . .

He hurt everywhere. His face, his head, his ribs, his stomach. When he swallowed, his throat burned like it had been cracked open and laid out under the hot sun. Jonah raised a hand to touch his neck, but there was a tug of resistance. He opened his eyes again to find a narrow tube protruding from a vein below his knuckles, secured in place with tape. Jonah followed the line up a silver pole, to a hanging bag of clear liquid.

He was in the hospital.

Jonah blinked. A half-second flash of a memory, so hazy it could have been his imagination, was gone as soon as it came: a wood-beam ceiling and a face, looking down at him while the water tried to pull him under.

The pain in his head spiked. Jonah pressed the heels of his palms against his temples, trying to alleviate the pressure, but it only sent the pain deeper. A broken noise slipped free from his throat, and when he opened his eyes again, he wasn't alone.

A woman peeked into the doorway of his room—a police officer, with a black button-up top and a gun holstered at her belt. Jonah pressed himself into the mattress.

She turned away and murmured something into the radio at her shoulder. Jonah's heart was pounding out of his chest, palms sweating as he clutched his fists around the hospital sheet pooled at his waist.

When Marcus appeared beside her seconds later, his heart nearly gave out altogether.

He stepped into the room as the uniformed officer ducked out, leaving the two of them alone. Marcus approached slowly.

Desperate words, a plea, a defense—*something*—bubbled in Jonah's throat. "I didn't. . . I didn't tell them. . . anything. I didn't—"

Marcus raised his hands, and Jonah flinched. Out of the corner of his eye, he saw Marcus take a step back.

"I know," Marcus said softly. "I'm going to get a nurse and let them know you're awake, okay? I'll be right back, just. . . try to take it easy."

Jonah only raised his head when he heard the sounds of retreat. He watched Marcus's back as he turned through the doorway, returning seconds later with a young woman in lavender scrubs. She greeted him in a warm voice and asked if it was okay that she examined him. Unsure of what other choice he had, he nodded.

The whole time she worked on him—shining a small flashlight in his eyes, pressing on the veins in his wrist with cold fingers—Jonah's gaze lingered on Marcus, who stood just outside the doorway. If the nurse sensed the tension in the room, she gave no indication as she finished up her examination and snapped her rubber gloves into the trash bin.

"How are you feeling, Jonah?" she asked. "How's your pain level, one-to-ten?"

Jonah, not Leo. He shot a nervous glance at Marcus, who didn't react at all.

"Four," he lied. The look on her face told him he wasn't as convincing as he'd hoped.

"Okay. Let us know if that changes," she said. "The doctor will be in to see you in a bit."

"Thank you," Marcus murmured to her as she passed him on her exit.

When it was just the two of them again, Jonah felt himself shrinking back, but Marcus didn't crowd his space. Instead, he considered him from across the room, stepping just inside the threshold.

He pointed to a chair near Jonah's bed. "Do you mind?" he asked.

Jonah had never been allowed to tell him *'no'* before; he assumed that much hadn't changed. He nodded, and only then did Marcus pull the chair up and sit down.

"How much do you remember?" he asked.

Jonah blinked a few times, trying to make sense of what was really being asked of him. It felt like a trap. There was always a trap.

He shook his head. "I don't know," he said.

Marcus studied him. "About Shepard," he nudged. "About what happened at the house. In the basement."

Wood beam ceiling. A face overhead.

"You were there," Jonah whispered.

The memory began to take shape: A photo of Liam on Shepard's phone. A threat. An ultimatum. Bloody knuckles across his cheek. Hands around his neck. A loud bang. Someone beside him. The voice he couldn't quite access but some part of him recognized right away.

"In the basement, you. . ." Jonah blinked as the threads between the images pulled taut. "You killed him. Shepard. He's. . . ?"

He couldn't bring himself to say it, as if forming the thought out loud would crush the possibility to dust.

"Yes," Marcus said, "Ross Shepard is dead."

Jonah couldn't wrap his mind around the words, let alone allow himself to do something as fundamentally reckless as believe them.

"I don't understand."

"He was killing you," Marcus said slowly, deliberately, as if this was something he had rehearsed. "I did what needed to be done."

Jonah almost laughed. "Don't." The word was intended as a snap, but it came out shaky and weak. "Why are you. . . Why would you tell me that?"

"Because it's the truth."

"Since when do you care about what happens to me?" Jonah shot back.

Marcus shifted in his chair, an agitated movement that put Jonah on edge. "There's a lot you don't know, because you weren't ever supposed to. I'd like the chance to explain it." When Jonah only stared at him blankly, he continued. "The name Marcus was an alias assigned to me by the Bureau. My real name is Antonio Ellis."

"The Bureau," Jonah echoed numbly. He heard the words from a perspective outside of his own body. "You're. . . ?"

"I'm a special agent for the FBI," he said. "I've been working undercover for the past three years as part of a joint task force."

Jonah shook his head, failing to process the information he was being given. He pinched his thigh beneath the thin sheet, trying to wake himself from whatever strange dream he had fallen into.

"The assignment was 'as long as it takes' from the get, but none of us. . ." Marcus trailed off, shaking his head. "It took longer than we initially thought to get close to the target."

"What are you talking about?" Jonah finally found his voice. "You were there every single day. You were *part of it*. How was that not close enough?"

Marcus—*Ellis?*—grimaced. "Ross Shepard wasn't the target," he explained. "He was a link in a whole network of connections, nowhere near the top of the food chain. He was a means to an end."

When he caught Jonah's eyes, there was an apology there. He heard the part Ellis didn't say out loud: Jonah was just collateral damage.

"Who was it, then?" Jonah demanded. "Who was so important you could look past everything Shepard did?"

Ellis's eyes fell shut. "I can't tell you that," he said. "I'm off the case—I compromised my cover, and I don't regret it—but the investigation is still ongoing."

To his horror, Jonah felt the sharp prickle of oncoming tears and tried to blink them away.

"For what it's worth," Ellis said, "there wasn't a moment of what happened to you that I didn't detest."

"It's worth nothing," Jonah spat. "You sat there every night while it happened. You drove me there, to all of them, you. . ." His voice broke off, but he was too angry to be embarrassed. "You saw what I. . . when I got in your car every night, you *saw*."

Something fierce flashed behind the older man's eyes. "I was doing the job that I was given, in hopes that we would save hundreds of lives in the long run. I did what I could within my tight limitations. It was never enough to make it better, I know that, but I never tried to make it any worse. I. . . I never touched you," he finished weakly.

Jonah scoffed, a bitter, hateful sound that cut through the sterile room. "You think that absolves you? That you didn't try to fuck me, you think that makes you a *hero?*"

Ellis was shaking his head before Jonah finished speaking. "No," he said. "I don't."

"You. . ." Jonah began, but he trailed off, a chill settling over him at his sudden realization. He looked at Marcus—*at Ellis, at Marcus*—trying to spot the lie. "No." He shook his head. "You're not a cop. You can't be. You're lying. The body. You. . . The man I. . ." Jonah squeezed his eyes shut, trying to push away the memory of a hotel room covered in blood. "He was dead, and you helped Shepard get rid of a body. You wouldn't do that if you were a cop."

Ellis sat back in his chair, scraping a palm roughly over his stubble. "There was no body, Jonah," he whispered. "You never killed anyone."

The world tilted off its axis. Jonah stared at him, willing the words to converge into some sort of sense.

"What?" The word left him in a breath.

"Henry Becker is alive," Ellis said. *No. No. No, no, no.* "He was injured, yes. But Shepard had more than enough dirt on him to keep his mouth shut, and it kept the incident away from the police. I. . ." He paused, looking at Jonah then away. "Helped convince Shepard it was wise to keep him away from you, going forward."

Jonah couldn't breathe. "It was your idea?"

"To fabricate a murder to hold over you? No. That was him," he said. "But I couldn't stop him."

"Bullshit," Jonah snapped. He almost thought he saw Ellis flinch. "You act like you were helpless, but you could have *done* something."

"It's not that I didn't try," Ellis admitted. "I brought it to my higher-ups. I asked for a way to get you out of there, to find some sort of legal recourse that wouldn't compromise the investigation. But I was building Shepard's trust, and doing that was the only way to get closer to his circle. Sabotaging his twisted fucking operation would have raised too many flags. And even if I managed to get you out. . ."

"There would have been someone to take my place," Jonah finished flatly.

Ellis, at least, had the good grace to look ashamed. "It was always my plan to get you out, in the end," he said. "I didn't know when that would be, but I knew that when I was done with my assignment to Shepard, I was taking you with me."

"A year," Jonah said, the words cutting him on the way out. He had never spoken the quantity out loud. "A year of my life I spent under him. How much longer would it have taken? My court requirements were up after six months, and then he had blackmail to keep me around. It would have always been something. He would have kept it going until I was too fucked up to make him any money or I was dead."

"I didn't let him kill you," Ellis asserted.

"Yeah," Jonah said. "I hope that helps you sleep at night. Because if it's absolution you came here looking for, you can't have it."

"I don't expect you to forgive me."

"I don't."

"That's okay." He was placating him, throwing kerosine on the fire.

"Then what are you doing here?" Jonah asked.

Ellis was quiet for a few moments. "You deserved to hear the truth from me. After everything, you. . ." he cleared his throat, keeping his eyes hidden. "Jonah, you deserve a lot more than any apology or explanation I could offer you. And I am sorry. I am so deeply sorry for everything that has happened to you, and everything I played a part in. And I will be, for as long as I live. I know it's not enough, and it never will be, but I needed to be the one to tell you that you're safe now."

Safe. The temptation to let the word swallow him into its warm embrace was right there at the edge, like heat glowing off a fire onto outstretched, frozen fingertips. Ready to bring him in from the cold, if he let it. Jonah hadn't felt safe in a long time. A part of him knew he might not ever again. What Ellis was offering him was a cruel lie.

Jonah closed his eyes. He used the silence to draw in a few deep breaths, but on the third inhale, his injured throat spasmed, sending him into a coughing fit.

In his periphery, Ellis rose from his chair and crossed the room. He returned to Jonah's side moments later with a paper cup of water.

With little room for rejection, Jonah took it in his trembling hands and pressed the rim to his lips. The cold water was soothing. He drank slowly until the cup was empty and his coughing subsided.

"Do you want more?" Ellis asked.

Jonah swallowed, feeling the immediate difference in the reflex, and shook his head. He sat the cup down on the plastic tray beside his bed and watched as Ellis lowered himself back into the chair.

"So, it's just over," Jonah said, strained. "Just like that. He's dead, and after all this time, I'm just supposed to. . ." He blinked, realizing he had no idea how to end that sentence. "What happens now?" It came out in a whisper.

He hated having to ask, hated the uncertainty in his own voice, but the fear was creeping in quickly behind the realization. In many ways, Jonah was back at square one. The monster was dead, but that didn't change the fact that Jonah was still alone in the world, without a dime to his name.

"The house is shut down," Ellis said, confirming his suspicion. "The rest of the residents will have to work out their individual cases with the courts, but most of them have family they can stay with."

"How nice for them."

"Is there anyone you can call?" Ellis asked, more gently than Jonah had ever heard him. His pity added insult to injury.

"If I had anyone, I wouldn't have ended up here in the first place."

"Your parents...?"

Are the reason I was on the street at seventeen, he didn't say. Instead, he shook his head.

Ellis nodded, his expression carefully blank. "Look," he said. "I'm not going to pretend I can understand what you're going through, or the situation you're coming from, but you're going to need a support system in place while you get back on your feet."

"And if I don't have it?"

Ellis leaned forward, his eyes intent. "I'm not dumping you back on the street, Jonah. We will figure something out," he said. Then, after a pause, "I owe you that much, at least."

Jonah looked away, biting down on the urge to tell him he didn't want anything from him, of all people. It was terrifying to find himself in a position, once again, where he couldn't afford to turn down help—in whatever form it came.

"I'm going to give you a minute alone to process everything, but I'm not leaving the hospital." He rose from his chair, but paused before he walked away. He pulled the cell phone from his pocket and laid it on the tray next to the bed. "I'll be back," he said. "If there's someone in your corner, Jonah, I suggest you call them."

The silence left behind in his absence was too heavy.

Jonah stared down the phone on the table like an insult. He thought about all the possibilities that could come from dialing his mother's number, telling her he was in the hospital, that he had almost died, that he was coming off the worst year of his life and had nowhere to go.

She had never been a cold woman. She had cried, the day the pastor sat them down at their kitchen table and discussed Jonah's "options." She had screamed the first time Jonah's father put his hands on him. Despite everything, Jonah still believed that she loved him, even if it wasn't in the way that he needed, or the way she was supposed to.

Somehow, that made it hurt more—the idea that if he called her now, he would hear her tears on the other end of the line, and it still wouldn't be enough.

Maybe he couldn't avoid that conversation forever, but he could at least give himself the grace to put it off for now.

If there's anyone in your corner, Ellis had said.

In the entirety of his life, Jonah had only ever memorized three phone numbers: his mother's, his own, and the one he had carried around in his pocket for weeks.

Shepard might have stolen the note from him, but Jonah had committed the digits to memory the very first night he got them.

He picked up the phone.

CHAPTER 30
Liam

The Chicago police station was draped in tacky Christmas ornaments, faded from decades of living in storage between winters. Their presence added more melancholy than the intended holiday cheer, but Liam found that to be a more appropriate setting for the mood anyway.

Time had blended since the events of the dinner party. He could only string together a loose timeline: his mother scraping him off of the Bakers' garage floor, holding him in the backseat of his father's SUV, and gently rubbing blood stains off of his knuckles under warm water. She'd had a lot of questions, naturally, and Liam had tried to answer them as best he could, but the majority of his time had been split between inconsolable crying and drifting into fits of exhausted, restless sleep.

Now, the sun was golden-bright outside the single window of the precinct. Liam's mother was beside him; tense and strung tight with an anxiety that mirrored her son's in the form of a bouncing knee and rigid shoulders, but she was there. Something in Liam hadn't quite expected that, nor was he prepared for the warmth it brought in the midst of so much cold.

It hadn't been an easy decision to come here, and he still wasn't sure it was the right one. His eyes flicked toward the exit every few minutes, weighing the option of running away against staying.

Helping Jonah or hurting him.

The push-and-pull was a physical strain in his chest. Liam pitched forward and buried his fingers in his hair, still damp from the shower his mother had made him take before driving him into the city. A sound that might have been a precursor to throwing up clawed its way from his throat. A warm hand landed on his back.

"Breathe, Liam," his mother repeated. "It's going to be okay."

"What if it's not?"

Her hand paused, but no answer came.

Liam couldn't reasonably expect a solution from her, but still some childish instinct doubled down on the panic at the realization that this problem couldn't be solved by any motherly reassurance.

The soothing movements resumed in silence. Liam focused on breathing, tracing the line of grout between the tiles with his eyes.

"Mom?" he spoke up after a minute. "Are you mad at me?"

The tension in his back grew tighter the longer her silence stretched, until finally she pushed her fingers into his hair. "No, Liam," she said. "I'm not mad at you. I'm worried about you. I'm trying to... to make sense of all of this. If anything, I'm upset at myself for not seeing that you were clearly going through something."

Liam sat up. "I'm not a kid anymore," he said. "You shouldn't have to clean up my messes."

She smiled at him, and for the first time he noticed the signs of age around his mother's eyes. "I'm sure you think that's true. But you're *my* kid. I'm always going to feel the pain when you're hurting."

The glow in his chest grew a little warmer, but it only seemed to loosen whatever valve was holding his composure together. Liam swallowed, trying to force the tears back. "He's someone's son, too."

Not for the first time, Liam thought about Jonah's parents. It was hard not to harbor such a genuine hatred for two strangers he had never met, when all he knew of them was that their callous actions had pushed their son onto the streets that would eventually swallow him whole. If just one thing had been different, if they could have opened their hearts, just a little, to the boy who had come to them for love and acceptance, everything could have been different.

And maybe that meant he never would have met Liam, but he would have lived in his lonely reality a hundred times over if it meant sparing Jonah the miserable life he was living now.

"I know this probably isn't what you want to hear," he started, his voice weak. "But I love him." If there was any shred of certainty to be found in the madness that surrounded the situation, it was that.

"I know," she said.

There was no time to process her easy acceptance of his confession and all that it entailed, because a uniformed officer appeared in front of them, and Liam's heart bottomed out.

"Liam Cassidy? You can come with me."

Renewed terror flooded his system. He couldn't ignore the gravity of the choice in front of him now, nor the potential consequences that could follow. He didn't know how this would play out, but he hoped Jonah wouldn't hate him for going back on his word.

That was the best-case scenario; at least if Jonah was angry, he was alive. Liam wasn't sure how he could live with the alternative.

His legs were stilts under him, quivering as they took his weight. They followed the officer to an interview room off the main bullpen. It was a small, gray box of a room, with a single table and four chairs. Liam sank into one next to his mother, but the urge to run only doubled down inside the tight space.

The officer left again with a promise that her partner would be in to take his statement, but Liam was miles away.

The moment the door closed behind her, sealing them in, his heart took off like a rabbit.

"Mom." He struggled to speak around the fist-sized lump in his throat. "Mom, I— I can't... Is this the wrong thing? Am I making everything worse?"

Her eyes grew sullen as she watched him, perhaps only then registering the full extent of Liam's uncertainty. "Liam," she started to say.

But he never heard whatever reassurance she had to offer him, because the sudden buzz of his phone against the metal table seemed to shake the whole room.

Liam hadn't let it out of his sight all week. His plea to Jonah, that he should call him if he ever needed him, lurked in the back of his mind. Some part of him—maybe a larger part than he realized—held out hope that he would. It was improbable, and in a situation like this that hope could be poisonous. For a split second, he considered letting it go to voicemail.

The unlisted number could have meant any number of things that Liam couldn't deal with right now: a spam call, an overdue payment, a different police station calling to let him know that Nathan had decided to press charges against him after all.

Or maybe it was a hospital in Chicago.

Maybe Jonah's body had been found, and the only identifiable piece of information was a sliver of paper in his pocket with Liam's phone number on it.

But maybe he was alive.

He pressed the phone to his ear. "Hello?"

There was a pause, probably not a long one in reality, but one that stretched an eternity as Liam listened for any sign of life on the other side. Then someone cleared their throat.

"Liam? It's me."

CHAPTER 31
Liam

The flicker of blue from the television was the only light in the room, giving a dreamlike glow to the scene: Jonah in a hospital bed, bruised but alive, and Liam in a chair at his side.

He was holding Jonah's hand.

Liam had scarcely let go of him since arriving a few hours earlier, sure that without the anchor of physical touch, he would wake from the dream that Jonah was here with him, safe and alive and real. Every few minutes, Liam felt himself hold on a little tighter, just to reassure himself. He took great comfort in the fact that Jonah returned the squeeze, every time.

Nearly every channel was playing back-to-back Christmas movies. It provided both a familiar backdrop and an unsettling reminder that the world continued to spin, even as their own stuttered to a halt, stuck in this quiet moment, just the two of them.

A glance at the clock told him that in just a few minutes, it would be the morning of Christmas Eve. He was sure this was one he would never forget.

It had taken some convincing for Liam's mom to drop him at the hospital entrance. She had offered to stay, to come up to the room with him or find somewhere to wait, but Liam had decided, before Jonah had ever hung up the phone, that he would stay with him for however long he needed.

He didn't know how long that would be, and his mother had already gone so far out of her way for him. Liam assured her, with a tight hug across the center console of the car and a kiss on the cheek, that he would be alright from there. That he wouldn't be alone.

The moment he had laid eyes on Jonah from the doorway of the hospital room, he knew he had made the right call.

He still didn't know everything. There were so many questions Liam wanted to ask, but the last thing Jonah needed in his state was an interrogation. Liam had gotten just enough information to understand the basics of how Jonah had gotten here: that the man who hurt him was dead, and that the fucking *FBI* had been involved in getting him out.

And hadn't that been a shock—arriving to find the man he had thought to be Jonah's abuser sitting in his hospital room? Liam had nearly re-opened his split knuckles before Jonah could explain.

Beyond that, Liam could only glean information from what he saw with his own eyes, and that was bad enough.

He watched Jonah's face in the muted lighting, no room left within himself to be guarded in the way he looked at him. Probably, he'd leapt past the point of no return long ago.

Every few seconds, the screen would flash brightly enough to illuminate the bruises on Jonah's face. Even on his worst day, Liam had never seen Jonah so badly injured. His face and neck were mottled in shades of red and purple, swelling one eye shut almost completely.

Jonah must have sensed him staring, because he rolled his head along the pillow to meet his eyes.

"Did Nathan do this to you?" Liam whispered.

Jonah blinked with his one good eye, looking a little more aware. "He told you?"

"Not in so many words," Liam said. "It's a long story, but I know he saw you Friday night. Did he really do all of *this?*" He gestured at the mass of bruising covering Jonah's face.

Jonah watched him through dark eyes.

"Not all of it," he said finally. "Liam, there's something I haven't told you. About Nathan." He hesitated, turning his eyes forward again. "I knew him for months before I met you. That night we found each other in the bar, I was there because Nathan asked for me."

Liam was sure he wasn't understanding. "For my birthday," he clarified, not quite a question.

Jonah shook his head. "No. The overnight with you wasn't part of the original plan. He wanted something quick and discreet at the bar. I had to borrow his phone to get permission for the rest."

Liam felt dizzy. "You were crying that night," he recalled. "And at the diner, you. . ." Horror swelled in him. "You didn't look at him. Oh, god. Jonah, I'm so sorry. I had no idea he was. . . I never expected. . ."

"It wasn't your fault," Jonah said. "Nothing he did had anything to do with you. I know that."

"I should have known something was wrong by the way he acted that night we saw him together. I might have never known what he did if it weren't for the giant fucking gash you left on him. Good on you, by the way. Made it much easier to break his face open a second time."

"You hit him?" There was something like genuine awe in his voice.

"He deserved a lot worse than what he got." Liam's smile was short-lived, falling quickly back into a flat line. "I don't know what to say. I don't know how to make this right."

"It's not yours to make right," Jonah assured him. "I've always maintained that you're much better than your friends."

"He's not," Liam said sharply. "He is not my friend." *If he ever really was.*

"Good. You deserve better," Jonah said.

Liam squeezed his hand. *Now I have it,* he thought.

"Are you going to press charges?" he asked, cautious. "Against Nathan?"

Jonah's expression went tight.

"I didn't mean to imply that you should," Liam added quickly. "I just wanted to let you know that I would support you if you did. Or if you didn't. Whatever you do."

"No," Jonah said after a moment. "Pressing charges would open the door to months of dragging myself back to this place. To talk to police, to lawyers. That's on top of whatever trial may or may not. . ." He breathed a heavy exhale, as if the thought alone was exhausting. "No. I just want it to be over."

"I want. . ." Liam's voice broke off. "I want to kill him. All of them. Anyone who ever touched you."

"They weren't all bad people," Jonah said. "Most of them didn't know."

"Just because they weren't terrible doesn't mean it wasn't terrible for you."

Jonah didn't argue with him there.

They lapsed into a sleepy silence. The weight of the day was crashing over him, and Liam felt his eyelids starting to droop. Without letting go of Jonah's hand, he tilted his head against the bed rail and let his eyes shut for just a few seconds.

When he woke, probably several minutes later, it was to gentle fingers in his hair.

"Hey," Jonah whispered. "C'mere."

Liam sat up blearily, wiping at an embarrassing string of drool at the corner of his mouth. "Come where?" he said.

Jonah shifted his body, with what appeared to be no small amount of effort, to make room beside him. Liam looked at the empty space on the bed, then back at him. "I don't want to hurt you," he said.

"You won't."

It required a level of coordination that Liam didn't possess on his best day, but eventually he managed to slot himself beside Jonah without jostling him too much.

"Are you sure this is okay?" he asked, lips brushing Jonah's hair. He felt the answering nod against his shoulder and allowed himself to relax.

Sleep was just beginning to claim him again when Jonah's voice brought him back to the surface.

"Liam?" he said. "How did you get here so quickly?"

Liam opened his eyes.

"After I called you," Jonah continued. "You were here in under an hour. I've ridden in a car with you, remember? I know you don't drive that fast."

Liam took a breath, relishing in the close proximity, in case it wouldn't be welcome after this. "I was already in the city," he forced himself to say. "I'm a little afraid you'll hate me if I tell you why."

The mattress dipped as Jonah leaned back, just far enough to see his face. There was apprehension there, but it sounded like he meant it when he said, "I could never hate you."

Liam wasn't sure if that was true, but Jonah deserved the truth regardless.

"After I found out about Nathan, I sort of... broke." There was no better word for what had happened that night. "I was already at the end of my rope after a week of worrying about you and feeling so... so fucking *awful* about how everything went down—"

"It wasn't your fault," Jonah cut in. "I hated the way we left things, too. I could see that you blamed yourself, and that wasn't my intention."

Liam shook his head. "I never should have risked bringing you home with me in the first place."

"I took the risk, too," Jonah argued. "I chose it just as much as you did."

"Well." Liam swallowed back the urge to plead his guilt further. "Regardless, I hit a breaking point, and I ended up telling my mom. Everything, I mean. About you, and about how scared I was that I hadn't done enough to help you, and. . . I don't know. After hearing it all out loud for the first time, I. . ." He made himself look Jonah in the eye when he said it. "I was at the police station when you called me. I was going to make a report."

Jonah was quiet for a long time, nothing but the near-silent buzz of the television and the sounds of medical machinery in the background. Liam was braced for outrage and betrayal, braced to be kicked out of this bed and this room and this hospital and Jonah's life, so he nearly flinched when he felt a hand close over his.

"He was going to kill me," Jonah said. "He would have, I think, if Ellis hadn't intervened. And if not then, eventually. I don't hate you, Liam. You were right to be afraid for me. And I'm sorry I made you carry that weight for all this time."

"You were never a burden, Jonah."

Jonah smiled, kind but sad. "I know you're too nice to see it that way, but I'm still sorry."

"Maybe," Liam began cautiously, "between the two of us, we've had enough apologies for now?"

Some of the tension seemed to leave Jonah's body. He relaxed against Liam once again, resting his head on his shoulder

"So, you told your mom everything," Jonah said. "How did she take that?"

Liam thought about it. "Honestly?" he said. "Better than I expected. She drove me here, you know? I mean, she wasn't thrilled at the idea of me putting myself in potential danger, but she seemed to get it when I told her that I—" He bit his tongue, ears warming. "When I told her about you."

Jonah went quiet again, long enough to make Liam nervous. Then he said, quietly, "She loves you."

"She does," Liam agreed, his voice going a little watery. "I think she's more understanding than I give her credit for. And Jonah?" He squeezed his hand to make sure he had his attention. "I think that would extend to you as well. If you need somewhere to stay until you figure things out, or for however long. . ."

"I don't think you can make that offer on your parents' behalf," Jonah said.

"I'll call them right now, if you want," Liam insisted, already reaching for the phone in his back pocket. Jonah stopped him.

"I don't think they'd appreciate the midnight phone call, either."

He could hear the tick of amusement in Jonah's voice, but Liam was overcome by a tidal wave of grief. They hadn't yet talked about Jonah's plan forward from here, if he even had one, but Liam was suddenly, keenly aware of just how few people Jonah had left to turn to, and keenly aware of how that had landed him in such an impossible spot in the first place. Liam wouldn't let him be left out in the cold again. He refused.

"Jonah, I'm not going to abandon you," he promised. "I won't."

"I'm not asking you to."

What are you asking for, Liam wanted to beg. *Anything.* He couldn't imagine denying Jonah a single thing.

But he couldn't put that on him now. Not in a hospital bed, in the middle of the night, when his life had just been ripped out from under him *again.* There would be time to figure out the next step, but for now, Liam's job wasn't to plan for Jonah's future. It was simply to be there for him in the moment. That much he could do.

"Liam?" Jonah whispered, so small that he felt the name against his chest more than he heard it. "I think I want to call my mom."

CHAPTER 32
Jonah

It was almost poetic, how it ended the same way it began: in a nondescript hotel room, with Jonah's stomach in knots.

The hospital discharged him that morning, and Antonio Ellis stuck to his word about finding temporary arrangements for Jonah.

The hotel the Bureau put him up in was decent, and it was in a nice part of the city. Not that it mattered. It was only for a handful of days, while the agents and the local police needed easy access to Jonah for questioning. There were talks of a trial further down the road, where Jonah would be expected to come back to Chicago to testify against associates of Shepard whom Jonah had been unlucky enough to meet, but nothing was set in stone.

Something no one seemed to consider was how difficult it might be for Jonah to be confined to a room that mirrored so many of his worst memories.

A SERIES OF ROOMS

Hotel rooms, give or take a few hygiene standards and choices in decor, were largely the same. It was Jonah's personal Groundhog Day of off-white walls and mass-produced paintings, sheets that never quite felt clean enough and AC units that always, always ran too cold. There was something about the buried-deep smell in the carpeting, the remnants of stale smoke and mildew the cleaners could never quite shake. Jonah thought that scent might cling to him for as long as he lived.

It was made easier by Liam's presence. He hadn't left Jonah's side since arriving at the hospital, and he had promised that he would stay with him until Jonah sent him away.

A few days ago, Jonah would have given anything to share one more night in a hotel room with Liam. Now, he was too much of a mess to truly relish the moment, because Jonah's mother was due to arrive at the hotel in less than an hour.

The last time he had seen her, under the dimmed kitchen light of his childhood home, his mom hadn't been able to meet his eyes. At the time, he'd felt the scorch of her shame like a physical burn.

Later, he'd wondered if that avoidance had anything to do with the bruise forming beneath his orbital bone in the impression of his father's hand. Maybe she hadn't been able to stomach seeing her own betrayal reflected back at her.

If that was the case, he couldn't imagine her reaction to seeing him now.

Months ago, Jonah had begun to resign himself to the reality that he would never see his family again. As time went on, it had become easier to operate under that assumption than hold out any hope for the alternative. His sins began to pile up: the crimes, the strangers, the drugs. So many betrayals of his own body, his faith, his upbringing, pushing him farther from the light of the affection his parents had once held for their eldest son.

After a while, the thought of seeing his family again, the thought of his family seeing *him*, became a fear rather than a comfort. How would it feel to look them in the eye now, after everything he had seen and done?

It was the nightmare that had haunted him for so long, and now it was a monster come to life, staring him in the face.

Making the call hadn't been easy. He'd gone into it with the full expectation of rejection, either outright or in the form of a dead line and a blocked number. Liam had lent his phone and sat beside him in the hospital bed as he dialed, holding Jonah's sweaty hand between his own.

The moment he heard his mom's voice on the other end, however, her familiar cadence of skepticism at the unknown number, Jonah had lost all ability to speak.

Liam had stepped in, after a pleading nod from Jonah.

"Mrs. Prince?" he had said. "I'm here with Jonah."

Entire lifetimes had passed in the few seconds of silence that followed. Then, barely loud enough to be audible, she had echoed his name in an exhale that couldn't have been anything but relief.

It wasn't a long call, mostly because Jonah couldn't manage to string more than a couple of words together, but they had ended it with the exchange of a hotel address and a meeting time.

The constant anxiety since then had rendered him exhausted, but Jonah couldn't sleep. He turned on the TV, then turned it off again. He showered, but he was forced to put on the hospital-issued sweats afterward, making the whole thing feel like a waste.

He avoided the bed altogether, opting instead to sit in the stiff armchair by the window, hugging his knees tightly to his chest. A lukewarm cup of coffee sat beside him on the windowsill, untouched. Liam had prepared it in the cheap coffee maker solely as an attempt to drown out the other smells of the room with a comforting one.

Several times, Jonah tried to give Liam an out. He was aware, however distantly, that it was the day before Christmas. Liam was undoubtedly skipping out on his family traditions in favor of rubbing Jonah's back as he knelt in front of the toilet, losing his battle to nerves every time he tried to eat something. After everything Liam had already sacrificed for him, it felt wholly unfair for him to give this up, too.

Of course, Liam shut down every attempt. And selfishly, but maybe not so secretly, Jonah was grateful for one man's unwavering determination to stay.

***

In the elevator to the lobby, Jonah curled his fingers around the handrail and tried to level his breathing. Liam stood at his side, a silent pillar of support.

Agent Ellis had reserved the hotel's conference room for the reunion. *Neutral ground*, he had called it. He wanted to give Jonah privacy while retaining the option to escape to his room if he needed to. Jonah was still too resentful to feel properly grateful, but he couldn't deny that the safety net was a comfort.

When the elevator doors chimed open on the ground floor, Jonah's breath caught, as if someone had kinked his oxygen line. He stood frozen for so long that Liam had to wave his hand in front of the sensor to keep the doors from closing.

"You sure you're ready?" Liam asked.

Jonah forced his eyes to move to him. "She's already here," he said weakly.

The line between Liam's brows pinched tighter. "The choice is still yours."

That was true on paper, he knew. Shepard was dead, Jonah was a legal adult, and he hadn't spoken to his parents in over a year. There was no one left to control the trajectory of his life but him. But at that moment, the freedom of choice was just one more burden to shoulder.

Here he was, alive despite everything, standing at the edge of what could have been a new beginning, and he was more terrified than ever.

"I need to see her," he said finally, forcing himself off the wall.

Liam nodded, falling into step beside him.

When they reached the end of the hallway just off the lobby, Jonah spotted the door to the conference room. It was a warm, dark wood, with a single pane of glass showing through to the other side. There, within the small rectangular frame, Jonah caught a glimpse of silver-streaked brown hair tied back in a bun.

She was turned away, staring out at the overcast sky through the window on the opposite wall. Her body was cloaked in a bulky sweater, but Jonah recognized her immediately.

He moved, stepping past Liam and closing his hand around the doorknob. It was as if there was a magnet connecting his heart to hers, a bond pulling him toward her that no amount of time passed or betrayals committed could have broken. It fueled his body with the courage to push the door open and step inside.

"Mom?"

She turned instantly. The eyes that stared back at him were sunken into the ghost of a face he had once known better than anyone's. It was so different and every bit the same as he remembered, and both realizations ached.

"Jonah." Her voice was a wispy nothing from behind her fingers.

Standing before her, even sheathed in the bulky material of his oversized sweats, Jonah was stripped down to the bone. It was as if every memory was painted onto his skin, an open gallery of his shame. Regret knocked into him, nearly staggering him back. He was overwhelmed by the urge to fold into himself and disappear.

This had been a mistake. How could he have ever thought there was a chance they could come back from this?

She took the first step forward, leading with a hand outstretched, but it dropped to her side before she made contact. "Your face," she whispered.

He didn't know what to say. *"It's not as bad as it looks,"* would have been a lie. *"I'm okay,"* would have been an even more egregious one. Before he could grasp at a response, her gaze trailed higher.

"Your hair," she said.

He reached up to run his fingertips over the short, soft buzz. It had taken a long time to get used to, but even longer since he had really thought about it. Shepard had made him shave it the first time he'd caught lice from a client's dingy hotel room. *The last thing I need is another outbreak in the house.* Jonah had felt so filthy, like a plague of disease to the others. He had kept it short after that.

"It will grow back," he said, hating how it sounded like an apology.

As if hearing his voice broke the final thread of her control, she closed the distance and threw her arms around Jonah, startling him to momentary stillness. His arms hovered close without touching, eyes wide and blinking over her shoulder.

"I'm sorry," she cried against his chest.

They were the words he had wished for. Words he had long abandoned hope of ever hearing. Now, on the receiving end of them, after too much time, he only felt numb.

Could it really have been that simple? After all this time, could she really cross the wasteland between them in only a few steps?

Torrents of conflicting emotion warred inside him as his hands came to rest on the back of her sweater. He caught Liam's eyes over her shoulder, an unobtrusive observer against the far wall. Liam smiled at him, but Jonah thought he sensed a current beneath the surface; something wary and concerned.

When his mother's legs buckled beneath her, it was Jonah who was left to hold their weight off the ground.

CHAPTER 33
Jonah

Liam,
Went out to get some air.
Be back soon.
Your friend,
Jonah

He left the note on the nightstand, just as he had the first night they met.

He still remembered it well: sitting up with the rising sun to watch a stranger sleep while the clock ran out. He remembered hating having to write the note, knowing he had to run back to a life outside of that room when morning came.

Jonah wasn't running now. Not far, anyway. The hotel had a rooftop accessible to guests, and Jonah needed space to breathe.

He was careful not to wake Liam, stepping noiselessly across the carpet in his socked feet. In the hallway, he moved quickly past the row of doors, knowing his mother lay sleeping behind one of them, Agent Ellis in another.

The reunion had taken more out of Jonah than he'd had to give. There was already more than a year of distance between him and his mother, but the one thing Jonah craved most, once they'd both gotten their bearings, was space.

He was grateful when she had opted to get her own room for the night, but a part of him couldn't help but wonder if he wasn't the only one who needed a moment.

Somehow, they would need to learn to navigate this precarious dance between them, because tomorrow morning, Jonah would climb into the passenger seat of her car and make the three-hour journey back to his childhood home.

It wasn't a comfortable choice or an easy one, but it was one of the only few available. Jonah had no money. He had no credit and no prospects, a resume more likely to land him in a jail cell than a job, and Jonah never wanted to have to take his clothes off for someone again in order to secure his next meal. This year had made him vulnerable in entirely new ways, and Ellis was right when he'd said that Jonah would need support. This was what he had.

"Your father and I are taking some time apart," was one of the first things Jonah's mom had said to him in the aftermath of their reunion. He'd heard it for what it was: an explanation for her husband's absence and perhaps a token of good faith;

a declaration that she had finally come around to taking her son's side, if only a year too late.

It was a lot to process, packed into a singular statement of fact, and Jonah still wasn't sure how to feel. The idea of his mother being on her own for the first time since she was eighteen years old was hard to wrap his head around.

His entire life, his mother had been meek and quiet and at his father's side, falling in line with his decisions about how to run his household, conforming to the traditional role that had been passed down through generations of preachers' daughters before her. Knowing that Jonah himself had been the fault line of that separation was a double-edged sword.

It was a start, he thought. If she was willing to extend the olive branch, Jonah could find it in himself to try. He would get in the car and return to a home that no longer felt like his own. He would keep his head down and try to find some way of regaining control over a life that had been taken from him.

Beyond that, his future was a wall of solid gray. There was nowhere to go except toward it, with the feeble hope that the opacity would fade with time. That maybe, one day, it wouldn't feel like he was taking every step in the dark.

The rooftop was empty. He had been counting on that, given the hour and the temperature. The vapor of his breath swirled around his nose and mouth as he moved slowly toward the edge.

The expanse of the city around him made him feel overwhelmingly small, like he could be crushed by the sheer vastness of it on all sides. He gripped the railing, letting the sting of cold metal on his palms ground him.

Chicago was quiet from this high up. In the dark hour of the early morning—so early it was really still night—it glowed back at him with a hundred little signs of life: the flicker of light from an apartment window, the rev of an engine on an empty street. Jonah closed his eyes and wondered what it would be like to see the beauty of this city through the lens of someone who hadn't seen its ugliest parts.

There was no chance of him separating the negative associations. When he opened his eyes, all he could see was the penthouse floor of the luxury hotel three blocks west where he had once spent an endless Saturday night with one of Shepard's friends. He saw the glow of a corner store where his last few dollars had bought him a cheap imitation of dinner that had left him hungry and wanting. He saw the bus stop bench where he had sat at three in the morning, wiping blood from his nose with the back of his sleeve.

Maybe they weren't the exact spots, or maybe they were, but it was all the same in the end. So much of his time here had gone by in a blur, except for the moments that dragged on in excruciating detail. Jonah had seen every dark corner this city had to offer—the same city he had run to for escape— and even as it glowed around him now, in all its sparkling glory, he hoped to never see it again.

A cough from behind him made Jonah jump. He spun, scanning the darkness until he spotted Ellis by the entrance.

When their eyes met, Ellis was already moving to retreat. "Sorry," he murmured. "I didn't realize anyone was up here."

"It's fine," Jonah said before he could slip back through the access door. "I don't own the rooftop."

Ellis studied him for a moment, then let the door close behind him. "It's cold up here," he commented, retrieving a pack of cigarettes from his jacket. He walked to the railing, keeping a solid ten feet of distance between them.

Jonah shrugged, averting his eyes toward the city once more. They fell into a surprisingly comfortable quiet, broken only by the flick of a lighter and the occasional exhale of smoke.

"I put in my papers with the Bureau today." Ellis broke the silence without looking his way. "I'm done."

Jonah blinked, letting that sink in. When he cast a glance at Ellis, he was met halfway with a rueful grin.

"I don't know why I'm telling you. I know it doesn't make a difference."

"It doesn't," Jonah agreed immediately. Then, after a beat: "What are you going to do now?"

Ellis took another drag and let it out into the cold. "For work? I don't. . ." he trailed off. "I don't know. My mom passed away earlier this year. She left me her grandmother's house in Queens. Inherited, paid off. It's too big for a man living alone, but it should give me a place to lay low until I figure things out."

"Queens?" Jonah asked. "New York?"

Ellis nodded. "It's where I grew up."

He had never considered a version of this man that required "growing up." To Jonah, he had always been an immovable force; a part of the structure that imprisoned him, that would remain long after Jonah was gone.

"Can I ask you something?" Jonah heard himself say.

"Yes."

"Are you actually sorry? Not for me, but for your part in all of it. For taking the job at all."

Seconds ticked by, but Jonah refused to be the one to break the stalemate. He waited him out, tapping his thumbnail against the metal. Finally, Ellis said, "I don't know how to answer that. Would it make a difference to you, either way?"

No, Jonah thought. It probably wouldn't.

"Can I ask *you* something?" Ellis returned after a beat. "I meant what I said about the need for a support system, but I also realize I don't know your history. I imagine things weren't great at home, for you to have been on your own so young."

Jonah flicked him a look, a silent demand to get to the question.

"I just want to make sure that you feel safe going home with your mother tomorrow."

"What would happen if I said no?" Jonah asked, part irritation and part genuine curiosity.

Ellis looked out at the city for a few long seconds, then reached into the pocket of his leather jacket. He shuffled closer to Jonah, still keeping himself at arm's length, and held out a small rectangular card.

"I know you don't have much reason to trust me," he said. "If we never speak after today, that's okay. But if there ever comes a time when you need help, you can call me, day or night. That's an offer with no expiration date, and no strings attached."

Jonah eyed the card warily. "What would I want from you?"

"Maybe nothing." Ellis shrugged. "But I'll feel better knowing you have the option."

Jonah was about to reiterate how little he cared about Antonio Ellis *feeling better*, but he bit his tongue and took the card. On it was his name, number, and email. Jonah tucked it into the pocket of his sweatpants.

The door opened again.

"Jonah?" Liam stood at the entry this time, a blanket pulled around his shoulders. "Is everything okay?" The way he eyed Ellis spoke volumes about his own dubious feelings about the man's sudden redemption. Despite everything, Jonah felt a stitch of affection.

"I'm fine," Jonah answered.

Liam was already making his way toward them. "It's freezing," he scolded. He didn't miss a beat, lifting the corner of the blanket to pull Jonah under with him.

Ellis cleared his throat. "I'm going to turn in. I'll leave you to it." He stopped as he passed them, leveling a meaningful look at Jonah. "Day or night," he repeated. "I mean it."

Jonah pulled the blanket tighter around him, watching as the man rounded the corner of the entryway and disappeared from sight, wondering if it would be the last time he ever saw him.

"What was that about?" Liam asked.

"Nothing." Jonah blinked, coming back to the moment. "What are you doing out here?"

Liam smiled, producing the slip of paper from his pocket. "*Your friend, Jonah?*" he quoted, bumping their shoulders together. "Clever."

Jonah bumped back and didn't pull away after, leaving their hands brushing between them.

CHAPTER 34
Liam

Liam's teeth were at risk of chipping from chattering so hard, but Jonah seemed content to stand under the blanket on the rooftop with him, so he didn't dare nudge them inside. He would have stood out there all night if that was what Jonah needed.

The cold was a grounding force for Liam, too. The brave face he had tried to maintain for Jonah's sake was beginning to slip as dawn drew nearer, and he was clinging onto the last threads of his control.

In a matter of months, Jonah had carved out a place in Liam's life that couldn't easily be filled. Despite the circumstances that had brought them together, the bond they'd formed was genuine, and it was the kind Liam had spent his whole life aching for. Selfish as it was, he didn't want to let that go.

When he'd received that call from Jonah, less than forty-eight hours ago, he'd had no idea how quickly things would move. Now he was here, minutes away from Christmas Day and grappling for the words to say goodbye to the person he had only just gotten back.

Tomorrow, Jonah would get into a car with his mother—which Liam had his own feelings about, but dutifully kept to himself—and drive beyond state lines. There was no telling what that distance would bring.

What if this fragile, unnamed thing between them wasn't meant to last in the outside world? What if Jonah didn't even want to try? Liam couldn't blame him, if that was the case. There was a real possibility that Liam's presence would only serve as a reminder of the worst period of Jonah's life, that Liam was inextricably linked with this city and all the pain it had caused him. No one was more deserving of peace, and Liam would rather lose Jonah than stand in the way of his healing.

But if there was a chance—even a small one—that Jonah wanted to keep him in his life, this might have been Liam's last chance to try.

"I know I already made the offer," Liam said, "but I need to hear it from you one more time. Are you sure you don't want to stay with me for a little while?" He felt Jonah turn to him, even as he kept his own eyes forward; there was only so much courage he could muster at once. "I'm glad your mom is willing to try and fix things between you, but it's hard to watch you with her, knowing what your family did to you."

"It's hard for me, too," Jonah admitted.

It wasn't the honesty he was expecting, but it only drove Liam's urgency. "We could figure something out," he promised. "I know my mom would be okay with it, even if it's just for a little while, and then we could figure out something after that. I want to help you, Jonah. I want you to be safe."

"I can't do that, Liam." Jonah angled his body toward him under the cover of the blanket, softening the blow of his gentle rejection. "I don't want to be something you have to 'figure out.'"

"I didn't mean that—" Liam began, but Jonah shook his head.

"Sorry," Jonah said. "No, I know you didn't. I didn't mean for it to sound that way. It's hard to put into words." Liam waited patiently as he took a breath and started again. "You've done so much for me already. You helped me when I had no way of repaying you, but I don't want that to be the dynamic between us anymore."

"I don't want to lose you," Liam whispered. "I know it's selfish. I don't have any right to make demands on your life, and I'll completely understand if you want, or need, a clean break from. . . from all of this, but I. . ."

I love you.

The words caught in his throat. Not because they weren't true, but because they *were*. He had known it for a while now, and there was no doubt in his mind as the words clicked into place. They still had a long way to go in getting to know each other, and Liam wanted nothing more than to have the chance to do just that. But dropping that declaration on him now might have swayed a decision that should have been all Jonah's.

Before he could think of a way to reroute his sentence, Jonah's warm hand closed over his, gripping tight.

"I don't want to lose you either," he said. "That's what I'm trying to say."

"It is?" He didn't even care that he sounded pathetically relieved.

Jonah smiled. "Rather poorly, it would seem," he said. "But yes."

They turned to each other, closing the huddle of their blanket even tighter around them. For a brief flash, Jonah's eyes dipped to Liam's mouth, and Liam was sure he was about to kiss him. Instead, Jonah dipped his chin to hide his face away.

"Liam," he said. "I don't know how any of this is going to play out. I don't know what I'm supposed to do when I get to Indiana, or if I'm making the right decision by going in the first place, and I'm—" He stopped to breathe, closing his eyes for a few seconds. "My whole life is a mess, and I don't know how much I have to offer you. I don't know if I can be what you want me to. Yet. Ever. I don't know. I don't *know*."

"Hey," Liam interjected. "Just take a breath."

Jonah struggled to comply. It reminded Liam of the string of nights he had spent coaxing Jonah out of night terrors, slowly bringing him back to earth. Jonah had one fist clutched around the edge of the blanket, the other tangled in the front of Liam's shirt.

"I just don't want to lead you on," he said desperately. "Or string you along, or. . ."

"You're not." Liam shook his head firmly. "You aren't doing any of that. The fact that you want to be in my life at all is more than I could ask for." He dipped his head to the side, trying to catch Jonah's eyes. "Hey, you're my friend first. Okay? The best one I've ever had. Anything else. . ." He waved his free hand in front of him. "We've got time to figure out the rest."

Jonah nodded, and Liam could see the desperation with which he clung to Liam's words.

"What if I'm not okay?" Jonah asked. "What if I'm not okay for a long time?"

Liam tilted his head, resting it against Jonah's temple.

"I'm not timing you," he promised. "But you *will* be okay. And I'll be here for you while you get there. Call me. Text me. I'll invest in a carrier pigeon or tie two cups together with a really, really long string. Whatever."

Jonah smiled, and it was contagious.

"And you know what?" Liam couldn't help but add. "I can come visit. I happen to have accumulated a lot of hotel points over the past few months. Like, a *lot* of hotel points."

A warm puff of breath that might have been laughter tickled Liam's skin. A second later, a tiny pinprick of cold stung his cheek, then another. Liam blinked and lifted his head to find the sky speckled with falling snow. He chose to take that as a good omen.

A quick peek at his phone confirmed that it was after midnight now. Christmas Day.

"Would it be alright if I hugged you?" he asked Jonah, who nodded like he had only been waiting on the invitation.

Liam pulled him in tight, escaping into the warmth and solidity of his body. He never wanted to let go.

CHAPTER 35
Jonah

JANUARY

On his first night back in his childhood bed, Jonah didn't sleep at all.

The room had been largely untouched, kept like an exhibit in a museum—a living memorial for a boy who died young, his youth frozen in time inside four walls, a cautionary tale of a life derailed.

That night, as he stared at the ceiling above his twin bed, he was overcome by the gruesome mental image of thick, black sludge oozing from his pores. Spreading across the bed, the walls, the carpet—every move he made another blot he couldn't scrub out. Jonah had dragged his baggage back home from Chicago, like bringing a plague into a clean, quarantined space. His very presence was an insult to the person who used to live there.

He hadn't slept much in the nights that followed, either.

Jonah lost time, those first couple of weeks. Large pockets of it, chunks lasting several hours, would disappear from under his nose. He would close his eyes to the darkness of his bedroom ceiling and open them at lunch the next day, sitting across from his little brother, forcing a laugh at some joke that Jonah hadn't really heard. He would lose himself in the middle of a one-sided conversation with his sister, nodding along to the blur of words until he snapped into a new present several minutes later.

Something was building. Jonah could feel it in the back of his skull at all times, like a ticking clock inching toward the end of an invisible countdown.

During the days, he moved through the house like a ghost, caught behind some invisible haze that separated him from the rest of the world. He ate when food was placed in front of him. He pretended to watch whatever played on the television in the living room. But Jonah didn't really exist.

Nightly, during whatever wisps of sleep he managed, Jonah dreamed of gold wedding bands and tortoise shell glasses on hotel nightstands, wood-rot beams on a basement ceiling, and hands around his throat. He dreamed of clothes being pulled from his body and hands that didn't stop there, pawing and peeling at layers of skin until he was all blood-red muscle and sinew, raw and exposed. No longer human, just a human-shaped thing.

On the worst nights, he was plagued by the awful feeling of being watched during these violations. He would turn his head and see someone in the room with him, witnessing each horror in real time. Sometimes it was Liam. Sometimes his mom, his siblings. Once, he turned to find the distinct outline of his father's silhouette hovering in the doorway. In that dream, Jonah cried out for him. To help him, to do something. He would wake with a scream jammed tight in his throat and a hollow feeling that would follow him well into the daylight.

Often, when the nights were at their worst, he called Liam.

Jonah's mother had helped him reactivate one of his old, out-of-date phones from high school, stuffed in the back of their electronics drawer. The first thing he did was program Liam's number from memory.

Since then, they messaged every day, though Jonah knew his own conversational skills were lacking. It was hard to put his numbness into words, and even harder to put those words on a screen for someone else to decode, even though Liam never seemed to mind. But their phone calls were a reprieve.

Whenever Jonah called him, panicked and disoriented from a nightmare, Liam would stay up with him, no matter the hour. He would talk to him like he used to on Jonah's bad nights, chattering about whatever came to mind until Jonah was back in his body. Sometimes, they would spend an hour in silence, the only noise on the line their soft breathing as one or both of them drifted back to sleep.

He missed him.

Jonah made a point not to lean too heavily on him, even from a distance. Sometimes he would stop himself halfway through dialing his number and force himself to put down the phone.

He'd meant what he said to Liam on the rooftop their last night in Chicago: he didn't want to be Liam's burden anymore. He needed to learn to stand on his own.

And yet, as the days dragged on, Jonah found himself wondering if he had made the wrong choice in leaving.

It happened by complete accident.

His brother's car was in the shop for a repair and their mom was staying late at her new job, so neither one of them was able to make the Friday night custody drop-off at his dad's. Jonah just so happened to have stepped into the garage to find a spare bulb for his bedside lamp when the sound of tires coming up the drive startled him.

He brought a hand up to shield his eyes against the headlights, unable to make out the shape of the car beyond the glare. Then the engine cut out and the driver's door swung open.

"Hey, Matty, I got a call from the mechanic. He—"

Jonah went rigid as his father came to a stop in the mouth of the garage.

All his life, everyone had told Jonah how much he looked like his dad. He wondered if they looked identical now, sharing twin deer-in-headlights gazes across the empty space.

They had spent so much time in this garage together, once upon a time. Jonah's first baseball glove was somewhere on the wooden shelf just left of his shoulder, the same shelf he had helped his dad install when he was thirteen years old. Any of the grease stains along the ground could have been the very ones he'd made when his father had taught him how to change the oil on his first car. The room was a graveyard for the bond they once shared, and his father was a ghost standing before him in the flesh, coming to haunt him one last time.

"Jonah." He cleared his throat, pulling his shoulders back into the confident, collected pose Jonah had watched him assume so many times. "You. . . Wow, kiddo, you look so much like your brother. I can hardly tell you apart." He punctuated the end of his sentence with a weak chuckle.

Jonah bit down on the tip of his tongue and wondered if his father had even noticed that he'd said it backward. That Matthew was the one who looked like *him*, because Jonah was here first, no matter how hard his father might have tried to forget about his eldest son's existence.

Jonah didn't say that. He didn't say anything at all. He couldn't.

"You look. . ." His father seemed to be grasping for words. "You look good, Jo. Your mother said you weren't. . . Well, you know, at first. But now. . ." He cleared his throat again, dropping his gaze. It occurred to Jonah that his father had yet to look him directly in the eye. "You look well, is all I'm trying to say."

It wasn't even true. Jonah knew it wasn't true.

He didn't know what was happening. His jaw was locked up, his tongue so dry it stuck to the roof of his mouth. He couldn't have formed words even if he had the slightest clue what he wanted to say, but he couldn't run either. The ground beneath him seemed to have grown invisible roots around his legs, binding him in place.

"Hey," his dad said. "Listen, I know things were tense the way we left them, but I'm glad you made it home alright."

The words echoed inside his head like cannon fire.

Things were tense.

I'm glad you made it home alright.

Alright, he had said. Jonah was the farthest fucking thing from *alright*.

He was a shell of a person who couldn't keep down a full meal or get a night of sleep or have a real relationship with someone he loved. He was a gaunt figure in every passing mirror, a lifeless imitation of the person who used to wear his skin. But somehow, in his father's eyes, he was *alright*.

At least Jonah wasn't dead. *That* was what he meant.

At least his father didn't have to bear that on his conscience.

Jonah's anger was hot enough to melt through muscle and bone, atrophying his legs to keep him immobilized in the face of this assault. A swell of silence overtook the garage. His father had been given every opportunity to take even the smallest step toward making things right, and he had let them all pass by.

Jonah couldn't handle this. With every bit of strength he had in him, he forced his leg to move, testing his weight as he took a step back.

"I'll tell Matthew and Leah you're here," was the last thing Jonah said to his father.

Once he was moving, he couldn't stop. He might have heard his dad call after him, or maybe it was wishful thinking. Regardless, he didn't slow his pace until he had reached the top of the staircase.

"Jonah?" Matthew stuck his head out the door of his room. "Jonah!"

It wasn't until Matthew grabbed his wrist and turned over a bloody palm that he realized the lightbulb he was holding had shattered.

CHAPTER 36
Liam

Kim was sitting in her office when Liam tapped his knuckles on the door. She looked up from a stack of deposit slips and put them down on the desk when she saw it was him.

"He lives," she announced.

Liam slumped against the doorframe, sheepish. "Hi, Kim."

"*'Hi, Kim,'*" she mimicked in an unflattering intonation. "He comes in here after dropping off the face of the planet and says *'hi Kim.'* Hi yourself, Liam. Get in here and sit down."

Somehow, he couldn't help but smile as he dropped into the metal folding chair across from her. "I sent a text," he defended weakly.

"You might as well have left a ransom note made of magazine clippings, as cryptic as that text was." She was making light because it was Kim, but Liam had known her long enough to recognize the genuine concern. He had really worried her.

"I'm sorry," he said. "I really am. Things have been. . . It's been a strange few months."

"I've noticed," she said. "What made your absence all the more concerning was the way you walked around here like a zombie your last few shifts. It's hard to tell where your head's been at."

"I know," he said. "Did I mention I'm sorry?" He was trying to get better about saying that less often, but in this conversation, apologies felt warranted.

"You did," she said. "But I'm less interested in hearing how sorry you are, and more interested in hearing how you're doing."

I don't think I've gotten a full night's sleep in weeks.
I'm in a mild amount of credit card debt.
I miss my best friend.

"I'm. . . getting better," he said. "Am I fired?"

"Of course you aren't fired," she scoffed. "We're short-staffed as it is. Trust me, you're clocking in immediately after this conversation."

Liam huffed a laugh.

"In all seriousness, if you need to take some time off, you need to tell me," she said. "We can work something out."

"God, no," he said immediately. "If anything, I'd like to pick up more hours. Please."

"What, so I can watch you run yourself into the ground for another few months?"

"I'll have the availability this time," he assured her. Then, after taking a breath, he said, "I've decided to take the spring semester off."

It was strange to say out loud. Watching the registration date come and go without lifting a finger had been a nerve-wracking choice, but an intentional one. It was the first deviation from the monotonous path he had coasted since high school, and the first real step toward committing himself to the future he wanted.

Kim raised an eyebrow. "You're not dropping out, are you?"

"No," he said. "I want to get serious about art school. If I want to get to New York in the fall, I'll need to save up as much as I can."

A rare, earnest smile spread across Kim's mouth. "Now that's a plan I can get behind."

Returning to work was a jolt of whiplash. He likened it to the feeling of being immersed in a long book and being forced to reckon with the reality of life when he closed the cover. Except this time, it was his life with Jonah that had been the real thing, and now he was forced back into this two-dimensional world. The monotony of being inside the diner—of tending to unkind patrons and listening to petty gossip in the kitchen—was like trudging through wet concrete.

There was an hour left in his shift when the chime on the door signaled a new customer. Liam turned to greet them, but the words never made it out.

Ben met his eyes from across the room. Without acknowledging him, Liam turned on his heel and beelined for the kitchen.

"Liam, wait," Ben said before he could make it.

Against his better judgment, Liam stopped.

He hadn't seen Ben since the night of the derailed Christmas dinner. Liam was not particularly eager to revisit that memory. Especially now, in the middle of his workplace, where he was trying very hard to keep some semblance of his life together.

"Will this be for here or to go?" Liam forced a well-practiced customer service smile.

Ben leveled him with an annoyed look. "Liam, please. I want to talk to you."

"I'm afraid you'll need to order something or leave," he said, as coldly as he could manage. "Otherwise, this is called loitering."

For a second, it almost looked like he had won the battle, but Ben crushed his dreams, as he stepped forward and pulled out one of the stools along the bar. "Fine," he said, taking his seat. "One black coffee, please."

Liam's smile wiped clean from his face. The customer service voice dropped. "Ben, this is my job. You can't just come here and corner me into talking to you."

"You wouldn't answer your phone," Ben said. "I was worried."

"I've been busy." Liam dipped behind the counter, getting to work on the sham of an order. He turned back to Ben with the steaming mug, but didn't set it down. "Over there." He motioned with his head to an empty booth. "I'm not having this conversation where everyone can hear."

Ben conceded, looking relieved. Liam followed, calling over his shoulder to Kim at the register. "Taking a fifteen."

Alone in their booth, Ben was suddenly quiet.

Liam stared at him expectantly. "In case you missed that," he nudged, "I only have fifteen minutes."

Ben took a sip of the coffee, wincing as the heat met his lips. "I know," he said after another long moment. "I'm just. . . trying to figure out where to start."

Liam's defensiveness began to lose some of its bite. He nodded, once, giving him a second to gather his thoughts. Finally, Ben nudged the coffee slightly away from him, meeting Liam's eyes.

"What happened?" he asked, a little exasperated. "At dinner, I mean. I've never seen you like that. Not anywhere close to it, really. I'm not saying Nathan didn't have it coming," he added quickly, apparently unwilling to lose Liam's momentary good graces. "I'm sure I could think of a dozen reasons off the top of my head he had a good punch coming his way, but. . ."

But, indeed.

It was Liam's turn for silence. He picked up a discarded straw wrapper that the busboy left behind and began picking it into tiny pieces.

"Liam—"

"I'm not. . . ignoring you," he said. "I guess I don't know where to begin either."

It suddenly occurred to him that maybe Ben had reached out to his mother, or to Nathan himself, for answers. And while he doubted Ben would have gotten a straight answer from either of them, it would have been nice to know where he stood.

"How much do you know?" he asked.

"Only that Nathan showed up at Christmas dinner looking like that, and not twenty minutes later you're flipping tables and throwing punches. I'm assuming there might be some correlation there, but—" he tossed up his hands, "—please, feel free to fill the gaps for me."

Liam let out a long, slow breath, flattening his palms on the table.

"I assume you recall my birthday," he said, carefully measuring his words. "And the unwelcome idea of a *gift* you both chipped in on."

Recognition flickered in Ben's expression just before it was replaced by something like discomfort. He shifted in his seat, the sticky vinyl creaking beneath his weight. "It was Nathan's idea," he said.

"Yeah, that's not... Look, I've been seeing him," Liam blurted, probably a little too loudly. He shrank down into his seat. "Sort of," he amended softly.

Ben's eyes widened. "What? Really?"

Under the table, Liam's hands curled into fists. He opened his mouth, and then a thought occurred to him: in telling this part of the story and exposing Nathan for the monster that he was, Liam would also be outing him. Out of everyone in their immediate circle of friends and family, Liam was confident no one suspected it. Surely exposing Nathan would come to a shock to everyone, and definitely to Ben.

Then he remembered what Jonah had said to him at the hospital, about how he couldn't bring himself to press charges against Nathan for what he had done. How Jonah was forced to choose between his own mental well-being and a shot at seeking even a sliver of justice. Suddenly Liam's moral ambiguity didn't feel quite so hazy. The rage cut straight through the mist and made him see that he wasn't outing Nathan as a gay man, he was outing him as a predator.

"Nathan hurt him," Liam said simply. He heard the gravel in his own voice and willed himself not to start crying here. Not now. "He saw us out together a few weeks ago. He probably suspected something was going on, and that's what he was goading me about at dinner, but..." He swallowed back his disgust. "The point is, he tried to take advantage when Jonah was in a vulnerable position."

Ben was quiet for a long time. Liam wasn't looking at him, but for an anxious moment he thought maybe he had lost him. Like maybe he was going to side with Nathan after all, or tell Liam he was lying, or maybe blame him for keeping such close proximity to a dangerous situation. But to his surprise, Ben sat forward, placing a heavy hand on Liam's forearm.

"Liam," he said. "I didn't know."

"I know that," Liam muttered, treading carefully around the rare display of emotion.

"Is your friend. . . Or your, um," Ben seemed to struggle a bit with the verbiage, "Boyfriend or whatever? Is he alright?"

Liam had to press his knuckles against his leg for a few seconds.

"Bit of a loaded question," he said. "But he's safe now. He got out of the situation he was in."

"That's good." Ben nodded.

And it was. It *was* good. Liam's world might have been temporarily reduced to picking up the pieces of himself that broke along the way of seeing Jonah off, but it was a *good thing* that he was home now. He had to believe that.

"I'm sorry, Liam."

"You said."

"No." Ben shook his head, frustration peeking through his expression. "I mean, I think the apology I owe you probably goes a lot further back than all this. I haven't been a good friend to you. A good friend never would have set you up for something like that on your birthday when I knew you weren't comfortable with it. It's none of my business if you wanted to like. . . be a virgin 'til marriage or whatever."

Well, this was quickly going off the rails.

"Benjamin."

"Sorry," he said, and it sounded like he actually meant it. "For real, though. You've always been a good friend to me, and I should have been better at showing that I care about you, too."

Before Liam could fully lose his cool in the face of that unexpected emotional onslaught, the kitchen window bell rang—repeatedly, loudly, and pointedly.

Liam sighed. "I gotta get back before I am well and truly fired," he said, sliding out of the booth and onto his feet. "Look, I appreciate you checking in after. . . everything. Coffee's on the house."

Ben nodded, stuffing his hands into his pockets once he slid out of the booth as well.

"So," he said, rocking onto his heels. "It feels like we should, like, hug or something."

Liam raised a brow. "Do you want to hug me, Ben?"

"Not, like. . . in a gay way."

Well, Rome wasn't built in a day.

Instead of a hug, Liam opted for a pat on the arm. "We'll work up to it," he said.

He walked over to the window and delivered the line of plates to their respective tables, but the rest of his shift was knocked off-balance by the strange gravity of his conversation with Ben.

When he finally had another moment to breathe, he collapsed back against the wall behind the kitchen door and checked his phone.

There was a text from Jonah; a reply to the thread they both tended to throughout the day.

Got your book in the mail. I'll start reading tonight. Thanks.

Liam smiled. Before he could finish typing his reply, another text buzzed into the thread.

I miss you.

His first shift back was a short one, and it didn't bring in an abundance of tips, but there was something satisfying about working with a goal on the horizon.

When he got home, Liam changed out of his work clothes and collapsed into the swivel chair at his desk. It was still difficult, weeks later, to look around his room without seeing the impression Jonah had left behind.

For once, that might work in his favor.

He sat back and scanned the art-covered walls, remembering the care Jonah had taken to study each individual panel on his self-guided tour of Liam's past. At the time, it had been a mortifying ordeal to reveal himself like that, to be seen at close range. Now, he was able to look at his art through someone else's eyes, and for a moment, he could glimpse the potential that Jonah saw in him.

Liam used his legs to pull the chair toward one of his oldest drawings, the one Jonah had pointed out the night he was there. Carefully, he plucked it off the wall, trying not to chip the paint with the years-old tape. He set the drawing down on his desk like it was an ancient artifact. In the story of his own life, he supposed it was.

For as long as he could remember, Liam had only ever felt a vague sense of sadness when he thought of his childhood self—for the tough years of adolescence ahead of him and the deep yearning for friendship and belonging that he could never quite find.

Now, looking down at the depiction of his own childlike face, at the desperate way he held onto his friends, as if he knew, even then, that they weren't his to keep, Liam felt something like hope amidst the melancholy.

The three little boys in the picture and the bond between them no longer existed, reshaped entirely by the people around them, by societal expectations, and by each other. It was something Liam couldn't have back, and something that hadn't been his for a long time.

He was only just coming to terms with the idea that he had never been the dead weight in that friendship. Liam had always deserved better, and now he knew what *better* looked like.

He set the drawing to the side and cast another long look around the room. There was plenty there to work with, and time to make more. Applications for the fall semester were due at the end of February. Liam had a checklist of his top four programs in New York pinned to the corkboard above his desk, and a renewed determination to make that little kid in the drawing proud.

CHAPTER 37
Jonah

MARCH

It was cold when Jonah stepped outside a little past two in the morning. His thin cotton pants didn't hold up against the punishing chill, but he welcomed the bite. Tonight, the cold was the whole point.

He had spent hours turning over in bed, long past the time the rest of his family had fallen quiet behind their closed doors. The air inside his old bedroom was too warm. The street outside his window was too quiet. The comforter was too soft, too big, too clean. This endless state of half-awakeness he had been trapped in for weeks was eating him alive. Even true unconsciousness failed him as a means of escape, either evading him entirely or plaguing him with images of half-formed memories that left his skin crawling for days. He didn't have a preference for either.

It was that gnawing feeling that propelled him out of bed tonight, shucking off the bedspread and clambering to his feet.

He had just stood there for a moment, in the dark, in the middle of his room. His fingers had twisted into the hair on either side of his head—when had it grown?—pulling tight, tight, until the sting of his scalp blurred his vision with tears. He squeezed his eyes shut and wondered, not for the first time, if he was going out of his mind.

Outside, he thought. Just needed some air. Just needed some room to breathe.

He hadn't even stopped to pull on socks, and now the concrete patio was an icy anchor beneath his feet.

Jonah pulled in a deep lungful of air and held it, praying for the cleansing burn to shake loose his internal claustrophobia. It swirled around him when he let it out. He watched as the last trace dissipated into the darkness before he sank to the ground.

The backyard pool was stretched over with the tarp they used to cover it in the off-season. From this vantage point, it was hard to imagine the days he had spent out here as a child, his skin glowing into a golden tan in the sunlight. He looked down at his arms, turning them over to see the pale reflection of moonlight staring back up at him.

Looking away, he folded his knees into his chest and stared out at the pool, thinking about how shockingly cold the water must be beneath the cover. Maybe there was even an inch of ice on the surface. He remembered one summer, when his dad let him help open it for the season. They had removed the tarp together, freeing the hooks from the anchor points around the edge, and he had let Jonah dip his hand into the murky, green water. He remembered the way the cold shocked him, like ice down his back. Cold enough to hurt.

He wondered if he would feel the same sting now. If that sting would finally be sharp enough to cleanse his insides. Or if it would be lost like all the other sensations to his endless well of numbness, and apathy, and non-existence.

Sometimes he wondered if he really was alive at all.

It would have only taken a few steps, really. In a matter of seconds, he could have cleared the few feet to the pool's edge, could have freed the cable that held the corner of the tarp taut, just enough to give him room to slip his body over the lip of the pool, to slip beneath the surface and feel the cold shatter him. To break up the numbness, if only for a moment.

To disappear.

Jonah blinked, coming back to his body to find his toes at the edge of the tarp. He flinched, stumbling back.

"Jonah?"

He hadn't heard the back door open. His mother stared at him from the patio. The first thing he registered wasn't the deepened crease in her brow or the way she stood with one arm poised away from her body, as if preparing to reach out and yank him back from the edge of the water. It was the oversized shirt, faded from years of wear and hanging loosely on her frame.

His father's shirt.

His instinctive reaction was quick and fleeting, but he recognized that flare of heat in his chest as anger. Hot enough, if only briefly, to break through the fog and make him feel its burn. Jonah grasped after it like a starving man with a fish.

"Jonah?" she repeated, taking a step forward. Her slippers stopped at the edge of the deadened grass. "What are you. . . ? Baby, it's freezing out here."

"Sorry," he murmured.

He was braced for the usual reassurance, the promise that there was *no need to be sorry, Jonah*. But she was silent, eyeing him like he was every bit as crazy as he felt. For a long time, the only sound between them was the whistle of wind through the naked tree branches overhead.

"I wish you would talk to me," she said.

There was something different in those words, all falsehoods and optimism stripped from her voice. For the first time since Jonah had returned to Indiana, he heard the exhaustion that lay behind the façade.

Jonah ducked his head forward, the vague sense of frustration burrowing deeper.

"I don't know how to help you, Jo. I'm trying my best, but I can't reach you when you close yourself off like this."

Maybe they were both done pretending. Maybe they were both too tired, now, to keep dancing around the elephant in the room.

"What do you want me to talk about?" The calm in his voice was that of a smooth surface over a dangerous rip current.

"Anything," she said, and wasn't that a load of bullshit? "What you're thinking about, what... What happened to you."

"You don't want to listen to that," he snapped.

"If it would help you, of course I—"

"Trust me," Jonah said. "You don't want to hear the details, Mom. You can barely look at me as it is."

She flinched, but Jonah didn't feel compelled to retract his words. The anger had taken hold, and he wasn't about to fight it now.

"You know I don't..." She couldn't look him in the eye when she lied to him. "I don't think any differently of you."

"I *am* different!" he shouted. "Stop pretending like I'm this person you used to know. You won't say it out loud, but I can feel it. You're just waiting around for your son to show up, but he's not coming. He's never coming back."

"You—" She matched him for fierceness now, her slippers stumbling into the grass to meet him. "—are my son. You will always be my son."

"Where was that conviction when I needed you?"

He might as well have slapped her. She stepped back, shaking her head. Her silence only drove his anger forward.

"You wanted to talk about it," he threw back at her. "That seems like a good place to start. What did you think would happen to me when you kicked me out? Did you even care?"

Tears tracked down her face, just as they had the night Jonah left. "Of course I care," she cried. "I always cared. Your father—"

"My father," Jonah spat, "isn't here. I'm asking you. You're my *mom*. I needed you and you didn't help me."

Silence rang out through the darkness around them. The night sky had never felt so dark or so permanent overhead. In that moment, Jonah was sure he would never see the sun again.

"It's late," his mom said finally, her voice wavering. "And you're tired."

"I hated you," he whispered. "For months, I couldn't even think of your face because of how much I resented you for choosing him over me. And then. . ." He let himself pause, calculating how much exactly he was willing to divulge.

He thought about the time in the run-down clinic on the south side, getting tested for the first time, afraid that whatever diagnosis the doctor had for him would be a death sentence.

He remembered—only in hazy, grayed-out pockets—throwing up in the grass outside the car after a man had forced half a bottle of vodka down his throat, sure that the poison would kill him this time.

He remembered another man who had pulled out a gun inside the hotel room and made Jonah perform the full hour while thinking he wouldn't see the other side of it.

"I thought I was going to die," he settled for saying. "And that's when I realized that I didn't hate you. I loved you, still. Even after everything, I still loved you. And I didn't want to die never getting to see you again, because you're my mom, and you. . . and I. . ." He pulled in a deep breath. "I just can't make it make sense in my head. I can't understand how I could love you after everything you did, but you couldn't even love me enough to just accept me for who I am."

"Please don't say that," his mother begged. "Please, Jonah, don't ever say that I don't love you."

"Did you ever try to come after me? Even once?"

She was quiet, her eyes on the grass.

"I did," she said. "Once. It was a few weeks after you. . ." She shook her head. "It was a few weeks after. You were eighteen by then. When I talked to the police, tried to file a report, they said they couldn't open a search on a legal adult who wanted to disappear."

Jonah was momentarily stricken silent. "I didn't want to disappear," he whispered. "I didn't—" His voice broke off. He pressed a fist to his mouth, but the sobs sputtered out around it anyway. "I didn't want to. I didn't want this, mom, I didn't. . . I didn't. . ."

The fear that had turned to rage turned to despair and exhaustion, coming to a head as his knees found the grass. Jonah buried his face in his hands, and he screamed.

His mother's hands on his back, light and frantic, were peripheral. The consideration of his neighbors hearing him was peripheral. The only thing that existed in the world was concentrated in the fire that tore his throat apart in the backyard of his childhood home.

It was impossible to tell if the screaming continued, or if the sound only reverberated in his head. He was lost, and with every second that passed, he became emptier. Devoid of weight and intention and strength.

When hands pulled him forward, his body obeyed. He collapsed against his mother like a child, weeping into her chest. On some level, it was a parallel to their first reunion in Chicago, but something was distinctly different this time.

There was a desperation in this embrace, a finality, that wasn't there before.

He recognized, in that moment, that there was no world in which he could heal under that roof, sharing space with the ghosts of his past. Jonah clung to her this time because he knew it was a goodbye.

CHAPTER 38
Jonah

The view from the backseat of the cab was different than Jonah expected.

He had never been to New York. Every depiction in books and movies made it out to be a monolith of concrete and steel, but as the cab pulled away from LaGuardia airport, he saw a surprising amount of green.

It had taken him a full week after his breakdown in the backyard to gather enough courage to reach for the card—the one Jonah had shoved to the back of his nightstand drawer the first night back in Indiana. He could have thrown it away, and almost had, but perhaps some part of him had always known he would need an escape route.

He wasn't even sure what he had hoped to get out of making the call, only that Antonio Ellis had written him a blank check of his assistance, and Jonah needed out.

To his surprise, Ellis had kept his word. There was no hesitation when he offered Jonah a room in his newly inherited house in Queens—a private room, with a locked door, his own key, and no expectations.

On paper, it was the perfect plan: a fresh start in a new city, and a place to lay his head until he got back on his feet.

In reality, Jonah had been conditioned to look for the fault lines in kindness. The weak spot that exposed the ulterior motives. But in the end, the choice was simple.

He was in no position to turn down an extended hand. That sort of prideful naivety wasn't possible for someone like Jonah, who knew what it was like to lose everyone you ever thought was on your side. He wouldn't let that happen again.

Two hundred dollars in cash burned a hole in his front pocket, and there was a bank card with his name etched into the bottom in his wallet, which his mother had helped him set up before he left. Her way of showing support for his plan, he supposed. She had even driven him to the airport herself, teary-eyed and white-knuckling the steering wheel the whole way.

When she pulled him into a hug in the departures lane, she'd told him she loved him. She gave him the apology he needed and the one he deserved, and she said that she understood why he needed to leave, but that she would always be there if he wanted to return.

It was a start, Jonah thought. Maybe someday they would get there.

When the car ramped onto an elevated highway, Jonah got his first glimpse of the skyline in the distance. It was further away than he expected. He wasn't familiar with the city's layout, but now it made more sense why Ellis described his neighborhood as a "suburb in the city." Still, the view was nice. Jonah pulled his phone from his pocket and snapped a photo.

Meet me in the fall? He typed, then sent the message off to Liam.

From the back seat, he watched the dot on the GPS draw nearer to his new address, hugging his overstuffed backpack to his chest. It was hard not to think of the seventeen-year-old kid in the back of the Greyhound to Chicago, nearly two years ago to the day, freshly wounded and desperate for a soft place to land. From this perspective, it was easier to give that boy some grace for the things he had done when his back was against the wall.

Jonah was older now, and this time he was running forward instead of away. He wasn't responsible for creating the environment from which he'd fled, but he had left of his own volition. He had the opportunity before him to build the kind of life that he had already begun to mourn, and he wasn't going to waste it.

After twenty minutes, the car pulled onto a street lined with Tudor-style houses and brick driveways. He paid the driver with a wad of cash from his pocket and stepped out onto the sidewalk.

Looking up at the old house, with nothing but a small suitcase on wheels and a backpack slung over one shoulder, Jonah pictured a hundred different ways this could go wrong.

His phone buzzed in his pocket. He pulled it out to reveal Liam's reply.

It's a date, it said.

Jonah smiled.

Despite it all, he wasn't quite willing to write off the possibility that this was exactly where he was meant to be.

EPILOGUE

LIAM

On the morning of Liam's twenty-third birthday, he took the downtown train from Fordham University to 28th Street in Manhattan. He slung several large portfolio cases over his shoulder and trudged west, toward the Hudson River.

The space was part of an old industrial building, sectioned off for short-term rentals. Because of its distance from the train lines, it was one of the cheaper options, which also meant it was small. But Liam didn't need a lot of space, and even if his forehead was beaded with sweat from the long walk, nothing could dampen his good mood.

He shook hands with the venue coordinator, handed over the second half of the deposit, and then the space was his.

Once he was alone, he took a moment to just walk the perimeter, scraping his fingertips along the worn brick interior. The age of the place was apparent. There were divots here and there, little chunks that had been chipped away over time, and the wood floorboards creaked underfoot with every step.

It was perfect.

Liam dropped his bags in the corner and retrieved his phone and a Bluetooth speaker, scrolling until he found the playlist he had made for the occasion. Title: *"Baby's First Art Show."*

When the music started to play, he folded into a crouch and began pulling the canvases carefully from their bags.

The setup took him about an hour. It was in his nature to be indecisive, so he went through several rounds of arranging and rearranging every piece around the room until they fit just right. The paintings told a story, and that story just so happened to be one of the most important chapters of Liam's life. He felt duty-bound to tell it in exactly the right way.

Over the course of the hour, it became increasingly difficult to ignore the swell of nerves in his stomach. More than once, he had to ward off the compulsion to walk his paintings to the river's edge and throw them in, where they would never have to be viewed by the public eye—or one set of eyes in particular.

In the end, rationality won out. When the final canvas was displayed, he stepped back into the center of the room and spun in a slow circle, taking everything in.

For a moment, he was rendered breathless. Not by the paintings themselves, which he had stared into the face of for the better part of a year, but by the culmination of all of them, here, in this place, where he had dreamed of standing for so long. Nearly two years to the date since the idea had been born.

Over a year in the city, and Liam still wore the rose-colored glasses he'd had on the day he'd arrived. Something people never told you about watching your dreams come true was how surreal it would feel most of the time. Sometimes it was hard to believe he was actually here, but it was in the quiet moments, like this one, that he could believe he'd made it.

JONAH

New York had never been Jonah's dream.

But then, his future had always been something of a faceless monster; just fragments of ideas that refused to take shape.

He had gone from a lifetime of molding himself into a persona that would please his parents, directly into a place where any concept of a future at all wavered, even on the best days. Moving here had not been the result of years of dreaming and pining, like it had been for Liam, but the product of desperation. It was a place with a singular anchor to offer him safety, and Jonah had grabbed onto it with both hands.

He hadn't come here seeking a dream. He had come seeking refuge.

In time, though, he had found himself folded into the city's anonymous masses as if he belonged there.

A couple months in, Ellis got Jonah his first job. An old buddy of his who worked construction on Long Island was looking for day workers to demolish a house. Ellis was antsy after his abrupt departure from work, and Jonah needed to learn how to function like a person again, so he'd agreed to give it a try.

It had been ninety degrees on their first day, with the kind of humidity that had Jonah's shirt clinging to his back before they even arrived on site. He had a bagged lunch in his fist, a too-big pair of Ellis's steel-toed boots on his feet, and no clue what he was doing.

The guys on the crew were loud. Their fingers were thick and calloused from years of wear as they gripped Jonah's hand, and he felt himself squeezing back firmly, strangely motivated to make a good impression.

His first task was to tear down a wall that separated two small bedrooms. Ellis grabbed a couple of large hammers from the kit and handed one to Jonah. The surprising weight of it pulled his arm down.

"You want the first strike?" Ellis asked.

"Anywhere?" Jonah asked.

"The wall would be ideal."

Jonah fixed him with a flat expression and Ellis smirked back at him.

"Go nuts, kid."

Jonah tested the weight of it in his hand, shifting it from one to the other and swinging it up to shoulder height. He took a deep breath and let it out, narrowing in on a spot on the wall where two long scratches in the paint happened to intersect. *X marks the spot*, he thought.

In the moments before he swung, he felt a tingle in his arms, running up into the muscles of his shoulders; a burst of adrenaline that ached for release. He stared at the center of the X on the wall and saw a flash of the faces that kept him up at night—Shepard's, Dominic's, his father's.

Then he struck.

As the hammer crashed through drywall, Jonah let out a grunt that was half exertion, half rage. Before he could let himself think, he pulled back the hammer and slammed it into the wall again.

"How did that feel?" Ellis asked when Jonah stopped to catch his breath.

Despite himself, despite the sweat that clung to his eyelashes, his thumping heartbeat, and the ache that was already starting to pulsate in his shoulders, Jonah found that he was smiling.

"Fucking incredible."

That night in bed, after a long shower, he could still feel his pulse in his arms and legs as the endorphins settled, the weight of the day pressing him down into the mattress. It was a silent epiphany, as he stared up at the ceiling. It was the first time in recent memory that Jonah had felt strong in his own body.

If Chicago was the place where Jonah had learned how to survive, New York was where he learned how to live.

On the weekends and odd evenings, he began volunteering at a meal center downtown. It was partly to fill his time, never letting his hands sit idle for too long, and partly to prove to himself that he could.

At first, he worried that there would be too much negative association between his volunteer work and the work he had done under Shepard's Fold, but he refused to let that prevent him from doing good in the world.

That time in his life had been so lonely, so void of light in his memory. It couldn't have been more different than Jonah's experience in New York.

When he worked his shifts, he found himself making connections with the people who came through the line. He would sit with them and eat, sometimes, after the last meal was served, rotating through the regulars until he knew most of the crowd on a first-name basis.

Jonah listened to their stories and, in time, learned to share pieces of his own. When he did, he wasn't met with pity or judgment, but a respect he seldom felt worthy of. It was hard to feel alone in a community like that.

It was during one such dinner shift in early October, well over a year since he first touched down in New York, that he encountered a ghost from his past.

Jonah was on drink duty, pouring gallon jugs of apple juice into Styrofoam cups at the end of the line.

"Do you have coffee?" a man asked, his head hung low and shadowed by the too-big hood thrown over his head.

"Self-serve, over there," Jonah directed him to the far wall.

But as the man looked up to thank him, the meeting of their eyes forced Jonah's world to a screeching halt.

The first thing Jonah noticed, bizarrely, was that most of his piercings were gone. The only one that remained was the curve of silver that hung from his septum, capped with two round bulbs. Looking at it, Jonah could still feel the way it had brushed against his skin when they kissed.

"Dominic," he whispered.

It didn't feel real that he could be standing there now, states away, a *lifetime* away from the last time they had seen each other.

Dominic went still, his eyes widening. He stared for a few moments, a deer in headlights.

"It's Jonah," Jonah supplied numbly. "Prince."

"I know." Dominic shook his head, a rapid, jerky movement. He took a step back, tucking his hands into his pockets. "I should go," he said, and pivoted on his heel.

"Wait," Jonah heard himself say.

With what appeared to be some effort, Dominic turned back but didn't respond. Jonah's tongue was plastered to the roof of his mouth, but he forced himself to speak.

"You came here for coffee," he said. "You should take some. Are you hungry?"

He saw the internal struggle in the expression Dominic tried to tuck away, and for a moment Jonah was sure he would turn and disappear back into the streets. But instead, he said, "Yeah. Okay."

Jonah watched him from his spot on the line as Dominic received a plate of spaghetti and buttered bread, then grabbed a coffee and sat at one of the tables, alone. When the crowd began to thin, Jonah stepped out from behind his station and approached.

"Do you mind if I sit?" he asked.

Dominic didn't look up, but he paused with his cup halfway to his mouth. He gave the barest motion of a nod that Jonah decided to take as approval.

He could admit to second-guessing himself once they were seated across from each other. Jonah still couldn't quite process that it really was Dominic in front of him, let alone begin to traverse the minefield of history that lay between them.

For his part, Dominic seemed just as clueless, which was unnerving on its own. In the short time he had known Dominic, which had felt like a small pocket of eternity in the moment, he had never seen him be anything less than one-hundred percent confident.

Right up until the last phone call Jonah had shared with him. But that was the last thing to be thinking of if he wanted this to remain civil.

"How long have you been in New York?" Jonah was the first to breach the silence.

"Couple months," Dominic muttered between sips.

"Why here?"

He shrugged. "Wanted something new. Tried Detroit. Then Philly for a while. Hopped a bus here." Then, after a moment, "What about you?"

"About a year and a half," Jonah replied.

"What do you do?" There was genuine interest behind the question, which Jonah didn't know how to take.

"I'm in school."

Finally, Dominic looked up. The lines and dark circles around his eyes made him look older than he was. "School?"

"Yep," he said. "I'm studying to be a teacher."

Dominic looked at him long enough to have Jonah squirming. "You're a good person, aren't you?"

Jonah's first instinct—just past the surprise—was to bristle.

"I guess the bar is pretty low." The sudden clip in Jonah's tone startled both of them, but at least it drained the final remnants of pretense.

Maybe this had been a really terrible idea.

Dominic seemed to agree, because he was already scooting toward the edge of the table. "I should go," he said.

"Wait," Jonah said, reaching out just enough for his fingers to brush Dominic's wrist. He pulled back quickly. "I'm sorry. Please stay and finish your meal."

He must have really been hungry, because he settled back into his seat and endured the blistering tension between them.

After a few bites, Dominic began to fidget. "I..." he started, then stopped, snapping his mouth shut and shaking his head before beginning again. "I know it wasn't right, disappearing on you like I did."

The anger Jonah had kept buried for so long rose effortlessly to the surface. As much as he would have liked to sit there with a cool head and pretend that he had made peace with his past, that he was above it all now, that would have been a lie.

He couldn't count how many sleepless nights he had spent imagining all the ways their paths might cross again, and what Dominic would say to him. If he would grovel and beg for his forgiveness. If he would be harsh and cold and unrepentant. None of the scenarios in his head had landed them quite where they were now.

The man across from him ran a hand through his overgrown hair, and Jonah resented the fact that he could still feel the phantom texture between his fingers.

"You knew what would happen, didn't you?" Jonah asked quietly. "When you gave me his number, you knew you were throwing me to the wolves. That's why you disappeared."

Something changed in Dominic's expression. "I was eighteen when I met Shepard," he said. "It's true, what I told you about my parents. I never met my dad, and my mom. . ." He paused, snorting out a dark laugh. "She's so strung out she wouldn't recognize me if I was standing right in front of her. I started running for her dealer, just trying to keep the lights on, but I got caught. My public defender knew about his program and got them to cut me a deal."

"Are you trying to make me feel sorry for you?" Jonah's voice was dangerously close to breaking.

"No, I don't want your pity," Dominic said. "I'm trying to tell you that, yes, I knew what happened when I was under Shepard's roof, and yes, I knew that he would probably take an interest in you, too. I still thought it was better than you winding up in a jail cell."

"If you were so confident in your charitable decision, why did you take off running?"

"You think it would have been easy to get into that fancy New York college of yours if you were carrying around a criminal record?"

"He almost killed me." It came out louder than Jonah expected, drawing the eyes of a few curious tables near them. Jonah raked his fingers through his hair, which he had taken such pride in growing out since his time in Chicago. "He almost killed me," he repeated, softer.

Dominic curled in on himself. "I'm sorry, Jonah."

"I'm not interested in your apology."

Dominic looked up at him through bloodshot eyes. "That's all I have for you," he said. "I don't have anything else to give."

Every furious bone in Jonah's body wanted to kick him while he was down, but he forced himself to breathe through the anger. To remember to be the person that he was now, and not the frightened boy he used to be.

"Can you just tell me this?" Jonah asked. "Did you ever really care about me? Was it ever real to you?" *Because it was real to me.*

Dominic looked down at his untouched plate of food. "I know it doesn't matter now," he said. "But I did care about you. I was never any good at caring about people, though."

Jonah didn't know how to respond. The sudden threat of tears made him feel like the sliver of control he had over this conversation was slipping from his grasp, and he needed to step back.

Jonah cleared his throat. "You should finish your dinner."

Something like disappointment flashed across Dominic's face, but he seemed to pick up on the cue that the conversation was over. What was done was done. There was no going back, and the only forward for each of them did not involve the input of the other.

Jonah stood to leave.

"Thank you," Dom said. "For the food."

Jonah nearly gave into the urge to reach out and touch him; to feel the cold skin of his arm, to feel some solid proof that any of this surreal encounter had been real. But he thought better of it, dropping his hand.

"Take care of yourself, Dominic."

In the back kitchen, Jonah removed his apron and hung it on the door. He grabbed onto the counter as the adrenaline caught up to him, using it to keep himself upright. He closed his eyes and counted his breaths until they began to level out. Then, he stood up straight and combed through his hair with his fingers. He went over to the sink and splashed some cold water onto his face, and he slid on his jacket before stepping out into the cold.

He had an art show to get to.

The wind coming in off the Hudson chapped Jonah's lips as he turned the corner. The address was a brick building, clearly repurposed from a time when the neighborhood still clung to its industrial roots. Light from the windows spilled out onto the sidewalk, illuminating a cluster of students gathered outside, smoking. Among them, he caught a flash of red hair.

He spotted Liam before Liam spotted him, and Jonah allowed himself a few precious moments to admire him in his element.

The cold had turned the tips of his ears and nose bright pink, and he was laughing at something his friend said. In the half-light cast across his face, he looked radiant with joy, and the sight was enough to dampen everything that had come before this moment to background noise.

When Liam finally saw him, he passed the cigarette sheepishly and stepped out of the circle to meet him halfway.

"It was only a couple of drags, I swear," he blurted in lieu of a greeting. "Give me a break, I'm shitting myself here."

Smoking had been a habit Liam picked up—and mostly dropped—in his first semester of art school. He only ever reverted back to it when his nerves were higher than usual.

Of all occasions, his very first art show seemed worthy of a pass.

"People are going to love it," Jonah promised.

"You haven't even seen it yet."

"And I've been very patient," Jonah teased, then leaned in to plant a kiss on his cheek. "Happy birthday," he whispered, close to Liam's ear.

Liam caught his hand and reined him back in for a proper kiss. His lips were cold and tasted faintly of cigarette smoke and chapstick.

"I'm so glad you're here," Liam said. When he pulled back, he studied Jonah's expression. "Is everything okay?" he asked, running a thumb under Jonah's eye where the skin was still blotched pink. He'd hoped the cold would have covered for him. "How was your shift?"

That was a conversation better suited for another time, another place. Not on the sidewalk outside of one of the biggest events of Liam's life. Jonah could use some time to process it on his own first, anyway.

Tonight, Dominic Harris had no place in his life.

"I'm good," Jonah replied honestly.

"You're sure?"

"I am. Now, no more about me. I'm here to see some art."

A slow smile warmed Liam's face, but when Jonah took a step toward the door, he stopped him with a soft touch.

"Wait," Liam said. "I just want to say. . . if you hate it, it's fine. If it's too much, if it's. . . you know? You can leave. I'll set them on fire or throw them in the Hudson. Whatever you want."

Jonah had to fight to keep the smile off his face. Some things never changed, and his boyfriend's propensity to ramble when nervous was one of them.

Liam had told him about the project eight months prior, said that it was something that had been simmering on the backburner since a few weeks after they'd first met. And while Liam had kept the paintings themselves under lock and key, he had taken care to get Jonah's explicit consent on the subject matter long before it ever reached the concept of a public showing.

It was sweet that he worried about him, even now, but Jonah knew there was nothing to worry about. Not with Liam.

Jonah grabbed his hand, slipping his fingers between Liam's. "I want to see it," he said.

Liam's face cycled through several emotions before landing on something resolute. He squeezed Jonah's hand in return, then tugged him forward.

As soon as they cleared the doorway, parting the small gathering of patrons sipping complimentary champagne, Jonah's feet stilled beneath him.

All around them, propped on wooden easels and hung from aged brick walls, was a collection of painted rooms captured on canvas.

Not just rooms. Hotel rooms, specifically, defined by the matching sets of beds, always with a wired telephone and table lamp between them.

The rooms were painted in vivid realism, but in each one of them were the cartoonish outlines of two figures in a myriad of positions: sitting on opposite beds, perched in the window, lying on the floor. In each of them, the figures seemed to glow, brilliant and stark against the muted backdrops. The brightest things in the room.

In one of the paintings, there was an empty champagne bottle on the nightstand. In another, a spread of textbooks and paper across the bed. In each successive painting, the two outlines drew closer and closer in proximity, until the last one, where their figures tangled together into one unending, messy line on the bed.

Jonah's eyes found the stark black lettering printed above the collection.

"'A Series of Rooms,'" he read aloud.

"What do we think?" Liam asked. "Should I start tossing them off the pier, or can they stay?"

Jonah could feel Liam's gaze on the side of his face, but he couldn't tear his eyes away from the gallery of lived snapshots before him.

I love it, he wanted to say.

I love you, he thought, but the words weren't big enough to fill the feeling.

"Yeah," was the breathless response that made it to the surface. "They can stay."

ACKNOWLEDGMENTS

I've held Liam and Jonah's story close to my heart for over four years. Sharing it with you has been a dream come true.

I am forever grateful to everyone who read this story in its earliest form and saw something in it. I never would have been brave enough to put these words into print without your encouragement.

Huge thanks to Jessica Sherburn for the beautiful cover art. Another huge thanks to my editor Hilary Doda.

To my partner, who has listened to me ramble about these characters more than anyone should have to hear, and offered endless support along the way.

And to my writing mate, my shared consciousness in the simulation, the person I can always count on to read my stories first—you know who you are.

While *A Series of Rooms* is ultimately a story of hope and survival, it deals with some heavy subject matter along the way.

Content warnings below:

Sexual assault (including on-page depiction)
Trafficking
Physical & emotional abuse
Religious trauma
Homophobia from parents
Drug use

Printed in Dunstable, United Kingdom